RE-TERRIFY

EDITED
BY
KELLY A. HARMON AND
VONNIE WINSLOW CRIST

Pole to Pole Publishing
Baltimore

Re-Terrify
Horrifying Stories of Monsters & More
Copyright © 2018 Pole to Pole Publishing

Published by Pole to Pole Publishing
Edited by Kelly A. Harmon and Vonnie Winslow Crist
Cover layout copyright © 2018 Pole to Pole Publishing
www.poletopolepublishing.com

Cover Font "October Crow" by Chad Savage
http://www.sinisterfonts.com

ISBN: 978-1-941559-31-4

Túshūguǎn ©2014 Eric Choi, first published in *Ricepaper.*
Deadly Cargo ©2015 Geoff Gander, first published in *New Tales of the Old Kings.*
Bed-Time Story ©1987 Lisa Lepovetsky, first published in *Not One of Us.*
Lucky Clover ©2013 Kelly A. Harmon, first published in *Deep Cuts: Mayhem, Menace & Misery*
Snowbroth ©2015 Vonnie Winslow Crist, first published in *Potter's Field 5.*
Blood Born ©2012 Meriah Crawford, first published in *LocoThology: Tales of Fantasy & Science Fiction.*
Reanimated ©2015 Nicole Kurtz, first published in *Athena's Daughters, II.*
Uncle Sharlevoix's Epidermis ©2015 Gregory Norris, first published in *Dead Harvest.*
Gas ©1994 James Dorr, first published in *Eulogy.*
Under Two Moons ©2013 Jonathan Shipley, first published in *Phobus One: Zugzwang.*
Moonset ©2009 Steven R. Southard, first published in *Dead Bait.*
By Her Hand, She Draws You Down ©2001 Douglas Smith, first published in *The Third Alternative.*
The Monster Hunter ©2016 Gregg Chamberlain, first published in *Pulp Literature Magazine.*
Choop ©2008 Nancy Springer, first published in *Mystery Date.*
Bridge Over the Cunene ©2008 Gustavo Bondoni, first published in *The World is Dead.*
Brown John's Body © 1955 Winston Marks, first published in *Imagination Stories of Science and Fantasy.*
Short and Nasty ©1991 Darrell Schweitzer, first published in *Obsessions.*

Library of Congress Control Number: 2018967679.

RE-TERRIFY

The monsters of our childhood do not fade away...

- John le Carre

Table of Contents

Túshūguǎn

Eric Choi

*F**énshū carefully studied the boy with the book.*
The youth looked to be in his early teens, but it was difficult to tell. Contemporary Běiměizhōu children always looked much older than their years. This one resembled a skeleton, more bone than flesh, with grimy bug-bitten skin, laddered ribs, twig-thin arms and legs, and bloodied, swollen feet. His face was gaunt, topped by a tangled, greasy mess of long, black hair. He also stank, reeking like an oily, salty fish.

Fénshū looked into the boy's green eyes, and while it was impossible to get a sense of the boy's soul, she could discern a certain fire—perhaps of intelligence, certainly of strength.

"Nǐ jiào shén ma míng zì?" she asked. The boy was silent.

"Nǐ míngbái ma?"

Still no response.

"What is your name?" she said at last in English.

"Wu," the boy said. His yellowish-brown teeth were chipped and twisted.

"Hello, Wu. I am Dr. Fénshū Zhèng," she continued. "I am…an historical archaeologist. Do you know what that is?"

The boy fell silent again.

"How old are you, Wu?"

The boy did not answer, looking instead at his inquisitor and returning the question. "How old are *you*?"

Definitely intelligent. The boy's verbal language skills, at least in English, were excellent. Fénshū was quite impressed.

"I am sixty years old!" Fénshū cackled in a high-pitched voice, trying to smile.

Wu simply stared.

"Do you have something for me?"

Wu nodded, his calloused hands reverently handing over the book.

"Thank you, Wu." Fénshū gestured to the floor of the tent. "Please, sit down. My colleague will be back for you shortly."

Wu hesitated for a moment, then sat on the ground as instructed.

Fénshū pushed her spectacles up the bridge of her nose and examined the book. It was a brownish-black hardcover, about sixteen by twenty-four centimetres and perhaps three centimetres thick, enclosed within a clear sealable plastic bag of the type that had once been a common means of storing food in pre-Fall Běiměizhōu civilization. The book was in fairly good condition, except for a serrated gash that penetrated the pages from cover to cover. Also inside the plastic bag, collected mostly along the spine, were clumps of a white powdery residue. She held the book up to her nose and sniffed. Through the punctured plastic, it smelled faintly of camphor and another odd odor she could not immediately identify.

"Where did this come from?" Fénshū asked. "Where did you find this?"

The boy looked up.

"Where did you find this?" she repeated.

"In the old shit and piss!"

§

Over and over again, Wu's mother would ask him the same thing.

"What do you do if you see a Jiangshi?"

"Run," Wu would answer.

"Why?"

Sometimes, Wu would hesitate, and his mother would insist.

"Come on. Why?" she would repeat.

"Because a Jiangshi will hurt you, kill you, eat you."

§

The road upon which Wu walked was wrinkled and cracked like the skin of an old man. Weeds and wild flowers sprouted from every fissure, heaving apart the decaying asphalt. With slow certainty over the long years since the Fall, the pavement was being reduced to the constituent stone, gravel, and bitumen from which it had been formed.

For much of this day, Wu had been fortunate in his solitude. It was not to last.

Wu stopped in his tracks and squinted. In the far distance, a Jiangshi came into view. He recognized the brain-frizzed monster immediately, a stained and filthy figure slowly shambling in his direction with that distinctive jerky, unsteady gait.

He didn't think he had been spotted, but he wasn't about to stick around to find out.

Wu ran off the road, through the tall grasses, into the trees. Twigs and branches lashed his body and stones cut his bare feet, but neither slowed his flight. Deeper and deeper into the woods he ran, until his lungs heaved and his heart felt like it would burst from his chest.

Finally, he stopped…and stared.

Before him was a ruin of the old world. A house had once stood here, but it had long ago collapsed and been assimilated by the living woods. Only the chimney remained standing, but Wu could see that its bricks were dropping and breaking, little by little, as the mortar crumbled and powdered. Some kind of vine grew everywhere, climbing through the broken windows and up the bars and grillwork.

Wu circled about the stone tower, fascinated.

There was a shallow hill across from the remnants of the foundation. He walked to the hill and climbed. Suddenly, he stopped and looked down.

He had run over something.

Tracing back a few steps, he spotted a patch of dead leaves and twigs collected within a rough square. Resting on his knees, Wu swept away the detritus with his hands. A grey slab with a square metal handle imbedded on top appeared before him.

Wu stared in wonder, uncertain of what to do next. Finally, he reached down and grasped the handle with his small, bony hands.

Nothing happened.

He extended his legs and dug in his feet for leverage, pulling harder with all his strength, but still it did not budge. Exhausted, he released the handle and fell backwards, his legs splayed.

Something moved in the bushes.

Wu turned in the direction of the rustling noise, his eyes wide. He pulled a slingshot out of his pouch, his other hand frantically sweeping the ground for a suitable projectile. Grasping a stone, he loaded the pocket and pulled back the bands with trembling hands.

The leaves rustled again.

Wu drew back the bands a little further, then released.

§

The happiest times were when his mother told him stories about the things from before, the old world prior to the Fall.

"People flew?"

"Yes. In flying machines. Anywhere in the world, without fear."

And she would tell him about the music that came from a box smaller than your hand, and the heat and light and clean water that came with a touch, and the pictures that moved, and the buildings as high as mountains, and the places with piles of fresh food, and the artificial stars that let people talk to one another across the world, and most wonderful of all, the bound volumes upon whose pages were recorded the knowledge and beauty of Běiměizhōu civilization at its height.

"Books."

"Books," Wu repeated.

§

The boy emerged from the bushes a split second after Wu launched the projectile. Eyes wide, he instinctively ducked. The stone whizzed over his head, striking the trunk of a tree just behind him.

"What are you doing?" shouted the boy indignantly.

Wu grabbed another stone and reloaded his slingshot, drawing back the band and keeping it trained on the stranger.

The pale, skinny boy looked to be about Wu's age. With the exception of his short curly brown hair, Wu could have been looking at a reflection.

"What are *you* doing?" Wu challenged. He studied the stranger. The boy, though as emaciated as he was, did not slur his words, and he stood firm without the jerky twitches that were the stigmata of those who consumed the flesh of others.

"Are you a Jiangshi?" Wu asked rhetorically.

"Are *you* a Jiangshi?" the boy echoed in retort.

Slowly, Wu lowered his slingshot. "I am Wu."

"I'm Vancott," the boy said. He pointed at the crumbling chimney. "What's that ruin?"

Vancott walked up the shallow hill to join Wu, and the boys found themselves looking at the slab and handle in the ground. They took hold of the handle together and managed to lift the grey slab. Putting the lid aside, they went to the opening and peered down into the darkness.

Wu squinted. "Something's in there!"

A very faint odor wafted out of the opening. Vancott sniffed.

Recognition came to both of them at the same time.

"Stupid!" Vancott shoved Wu, sending him sprawling to the ground. "This is—"

"Old shit and piss," Wu said. He remembered his mother's words. "Skeptic tank."

The two boys sat silently, pondering their next move.

Suddenly, a flock of dark birds took flight from the trees, swirling noisily into the sky. Wu and Vancott turned.

There was a rustling in the bushes.

Vancott grabbed Wu's arm. "I saw a Jiangshi today!"

Wu shot Vancott a fearful glance. "I saw a Jiangshi, too," he hissed. "On the road."

The boys looked about, knowing they were badly exposed atop the shallow hill. At once, the same desperate idea occurred to both. They got up quickly.

Vancott slid the concrete lid partially over the opening, while Wu gathered up some dead leaves and twigs and piled them on top. It wasn't much in the way of camouflage, but it was better than nothing. Vancott squeezed inside first, followed by Wu. With great effort, they managed to get the lid almost closed except for a thin sliver.

Wu peered through the narrow slit, and before long saw the monster stumble out of the woods. The gangly, twitching figure, no longer really human, was the same one Wu had seen on the road.

Quietly, the boys drew the lid fully closed, and darkness enveloped them.

§

Wu and Vancott waited silently in the musty dark, for a sound, a voice, a sign…something.

They were sitting on a pile of flat rectangular objects. Wu felt around with his hands. The objects were all roughly the same shape but in different sizes. He remembered seeing something when they first opened the lid, but without light he could do nothing to identify the objects even whilst sitting amongst them.

Breathing was difficult, and the boys were getting sleepy. The stale air would not sustain them much longer.

Cautiously, they pushed the lid and opened up a small crack to look around. The brief inrush of fresh air hit their lungs with an almost icy sharpness, and it took all of Wu's willpower to not dash out right away.

Finally, they pushed the lid all the way open and climbed out. Wu moved to follow, but on sudden impulse grabbed one of the rectangular objects on his way up. Outside, the boys collapsed onto the sweet long grass of the shallow hill, lying on their backs, lungs heaving as they gulped fresh air, their mouths open and trembling like those of fish out of water.

After a long moment of rest, Wu rolled onto his side and saw the flat rectangular object lying on the grass. He sat up and took it with both hands, bringing it up to his eyes.

Wu stared at the object for a moment before recognizing it. "A book!"

"What?" Vancott asked.

Wu turned the book about, examining it from all sides.

It was brownish-black in color and sealed in a transparent pouch, probably made of the material that Wu's mother had called plastic. A hard seam ran along one side. Wu examined the seam and eventually figured out how to pull the pouch open. There was a faint medicinal smell, and clumps of a white powder fell out.

With deliberate care, Wu reverently extracted the book from the plastic pouch. There were symbols on the cover that he recognized as words, but like all contemporary teenagers he didn't read. He slowly flipped through the yellowish pages, each dense with indecipherable text.

"What is it?" Vancott asked again.

"A book," Wu repeated. "From the old world, before the Fall."

Vancott's eyes widened.

Wu was illiterate, not stupid. He had the sense to know, on an instinctive level, the importance of what he and Vancott had found. Somebody had done this on purpose, creating an improvised library—a túshūguǎn—either before or shortly after the Fall, in the hope that someone like Wu might find the treasure.

Wu put the book back into the pouch and resealed it. The boys covered up the hatch again with leaves and twigs before setting off. They would need to find a person who could read.

§

Wu and Vancott wandered aimlessly for days. Sometimes, they would walk for hours in one direction when Vancott would suddenly change his mind, and then they would turn about and retrace their steps. On other occasions, they seemed to be walking in circles. Wu began to doubt whether Vancott had any idea where they were going.

Beside him, Wu heard Vancott's stomach growl. His companion always seemed to be hungry. For such a thin little guy, he ate an awful lot. Not for the first time, Wu wondered how Vancott had managed to survive on his own for this long.

A feral rakunk bounded out of some shrubbery a short distance ahead. Vancott had seen the black masked fluffy tailed animal first, putting out his hand to stop Wu and signaling for silence. If nothing else, Wu was grateful for Vancott's sharp eyes. His companion may eat too much food, but at least he was good at spotting it.

Wu slowly knelt to pick up a rock, quietly pulling out his slingshot at the same time. He steadied himself, drew back the band, took aim, and fired.

Killing the game turned out to be the easy part. Starting the fire to cook it proved much more difficult. It had rained earlier in the day, and the boys had trouble finding dry grass and leaves for tinder. More than once, Wu saw Vancott eyeing the book. He pulled it closer.

Night had fallen by the time they got the fire going and cooked the rakunk. In the chilly dark, Wu and Vancott managed to find some comfort in the warming flames and meat. When they had finished eating, they lay on their backs and gazed up at the twinkling tapestry of stars above. Wu thought about his mother's stories of people in flying machines, soaring amongst the clouds and even out to the dark heavens beyond.

Wu closed his eyes, and as sleep came, the book slipped quietly from his arms and fell to the ground.

§

He dreamed.

It was a strange dream, the kind Wu knew was only a dream even while he was dreaming it, because he was seeing things that he could not possibly have known or remembered. He was in a vast cavern, within which were rows upon rows of shelves, each packed end-to-end with books. The volumes were all of different sizes, thicknesses and colors, with incomprehensible words along the spines. There must have been hundreds, if not thousands of books, stretching further into the depths of the cavern than Wu could see.

He reached out to a book at random and tried to take it off the shelf. The book came out about two-thirds of the way and then abruptly jammed.

Wu pulled harder, to no effect. He grabbed the book with both hands and yanked with all his strength.

The entire bookshelf began to fall towards him.

Wu let go of the book and stepped back. The bookshelf was still falling.

Walking backwards, he tried to quicken his pace. He looked up, and saw that the bookshelf appeared to be of infinite height, stretching upwards without end. There was nothing he could do to avoid getting crushed.

The bookshelf came down.

There was a scream.

Wu woke with a start. The scream had not been his.

Beside the smoldering remnants of the fire, Vancott was locked in a desperate struggle with a monster. His attacker had pinned him to the ground. Vancott squirmed, kicked, and punched, frantically trying to free himself. The Jiangshi was as emaciated as the boys, but he was taller and armed with two lethal weapons—madness and a knife.

Wu was frozen in momentary fear. He tried to yell, but no words came.

The Jiangshi brought the knife down—once, twice...

Before there was a third stroke, Wu sprang forth and launched himself at the monster. He ran into the Jiangshi's back and pounded the smelly, sore-ridden flesh with both fists. The Jiangshi grunted and took a swing, sending Wu sprawling to the ground.

Lying on his back, Wu looked up at the looming monster's gnarled, weathered face with its long, filthy, tangled hair, twitching unfocused eyes and rotting yellow-brown teeth. Wu backed away on his elbows like a crab.

He hit something on the ground.

The Jiangshi raised his knife to strike.

Wu grabbed the rectangular object and brought it up with both hands. The knife plunged into the book, piercing it from cover to cover, its point protruding out the back.

Grunting, the Jiangshi twisted and pulled on the knife, finally extracting it from the book, but stumbling backwards a few steps.

Wu threw the damaged book at the Jiangshi, hitting the monster on the side of the head. Already off balance, the Jiangshi fell onto his haunches. It didn't take long for the monster to get up again, but the delay gave Wu just enough time to load his slingshot and fire.

The mote scored a direct hit into the Jiangshi's left eye.

Screaming and clutching the bleeding eye with both hands, the Jiangshi dropped to the ground. The monster rolled side to side, shrieking and twitching uncontrollably as blood and vitreous fluid oozed between his fingers.

Wu got up and walked over to where Vancott's lifeless body lay in a pool of his own blood. Vancott was on his back, mouth and eyes still wide open. In silence, Wu simply stared at his dead companion with a lack of emotion that would have shocked his pre-Fall ancestors. He left Vancott where he lay, picked up the book, and simply walked away.

Behind him, the Jiangshi's screams went on and on, the cries of a wounded animal. Wu kept walking, book in hand, until he could not hear the inhuman noises anymore.

§

"I am sorry about your friend," Fénshū said when Wu finished his story.

Wu said nothing more.

"You are a brave young man," she continued, "and extremely lucky as well. We are the first expedition to work in the Vancouver ruins for years, and it is only possible because we were able to afford the armed guards to protect us from the Jiangshis." She put the book on the ground. "Did you see anything else down in that...um, 'skeptic' tank?"

The boy fell unhelpfully silent, once again.

A young woman entered the tent, carrying a small bundle of clothes.

Fénshū pointed. "Wu, please go with my colleague. She will give you some food. You need to rest, and when you are better, we will need you to take us back to this place you found. Do you understand?"

Wu nodded.

"Gēn wǒ lái," the young woman said, taking Wu's hand and leading him out of the tent.

Fénshū waited a moment, then picked up the book and took it outside. Near the centre of the expedition encampment, a small fire burned. She walked towards the campfire, and without a second thought, casually tossed the book into the flames.

The plastic wrap melted quickly, evaporating like water on a hot plate. Then the flames attacked the book itself, consuming it from the outside edges in. The words on the cover—A Novel, *Oryx and Crake*, Margaret Atwood—were legible for a few moments until the dust jacket blackened and crumbled away. Acrid smoke billowed briefly when the white residue ignited, causing Fénshū to cough and blink. The spine was the last to endure, but eventually it, too, yielded to the flames.

When the book had been reduced to ash, Fénshū returned to the tent and settled back in her chair. Pre-Fall Běiměizhōu texts were of academic interest and had some nominal value on the antiquities market, but her backers in Běijīng and Clavius had little interest in them. Excavating the Vancouver II site was a costly and very risky venture. Her expedition would need to find something of much greater value, and soon. The boy would take them back to the other site. For her sake—and to some degree, the boy's—she truly hoped that artifacts of real value were still out there, somewhere in the ruins of the old shit and piss.

Deadly Cargo
Geoff Gander

*T*homas de Raaf *cut his way through the boisterous crowd* at Picton's smoky and dark Sailor's Rest, and stepped up to the bar. Not for the first time, he wondered if he was doing the right thing. He rubbed his sweaty palms on his trousers. The *Polaris* would be his first ship; he needed this job. His tension eased as the men around him swapped stories about lives left behind, joked about old sailors' tales of lake monsters, and speculated about their captain. Everyone had heard something. Captain Harris was a defrocked clergyman; he had run guns to the Confederates during the Civil War; and he had even sailed in the South Seas in his youth, and made a fortune. Thomas's uncle had told him that Harris had been sailing Lake Ontario for years, and was a strict, but fair, man.

"Tom, lad, there you are," said his uncle. Charles Smythe cut through the crowd and wrapped a burly, tanned arm around Thomas's shoulders. "I trust your mum's well?"

"She is, Uncle," said Thomas. "And thank you for this opportunity."

Smythe shook his head. "It's the least I could do. It's not as though you'd get much of a share of the farm, anyway."

Thomas nodded. He had three older brothers, two of whom already had young wives of their own. His father had told him on no uncertain terms that he would have to make his own way. That was why he was here, thanks to a letter from his mother to her brother, who happened to be the *Polaris*'s first mate.

"There's just one thing I need to ask you, on behalf of the captain," said Smythe. "Are you a superstitious, lad?"

"How do you mean," asked Thomas.

"Do you put any stock in omens, Indian legends, and the like?" asked Smythe.

Thomas furrowed his brow for a second. "I believe in what I can see with my own eyes," he said slowly.

"Good," said Smythe. "Captain Harris likes rational men. Stow your belongings, then. We set sail tomorrow."

§

The next day the *Polaris* sailed for Rochester. She was a two-masted schooner, over one hundred fifty feet long and twenty feet wide, with a dark green hull and her name painted in large white letters along the gunwale. Her deck gleamed in the sunlight, and nothing— not even the shortest length of rope—was out of place. While Thomas learned his duties as a deckhand, he wondered yet again whether he was doing the right thing.

His family had been farming in Prince Edward County for generations, and had always been solid, down-to-earth folk. But for as long as Thomas could remember he had preferred imagining himself in the strange lands he had read about in his family's few books to tending the livestock or the fields. It was all very strange and had happened so fast; but it was an opportunity, and right now it was all Thomas had. He gazed nervously over the grey, rolling waves.

Thomas' reverie was interrupted by the arrival of Captain Harris on deck. He was thin, vanishing into his dark blue topcoat with its shining brass buttons. The points of his starched collar gleamed in the sun, and the breeze fluttered the ends of his long grey mustache. He straightened his white cap and surveyed the crew briefly before muttering, "As you were," and turning to Smythe, who came to meet him. The two men talked for a few minutes before Harris returned below decks.

Once the *Polaris* docked in Rochester that evening, Smythe ordered the crew to start loading coal for Toronto. Thomas was picking up his first sack when he noticed two men ride up in a wagon and unload two large crates. Something was stenciled on the side of each crate in large lettering, but from where Thomas stood, he was unable to read what it was.

As the men unloaded the second crate, one of them lost his grip. He leaped back with a shout just before the crate could crush his foot. Smythe bounded over, his face red. "Be careful with that, you fool," he shouted. "That's expensive cargo for an important customer, and if anything's broken it'll cost you your job!" Thomas perked up. He had never seen his uncle so angry before. What could be so important about that cargo? The man spluttered a hasty apology, but Smythe shoved some papers into his chest. "It's signed for—just go."

Every time Thomas returned to pick up a sack, he tried to get a better view of the writing on the crates, but his uncle stood guard over them and he had no desire to have that rage directed at him. Eventually, he had his chance, and saw that they were addressed to a "Dr. A. Winchester, University of Toronto." He dropped his load in surprise. Smythe glared at Thomas and he hastily snatched up the sack and scurried to the ship.

Dr. Winchester had written a book about the legends surrounding Atlantis and Mu. Thomas' teacher had given him a copy one year because he had been the most attentive student in class, and he had read it so often that it had fallen apart. In his most vivid imaginary journeys, Thomas had visited the sunken continent and explored its weed-choked cities. He studied the crates with renewed interest.

That night, Thomas tossed and turned in his berth. The thought that artifacts destined for Dr. Winchester's study could be sitting less than one hundred feet away was too much to bear. His mind raced with thoughts of barnacle-covered coins, rusted swords, and algae-encrusted statues. He had to see what was in those crates, but he didn't dare get up, as his uncle was guarding them even now. Suddenly quick footsteps came from the hold, and seconds later Smythe bustled past towards the captain's cabin muttering, "Noises."

This was his chance. Thomas crept to the hold, careful not to make a sound, and once there he grabbed an iron rod leaning against the bulkhead and studied the crates. Prying them open would make a lot of noise. There had to be another way. He looked more closely. The slats of one of the crates had split near the bottom corner. *This must be the one they dropped*, he thought.

He gently tugged one of the slats and it broke off, creating a hole just large enough for his hand. His breath caught and he reached in. His shaking fingers brushed nothing but rough straw, and his heart sank. He pushed further— there! He felt something hard, smooth and cold. Metal. He pulled it out, and by the yellow light of the single lantern looked at a golden wristband, almost as long as his forearm, inset with a mosaic of colorful stones.

Thomas paused to listen. All was quiet, aside from the pounding of his heart. He studied the wristband's images of fish, octopi, and what looked like giant worms or snakes, and a warm numbness crept up his limbs. The edges of his vision blurred, and the sea creatures seemed to begin twitching. He looked even more closely, and the creatures swam in a golden sea. A low humming seemed to come from the other side of the bulkhead, accompanied by a faint scratching sound.

The deck bucked under his feet with a loud crunch and Thomas fell to the ground. He lay there, dazed, while shouting could be heard on deck. After his head stopped spinning, he struggled to his feet and scrambled for the ladder. The scene on deck was utter chaos. Captain Harris stood in the middle barking orders, while Smythe was getting people to their feet. Only a couple of men seemed to be alert; the rest either staggered around or were lying about in a daze.

"Thomas," shouted Smythe, "Grab a lantern to check the port side. We've run aground. Check for damage."

Thomas picked up a nearby lantern and scrambled to the gunwale. As he lowered it over the side with a rope, the captain shouted to Smythe. "Did you not check the charts when you plotted our course, Mr. Smythe? Did you not take soundings?"

"Aye, sir," said Smythe. "The lakebed is many fathoms down. There should be nothing but open water."

"Sirs," said Thomas, "We're stuck in a sandbar at the bow, perhaps fifteen feet or so. I see great scratches in the hull, and," he paused, "I swear there are footprints in the mud surrounding the ship." He turned to the other two men, his eyes wide.

The captain went pale in the moonlight, and then seemed to get a hold of himself. He turned to Smythe. "Draw pistols from my cabin for the both of us, and the rifles," he said in a low voice, but loud enough for Thomas to hear. "We'll not end up like poor Sidley and the *Picton*."

Smythe went below and the captain turned to a dark-haired, stocky man. "Johnson, take some men, equip them with shovels and set to digging us out of the muck. You will be covered while you work."

Thomas stood on the port side a short while later with Smythe, rifle in hand, looking over Johnson and some other men, who were digging furiously and cursing loudly. "Uncle," he asked in a low voice after a long, tense silence, "What's this business about the *Picton*, and why are we armed?"

Smythe looked over his shoulder. The captain was standing guard on the starboard side with a red-haired man, and a gangly fellow kept watch at the bow. He leaned close to Thomas. "A few years back, in 1880 or so, there was a schooner—the *Picton*—captained by Jack Sidley. He was a great skipper; no one could run a ship as fast as him. One clear morning he was hauling coal from the States, and was eager to get underway. There were two other ships—the *Acadia* and the *Annie Minnes*—following the same course, but they couldn't get out as fast as Sidley. They were a couple miles behind, but only an hour after casting off the other two ships saw the *Picton*'s topsails coming off. They thought Sidley might be dropping sails for some reason, but then his ship just sank out of sight, in the blink of an eye. The others raced to get there, but there was nothing to be found. Nothing.

"Captain Harris knew Sidley, and had sailed with him under Marsh. But that event changed him, and he refused to sail that route again. He sold the *Acadia* and tried to forget it all, but his backers came back and convinced him to command the *Polaris*."

Thomas swallowed. "And the guns?"

"Let's just say the captain never believed that Sidley was done in by weather or bad luck," said Smythe.

"Does this have anything to do with those crates?" asked Thomas.

Smythe studied his nephew thoughtfully. "I've been with the captain for 15 years. Every so often there's a load of special cargo waiting for him. I don't know what that the stuff is, but Dr. Winchester pays the captain well to deliver it. I asked about it only once, and all the captain said was that the cargo was going to be taken to a place where it couldn't be used. And that he'd dismiss me if I ever mentioned it again." Smythe looked down to check on Johnson and the other men. "The only other thing I know is that Sidley sometimes picked up cargo like that," he added.

Thomas shivered, but his thoughts were interrupted by a shout from a bald man. "There's something out on the water!"

Smythe leaned forward to stare at the waves. "Can't see nothing," he muttered. "You, Thomas?"

Thomas squinted. Nothing seemed to disturb the surface of the lake. He turned at the sound of a splash to his right, and saw a man-shaped figure wading out of the water to the sandbar. Thomas raised his rifle. The moon emerged from behind a cloud, and the figure was revealed in the silvery light. Thomas gasped and dropped his weapon. The creature was the size of a man, with a flabby torso and spindly arms and legs. It was covered with dark green, glistening scales and its large head had a ridged crest that projected backwards.

The creature stopped and looked up with bulbous yellow eyes. It opened its mouth, revealing a row of needle-like teeth, and hissed. Thomas' heart was pounding, and a voice in his head screamed at him to pick up the rifle and shoot. His hands twitched, but he was frozen in place and unable to look away. The bald man turned at the sound and screamed. A deafening crack sounded in Thomas' ears as Smythe fired his pistol at the creature. The shot went wide.

There was a muffled shout from the captain, followed by another shot. Thomas ears rang and Smythe fired again. The coppery smell of gunpowder stung his nostrils, and smoke obscured his vision. Everything blurred and he grew dizzy. Suddenly he convulsed and blinked several times, and everything came into focus again. He bent over shakily to retrieve his gun.

"Another one to the left," shouted Smythe, and he turned to fire in that direction. Thomas' arms trembled as he raised his rifle and fired at the first beast, which was now out of the water and shambling towards a blond-haired man. He missed. The bald man, wild-eyed and shouting, jumped onto the rope ladder.

Gunfire was steady on the starboard side, punctuated by faint screams. Thomas reloaded and took aim with steadier hands. His next shot hit the beast in the head and the back of its skull exploded, raining bone shards and scraps of flesh and brain over the muddy ground. It hadn't finished flopping to the ground before more splashing alerted him to the arrival of more creatures.

"Cover them while I reload," barked Smythe. Another one of the creatures lay sprawled in a jumbled heap in the mud. Johnson slashed at the nearest monster with his shovel. The thing sprang aside and Johnson fell over. The beast leaped onto him and grabbed his throat with its webbed hands. Thomas fired, hitting it in the arm. It shuddered, but didn't stop its attack.

"Pull up the ladder! Those men are done for," shouted the captain.

A scream echoed from the bow. A broad, frog-like face had popped up next to the man on guard, who smashed it with the butt of his rifle. Another set of webbed hands reached up and grabbed one of his arms. The gangly man jerked back, but the creature's grip held, and the first monster seized the man's coat. Thomas whipped his rifle left and right to get a clear shot, but the monsters pulled the shrieking man overboard before he could fire.

Smythe called Thomas to help pull the bald man aboard. His bloodless lips moved soundlessly, and once they brought him over the side he crumpled onto the deck and curled into a ball. His eyes stared ahead, unseeing. Thomas shook the man's shoulder gently, and then more roughly, but he remained motionless. Smythe put a restraining hand on Thomas. "Leave him be," he said hoarsely, "He's gone." Thomas' vision blurred and his knees buckled, and he sank to the deck, but a pair of hands shook him roughly, jarring his eyes open once more. "Get a hold of yourself," Smythe shouted.

"Mr. Smythe," cried the captain, "The *Polaris* is lost. Go to my cabin and get the brass tube; I have already prepared a final message. Start a fire down below as well – they shall not have our cargo."

Smythe's shoulders sagged, and his grip on Thomas loosened. He looked at the younger man for a long moment. "Give me your rifle and ammunition, and take my knife. I'll do as the captain orders, but there's no sense in all of us going down. By my reckoning we're about half a mile off of Salmon Point. It's not as gentle as the Bay of Quinte, but if you swim hard you might make it."

More creatures had climbed over the bow, and the red-haired crewman next to the captain dropped his weapon and sank to his knees, weeping. The captain fired several rounds into the nearest beast, which collapsed onto the deck. Smythe ripped the rifle from Thomas' hands and put the knife in his belt before giving him a hard shove towards the gunwale. Thomas blinked and grabbed the ladder with numb hands, and swung over the side. He climbed down most of the way, but lost his grip a few feet from the bottom and landed on his backside in the mud. The gunfire was quieter down here, but there were other sounds—splashing water, hissing, and croaking. With a pounding heart he dove into the water and paddled madly. The crack of a rifle, followed by a shout, echoed in the night. He focused on the shoreline that lay somewhere to the north. *Half a mile*, he thought, *I can do this.*

Sometime later a loud crackling broke through the night air, and a reddish light appeared at the edge of his vision. He half-turned, and saw a tongue of flame erupting from the hold into the night sky. The unspeakable creatures swarmed up the sides like ants, and the gunfire became more intense. Thomas shivered in the summer night, and it was with difficulty that he tore himself away from the scene and swam as never before. There was a faint shriek, and another, and the gunfire died away.

Thomas swam on. His trembling limbs burned. The fire's red glow grew fainter as he put more distance between himself and the stricken vessel. After a loud splintering sound and a drawn-out hiss, the light went out. The moon provided enough light for him to see the jagged line of the coast ahead. He was almost there. He lengthened his strokes to eat up that distance as quickly as possible.

Suddenly, something clamped down on his ankle. Thomas kicked frantically, but failed to make contact with whatever was holding him. His assailant dragged him down. He gasped a deep breath before going under. It was too dark to see anything. Something tugged at his belt, and he flailed about. His hand closed on something cold and rough. His lower arm erupted in sharp pain, as though dozens of pins had been jabbed into it. He fought the urge to scream, and pushed his attacker with his other hand. One of his flailing feet made contact with something hard, but he was still trapped. He groped around his belt, hoping to unbuckle it, and his fingers brushed against the handle of the knife. He drew it and slashed wildly. His blade bit into something soft, and he drove the knife down again and again. The tugging stopped and he surfaced as fast as he could, filling his burning lungs with great gulps.

The rest of the journey passed like a blur. He emerged on the rocky beach and collapsed with a great sob, but forced himself to his feet again and staggered over a ridge, and kept walking. Once the lake was no longer in sight and the sounds of the surf died away, his body grew leaden and he tumbled into the long grasses and fell into a deep sleep.

§

The sun was high in the clear blue sky when Thomas awoke, soaked and shivering despite the warmth of the day. He sat up and looked around. Nothing but tall grasses and shrubbery as far as the eye could see in every direction but south, with a faint plume of smoke far to the north. A farm, perhaps. To the south the land rose into a grassy ridge, beyond which would be the rocky beach, and the lake. The wind changed direction, and brought with it the smell of seaweed. Flashes of memory from the previous night bubbled up—fire, smoke, screaming, a bald man slumped on the deck—and he shuddered.

"It can't have happened," he mumbled to himself. Somehow, he must have fallen overboard in a storm–it happened often enough. But maybe someone else was on the beach. Maybe his uncle was there. Thomas shuffled painfully to the ridge. He couldn't believe how much his arm hurt. He held it up, and saw that the sleeve of his shirt was shredded below the elbow, and caked with dried blood. His arm was swollen and red, and it looked like something with a lot of sharp, narrow teeth had bitten it. Another memory flashed into view, of being dragged underwater at night. Thomas shook his head and walked on.

Patches of drying seaweed, and the occasional dead fish, dotted the rocky beach. A flash of white in one of the clumps of rotting vegetation caught his eye. He carefully slid down the slope and poked through the stinking pile, and found a large piece of wood almost twice as long as his arm that was charred and splintered around the edges. The green paint on it had bubbled and cracked, but enough of the white paint remained to spell out "POL". His stomach churned and he grew nauseated. He fought for breath and shook his head. A shipwreck. There could still be survivors somewhere else on the beach. He had to keep moving.

His pain forgotten, he walked briskly along the shore. A metallic glint drew him to a shallow pool, where a brass tube lay. He picked it up and turned it over. Clearly etched into the side were the words, "*S.S. Polaris* – Capt. N. Harris". His hands shook as he broke the seal, and pulled out a rolled piece of paper. The writing was cramped and precise, but easy to read.

"Final Log of Captain Nathaniel E. Harris, of the *S.S. Polaris* (Toronto)

"July 18, 1884:

"I write this final entry, and as God is my witness declare it to be truth. My vessel is stricken, as I knew it would someday be, by unwholesome beings that dwell in the deeper reaches of the Great Lakes. I neither know nor care about their intentions, save that if they were to be realized humanity's doom would be sealed.

"These 'Deep Ones' have been active under all the high seas for uncounted centuries, as I learned years ago while sailing in more exotic climes, and are in all likelihood the source of many of our legends about sea monsters, mermaids, and mythological places such as Atlantis. But in recent years they have established themselves in our own inland waters. I, and certain other like-minded captains, have been recruited by a number of notable scholars, including the eminent Professor A. Winchester, of Toronto, to hinder their activities.

"The professor informed me that these creatures intend to bring even worse terrors into our lakes, for which they need certain artifacts. The professor's associates have been, at great personal cost, acquiring these items for a number of years, in various parts of the world. Captains, such as I, are entrusted to deliver them into his care, at which point he renders them unusable.

"But the Deep Ones are clever, and have learned of our activities. Each captain who undertakes this duty does so with the knowledge that they may someday meet their end. Many already have, and so, now, do I.

"May God have mercy on my crew.

Nathaniel E. Harris"

The paper fell from Thomas's nerveless fingers. He sank to his knees on the rocky shore, and gazed in horror at the grey, rolling waves.

Bedtime Story

Lisa Lepovetsky

You *first."*

"*You* first. It was your idea to go in, so go. I dare you."

Diana hesitated long enough to tug compulsively at her blonde pigtails, then strolled through the door.

I was impressed, watching her push open the grimy, pink screen door of Wisterly's Funeral Parlor in Black Oaks, Georgia, as though she had no other care in the world than to pay her respects to the poor deceased. I followed closely, trying to appear as nonchalant as possible, but grace under pressure was never my strong suit. I could feel perspiration creeping down the center of my back and into my eyes. It wasn't simply the ninety-degree heat and lack of air conditioning in the dark lobby. What if there were somebody in the place—a son or brother of the deceased? What would they say about two twelve-year-old girls in shorts and halter tops?

My mind balked as my body continued. If Aunt Betsy knew where I was, she'd have me on the next flight back to New Jersey. Never mind that my parents had just gotten back from Europe. Never mind that I still had another week of vacation left before school. I'd be at the airport before I could say, "I'm sorry."

Aunt Betsy was my mother's older sister, a childless spinster (as my mother put it) who'd moved from Pennsylvania to Georgia when the cantankerous father she'd been taking care of for most of her adult life finally died. My mother sent me down to Georgia once a year for two weeks, purportedly so that Aunt Betsy could experience the joys of parenthood. However, I knew it was just to get me out of her hair for a while. Not that I was a problem in any way—except for my rather colorful imagination—but Mom was just not cut out to be a mother. So here I was, staying with poor Aunt Betsy, trying to find interesting things to do in Black Oaks.

Diana was the daughter of Aunt Betsy's best friend, so according to the old ladies, Diana and I were supposed to become best friends, too—at least while I lived with Aunt Betsy. So, we did. I felt like Oliver Hardy to her Stan Laurel, though we never mentioned the differences in our physiques to one another. I had always been chunky and awkward, and next to Diana's svelte twigginess I felt even more so. Now she seemed to glide wraith-like along the dusty faux Persian carpet, her feet noiseless in the artificial gloom, while I listened to my own footsteps thud like jungle drums. *Or was it my heartbeat?* I wondered.

My anguish was interrupted by Diana's annoyed whisper. "Alice, get your butt on in here. The coffin's not out there. He puts them here, in the back room. Jeez."

I hesitated at the arched doorway, unable to see her. The room was dusky from the velvet drapes pulled over the windows, shutting out the late afternoon light. I didn't need to look at a corpse to get the shudders.

"C'mon," Diana hissed. "You wanted to see a stiff, didn't you? Well, here's your chance. That's it over in the corner. Go on. I'll stand guard here by the door."

I dragged my feet over, wishing I hadn't let myself be suckered into this one. Seeing a dead person had seemed more interesting out on the sunny sidewalk than back in this dim, musty room. And it was Diana's idea, anyway. She'd bragged that she did this all the time. I was beginning to doubt that.

I turned away from the narrow finger of light pointing across the floor, and was confronted by a middle-aged man, apparently asleep in a grey, oblong box. As my eyes adjusted to the dimness, I was reluctantly fascinated by the still face. I could even see the changes in coloration where the makeup ended at his receding hairline. His pale hands were crossed on his chest, and he had some kind of large ring with lots of designs and letters on it. *Maybe Masons,* I thought. My father was a Mason.

"I dare you to touch him. Double dare you," Diana whispered loudly from the shadows across the room, near the open door. I sighed. I knew I would end up touching the doughy-looking flesh, but giving in too easily would be cheating.

"Do it yourself, Di. Double-darers go first."

"I came in here first, remember? Besides, I've done it before, lots of times, no big deal. What's the matter—you chicken or something? Probably sleep with a nightlight on, too…baby-baby-baby." She waved her elbows up and down and made clucking sounds.

Diana had hit my weak spot. There was no way she could know I still slept with a nightlight, but I felt naked and embarrassed. I couldn't breathe (not to mention sleep) in a room filled with all that smothering dark when the lights were out. You just never knew what might be hiding in the shadows or under the bed. I felt my face flush, and muttered a brief prayer of thanks for the dimness of the funeral parlor.

The thought of touching the grey, painted skin was repulsive and at the same time oddly exciting. My tongue was dry, and my palms were damp. As my stomach growled, I wondered how I could be hungry in such a situation, but I was famished and I didn't want to drag the suspense out any longer than I had to. Di's razzing was just the excuse I needed to get my hand moving. I bit my lip and held my breath as I put my hand out over his face. Just as my forefinger stroked the cold, rubbery skin, Diana shrieked.

"Alice! Get out of here! It's him—he's coming. Out the back door."

I heard Di's sneakers padding down the hallway before I even turned around. *Who's coming?* My mind asked the question to the suddenly empty room. *What back door?* Disoriented, I had some trouble getting started. By the time I had built up some speed, I ran headlong into Abraham Lincoln and crashed to the floor.

At least that was what my mind saw. A gaunt giant with a black, shaggy mane and beard towered over me as I scrambled up from the filthy linoleum. The dingy chandelier glowed behind him, so I couldn't see his face. My mind wanted to run, but my body just stood and shuddered. Where could I go? I had no idea where the back door was, and the giant was between me and the front. If I just kept calm, I could make a break for it at the earliest opportunity.

"What're you doin' here, fat little girl?" Lincoln's heavily accented voice resonated so deeply, it took time for me to translate. He mistook my silence for insolence and continued, angrier: "I wouldn't want to call the po-lice, but you are trespassin' here. You'd best cooperate with me if you don't want to go to jail. Unnerstand?"

I nodded, my mind whirling. I'd been warned about men who took advantage of little girls. I was never quite sure what that meant, *take advantage*, but I knew it wasn't good, and I should avoid it at all costs. I thought it had something to do with what Aunt Betsy called "a fate worse than death." I stood in the musty hallway, surrounded by blue flocked wallpaper, wondering what fate could possibly be worse than death.

"I know what you're thinkin'," the man hissed, and I believed him instantly and completely, though I couldn't imagine how. "Now, what's your name? Where you live? C'mon, answer me."

In a burst of Technicolor, my terrified mind saw the place surrounded by flashing red and blue lights and screeching tires. Indecipherable orders were shouted through battery-powered bullhorns as I was led away in shackles by burly, faceless storm troopers with high-powered rifles.

"Harmon," I gasped. "Alice Harmon. New Jersey. Staying with my Aunt Betsy Wilson in Black Oaks. One more week. Please."

I didn't know what I was pleading for, but it felt right. I'd run out of breath, but I was prepared to tell my life's story in great detail as soon as it was asked for. He just stood looking at me—actually, I felt he was looking *into* me. I tried to appear unruffled, but my clothes were drenched with sweat, and each breath ended in a little sob. The old man suddenly, inexplicably grinned at me. His teeth had brown stains; cigarettes, I figured.

He gripped my shoulder with his huge right hand. I had to swallow a rising gorge as I noticed a red raw stump where his thumb should be. The skin was so cold, my left side seemed to numb at his touch. A sour, rancid smell drifted around us, obviously coming from him. I braced myself for the "fate worse than death."

But he merely stood over me with his head tilted forward slightly. I couldn't see his eyes in the shadow, but I knew they were still boring into me. Then he spoke again, his voice now soft and gravelly.

"You ever hear of the bogeyman, fat little Alice Harmon?"

I nodded, unsure of where this was leading. But I figured it would be good to agree with him.

"I suppose you think it's just so much bull, don'tcha?"

This one was tougher. If I said no, he might think I was arguing and get angry. But if I said yes and he believed in the bogeyman, he might think I was making fun of him and get angry. I tried to shrug with my free shoulder. He leaned down closer, and I tried not to flinch as I felt spittle on my face and he went on quietly.

"You young'uns 're all alike. You think you have all the answers, don'tcha? You find out there's no Santy Claus and no Easter bunny, and you figger ever'thin's a story. Only babies and really old folks know the truth. That's why they don't sleep at night. They know what's out there waitin' for 'em."

I thought of my nightlight and my fears of the dark, but I still said nothing.

"And me. I know it's real, the bogeyman is. It's lumpy and oozy and smells like somethin's been dead for a long time. It creeps into your room late at night, after you've fallen into a nice cozy sleep. Maybe from the closet door you forgot to close, maybe from that dark corner behind the dresser, maybe from right under your bed—it crawls out and stands drippin' and slimy by your pillow with the hunger deep in its eyes, hunger for fat little girls sleepin' all soft and sweet in their warm beds."

He was close enough for me to see his features now. His eyes were luminous, pupilless yellow globes beneath shaggy brows. Thick lips jutted from the tangled beard, flashing those brown, ragged teeth. The stench from his mouth made my eyes water as he went on, still clutching my shoulder.

"And you know what it does with them children? Rape 'em? Murder 'em in their beds? Naw. It carries 'em back a long slimy maze of tunnels filled with crawly things and stuffs 'em into a cubbyhole. It likes to let 'em wander lost in there for a while till it's ready for 'em. Feeds on their fear for a while first. That's better than any meat. Then, ever' so often, when it's hungry, it finds 'em and rips off a ear or a foot—just enough for the moment, 'cause it wants 'em alive. Fresh meat's better'n old stuff. Finally, there's nothin' left in the cubbyhole 'cept a little old puddle of…somethin'."

He was almost drooling now, flecks of white foam at the corners of his mouth, and I could hardly hear him over my own sobs. "But that ain't the worst. Them that's et has it easy, 'cause the others, the ones that know about the bogeyman, become like it, draggin' off little children, that hunger a-gnawin' at their guts. It knows which ones has that hunger in em' and lets 'em alone after they see it, to live in their own darkness above ground. There's a little of the bogeyman in us all, just waitin' for the chance to come out. And you know why the bogeyman's there at all?"

I didn't think he really expected an answer, so I shook my head, just in case.

He continued anyway. "To punish young'uns who do bad things they know they shouldn't do—like disturb the rest of the newly deceased. The bogeyman knows you and where you are, 'cause it's inside you all the time. And it'll be comin' for you, little girl, little Alice. Maybe just the day you've forgotten all about it or the day you've decided it's just so much shit from an old man's imagination. Just wait, fat little Alice, it'll come, one way or t'other. Oh, yes. Oh, yesssss. You just wait."

He leaned back his head and started to chortle—the sound of metal scraping on stone. The spell broke and I jerked my shoulder away from his grip and I ran. I didn't stop until I was safe inside Aunt Betsy's house more than a mile away. I wouldn't let her turn off any lights all night, and wouldn't say why. Diana and I avoided each other for the rest of the vacation, and though we exchanged Christmas cards for a couple of years, that afternoon at Wisterly's Funeral Parlor was never mentioned again.

§

Six years later, I was back in Black Oaks again. I had come down in November for a month-long, in-school vacation. I knew this would be the last time I stayed with Aunt Betsy; she was getting on in years, and would soon be moving into a housing unit designed for the elderly. They didn't allow teenagers to stay for extended visits.

Diana and I hadn't been in touch since the last Christmas, but Aunt Betsy begged my mother to let me stay with her. Neither of them seemed to notice my lack of enthusiasm, and I couldn't explain my reluctance to see Diana again. I needn't have worried, because she was attending a rigorous private school in nearby LaGrange that winter, and her mother explained she had no time to visit. I tried not to show my relief.

While I was in Black Oaks, Diana disappeared. After a week's search, her body was found in the dense pine woods between LaGrange and Black Oaks. Three days before I was scheduled to go home, I found myself dragged to her funeral by Aunt Betsy ("It would mean so much to her poor, wretched mother, dear.")

The weather was bleak and raw that day, with sleet ticking on the windows and I couldn't seem to get warm, from the moment I got out of bed. Everything felt unreal, disconnected, and I decided I was coming down with the flu. But to please Aunt Betsy, I went to the funeral with her. The service was held in the dusty back room of Wisterly's Funeral Parlor, where I had touched the clammy cheek of an unidentified corpse six years before. Standing by the closed black casket and pointing to Diana's mother across the room, Aunt Betsy took my hand and twittered in my ear.

"The poor woman is a wreck. They don't even know why Diana was in the woods—a young girl, alone out there. Maybe there was a boyfriend, but nobody seems to know of anyone she was seeing. They found her body—or what was left of it—in the mouth of a big old sewer pipe. She must have been wandering lost for days before she died of exposure, which is odd, because she knew these woods so well. Anyway, it seems the animals got her. The body was chewed and she'd lost her...oh, dear, I'm so sorry, Alice. I shouldn't be telling you this. You look awful."

As she clucked her tongue at herself, my stomach churned. A memory gnawed its way through my defenses, and I had a glimpse of something terrible, something that leered at me and licked its lips when Aunt Betsy mentioned the big sewer pipe, but I forced it back with a violent effort of will. I felt disgust and horror at the image of poor Diana out there, her body chewed and mangled, and I felt something else...

Aunt Betsy grabbed my arm and pulled me around. "Alice," she said, "I don't think you've ever met the owner of the funeral home, Mr. Wisterly. He's been in charge of all Black Oaks funerals for the last twenty-five years, single-handedly. Mr. Wisterly, meet my niece, Alice."

My breath caught in my chest, and I bit my tongue. There was no escaping. I held out my hand, dreading the sight of that big, hairy, paw gripping mine. I saw before me Di's bloody blond pigtails dangling from the sewer pipe and heard her whimpers as she waited to be devoured. I knew who had killed poor Diana and eaten her warm flesh in the woods, and I trembled violently at Mr. Wisterly's cold touch and the smooth stump of this missing thumb rubbing obscenely against my palm.

Aunt Betsy blamed my breakdown on grief and physical exhaustion. Mom was very understanding when I insisted on sleeping with the lights on for my next years at home. All she knew was that they kept the nightmares away. And the screams in the night. She didn't know what else they keep away.

Would Mom and Aunt Betsy have been so understanding if I'd told them about the other feeling I had that day at Diana's funeral? The feeling that convinced me there were, as Aunt Betsy had suggested, "things worse than death?" The feeling of a gnawing, insatiable hunger deep inside as I remembered poor Di's mangled body and licked my lips?

I still sleep with the lights on.

Lucky Clover

Kelly A. Harmon

ean shook the accordion pleats out of the road map and **S**tried to find out how lost they were. Unfolding the map between the window and the gear stick proved nearly impossible with his seat pushed so far forward, though it couldn't be helped. Mick's boxes and bags, most piled high on the full-sized cooler in the back seat, filled the small hatchback to the top of the sagging headliner. The top-left corner of the map flapping in the gale-force wind blowing through Mick's wide-open window didn't help matters.

"Any idea where we are?" Mick asked before Sean could even get the map spread out. Mick took another drag off his cigarette, turned up the Ramones on his buzzing speakers, and pushed the accelerator to the floor. The car leapt forward in a burst of speed, then settled into a noisy rumble down the highway.

"Maryland," Sean answered, head buried in the map. He traced a blue line south to north across the center fold. That was Mick's problem: the road pitched north on the map, but Interstate 70 ran east to west. Thanks to Mick, they'd lost at least two hours.

"Smart ass," Mick said. "We've been in Maryland for almost an hour. Even I figured that out." He sucked hard on the cigarette, smoking it down to the filter, and then flicked it out the window. "This is the last time I'm taking you on a road trip," he said, shaking his head. "Can't take you anywhere without getting us lost."

Sean knew better than to argue. He already regretted having agreed to make this trip. He was tired of taking the blame for all that had gone wrong. And tired of shelling out dough for everything, especially gasoline, since Mick felt he'd done his part by driving. *At least Mick bought his own cigarettes*, Sean thought. Mick's two-to-three packs a day would have bankrupted him. No wonder Mick didn't have the cash to pay for anything else.

"We're not lost," Sean said, thinking, *but if you could read a frikkin' map, we'd be a lot further down the road.* "Take exit 53 South when you come to it." Sean looked up to see the ramp for exit 53 pass by.

"Dammit!" Mick said, pulling hard to the right and onto the shoulder, almost hitting the guardrail. Horns blared all around like the trumpets of Jericho. Tires squealed behind them as a car eked by their fender. The driver flipped Mick the finger as he roared past them on the left. Mick stomped hard on the brakes, shaking his fist at the other driver.

Sean pitched forward, his hands smashing into the dashboard, crumbling the map. He choked as the seat belt caught him on the side of his neck. The car stopped with a lurch, snapping Sean back against his seat.

"Jesus, Mick, calm down, will you? You nearly strangled me."

"I'd have bloodied your nose if you hadn't been wearing the belt," Mick said, laughing. "Aren't you glad I made you wear it?"

"And you'd be laughing then, too, you moron..." Sean shook his wrists, willed the tingling to stop. "You're going to get us killed. Quit driving like a maniac."

Mick shoved the gear stick into reverse and turned around in his seat, left hand on the wheel. With his right hand, he pushed Sean's duffle out of his field of vision and started backing up.

"What are you doing?"

"Going back to take the turn we missed, thanks to you." Mick jammed his foot down on the accelerator and reversed up the soft shoulder.

"Don't be a jerk, Mick. Just play the clover."

"Take the wrong ramp twice over just to get back on this road? No way. Reversing it is faster." He punched the accelerator again and the car leapt backward. Rocks and debris kicked up from under the front tires and a plume of dirt rose up and dusted the hood of the car.

"And illegal," Sean said. "Not to mention dangerous." He folded the map in half, then half again, and shoved it into the door panel pocket. "Play the clover, Mick."

"No way," Mick said, shaking his head, glowing ember on his cigarette emphasizing each jerk of his neck. "No cop, no stop." The car rumbled backward up the shoulder, dipping to the right once as it swagged off the tar-and-chip pavement and onto rutted dirt before Mick corrected.

Sean crossed his arms on his chest. "I'm not paying the fine this time if you get another ticket," Sean said. "Consider it lucky, Mick, to have to drive around a clover."

The car lurched to a sudden stop as Mick slammed on the brakes again, swearing under his breath while Joey Ramone screamed that he wanted to be sedated. Sean thought he wouldn't mind a little of that himself. This road trip wasn't going at all like they'd planned. He didn't know how much more of Mick's attitude he could take.

"You and your damned Irish superstition," Mick said.

"You ought to pay attention to it, being of Irish-descent yourself."

Mick stared straight ahead, his face hard as fossilized limestone from County Clare. He said, "Faith, hope, or love?"

"It's a four-leave clover, Mick, don't forget *luck*. Make a wish on your way around."

Mick shook another Camel out of the soft pack and pulled it out with his lips. He pushed the cigarette lighter in, and without even looking, merged back into the westbound traffic accompanied by the sound of horns.

Sean grabbed the dashboard and screamed at Mick, "Are you trying to get us killed?

The lighter clicked. Mick leaned forward and grabbed it, moving the glistering red cylinder to his face. He angled the cigarette down with his teeth and pressed the tip of it against the glowing brand. The sweet scent of fresh-lit tobacco filled the car. Mick filled his lungs and pushed the lighter back into place. He exhaled slowly, blowing the smoke in Sean's face.

"You're an ass," Mick said. "You know that?" He leaned forward and cranked the volume knob all the way to the right.

"Me?" Sean had to shout to be heard over the music. "I'm an ass because I don't want to get killed? Or, because I don't want to do anything illegal?" He turned to face the back of the car and waved a pointed finger. "Maybe I'm an ass because I don't want to piss off the guy behind us in case he has a gun?"

"Right on all counts," Mick said. He took another drag off the cigarette and blew more smoke in Sean's direction. "It would have been so much easier to back up—would've been on our way by now. Instead, we've got to play the cloverleaf round and round to get back where we started. What a waste of time." Mick laid on the horn as a driver merging onto the highway cut him off. "Asshole!" he yelled.

He punched the accelerator turning into the curve of the southbound exit ramp. Sean grabbed the armrest on the door. His left hand was pressed against the dash, bracing him into the seat, wrist white with the pressure.

"Get your hand off the dash," Mick said, smashing his fist against Sean's splayed one.

"Dammit," Sean said, pulling his hand back.

"I am *not* going to get us killed," Mick said, pulling the car back onto the highway. He sucked on his Camel, then, with an expert hand, guided the cigarette into the stream of air rushing by outside the rolled-down window, close enough to whip the ash off, but far enough away from the stream not to rip out the cherry. He returned it to his mouth, letting a little saliva stick it to his bottom lip. "This is the last trip we're taking together," he said to Sean. "After this, I'm through with you."

Sean laughed. "You think that's some kind of punishment? Depriving me of your sainted company? What a joke. You're damned right this is the last trip we're taking together. Just get me home in one piece so we can go our separate ways. The last thing we need is a frikkin' accident that smears us together for eternity. You know? Sometimes..." Sean pressed his lips together.

Mick punched the accelerator again, slamming Sean back against the seat. He laughed, then did it again. "Sometimes, what?"

"Sometimes..." Sean grabbed the dashboard again. "Slow down around the curve. You are so going to get us killed."

Mick laughed and pushed the accelerator to the floor around the final ramp of the clover. The Ford's tires squealed. Joey Ramone yelled right along with them.

Sean said, "You know, you're a good friend and all that, but sometimes you're so...I wish..." He shook his head, knowing what he said wouldn't make a difference to Mick. "You're so blind. You can't see..."

The turn faced them into the setting sun.

Blinding light blazed in through the windshield. Mick screamed, "I can't see!" and stomped on the brakes. The car careened around the final bend of the clover loop, tires hiccupping across pavement as the rushing forward momentum pushed the car in a straight line. They hit the short curb at the end of the pavement and jumped off the road, shearing through the guardrail. The Ford Escort turned over and over into oncoming traffic.

§

"You still feel guilt over Mick's death," the doctor said, pulling the visitor chair closer to the Sean's hospital bed. He propped a notebook on his knee and pulled out a mechanical pencil.

"I could have done more," Sean said, picking at the hospital-white blanket. "I could have tried harder to stop him."

"You said he was driving recklessly," the doctor said, "what could you have done? Grabbed the wheel? Put your foot over top his on the brake pedal?"

Sean sat silent for several moments. The doctor ceased writing in his tablet and waited.

"I wished him dead."

"Your best friend?" the doctor said, raising his eyebrows.

"Ever since fifth grade," Sean said, "when Mr. Baker gave us detention together."

"There's nothing like shared misery to bond friendships," the doctor said. "But it was more than that."

Sean nodded his head. "Class projects, sleep-overs." He laughed. "Sock fights." He lifted a hand to mimic a throw, then winced at the pain in his ribs.

"But you grew out of that."

"Mostly," Sean said with smirk. "Got our first jobs together at Jack-in-the-box. And got fired from there together, too. Girl chasing on Friday nights. Summer vacations." He sobered. "He saved my life once, at the pool. I dove in and pushed off the bottom...but my foot went through the filter grate at the bottom. He jumped in and busted the grate, loosed it from my ankle. Then, he dragged me to the surface 'cos I didn't have the energy to swim."

He hadn't told the doctor that part before. The doctor looked at him with an expectant expression on his face, waiting for Sean to speak.

Sean just closed his eyes and leaned back against the pillows. He couldn't say more. He was tired, needed to sleep.

"Well," the doctor said, laying down his pencil. "It seems we've come to the heart of it. It's not the guilt of Mick's death that's causing you grief, it's betrayal: he saved your life once, and you feel as though you've taken his."

Sean whispered, "What should I do?"

Was he dreaming, or did he hear the doctor say, "Wish him back." before sleep claimed him?

§

Bright sunlight glared off row after row of monuments in the large Catholic graveyard. Sean squinted his eyes, feeling the skin pull taught on the right side of his face where black stitches pulled the ruined skin together. He laid a bruised hand atop the carved lamb on Mick's tombstone.

"This wasn't supposed to happen," Sean said. We were supposed to part ways, like a divorce. Irreconcilable differences." He swallowed hard.

He let go of the lamb, limped backward to read the writing on the tombstone.

Michael Casey Dunn
b. July 17, 1991 - d. September 23, 2009.
Death is not a foe, but an inevitable adventure.

The sharp cuts of the chiseled epitaph created deep shadows on the face of the stone in the harsh glare of the afternoon sun. No comfort in that epitaph; Mick's father probably chose it. He'd remarked on more than one occasion that their road trips would get them into trouble. This kind of trouble he probably hadn't considered.

Sean wiped his eyes, careful not to touch his broken nose.

"I didn't even get a chance to say goodbye," Sean said. "They told me you died on impact—no pain. I hope so, buddy, 'cos I can tell you from experience that pain sucks.

"I hope your cloud is comfortable. It's just one more thing to pin on me if it's not. That's all I've been thinking about: you condemning me for this. Ever since they told me you were dead, it's played through my mind like a movie on repeat. That, and the fact that I'll never see your ugly mug again. I don't know if I can take that."

He took a deep breath, limped forward to rest his hand on top of Mick's tombstone. "I've been giving this a lot of thought—you may be partly right. The accident is sort of my fault." Sean brushed aside a speck of dirt. "I mean, you were driving way too fast, but I did make the wish, though I didn't realize it for what it was at the time. It all comes down to the clover, Mick. Four-leaf clovers can make wishes come true. I'll do what I can to make it right."

Sean limped to his car and got in.

§

He drove all night and half the next morning until he got to exit 53 on Maryland I-70. He slid a newly-purchased *Best of the Ramones* recording into the CD player and took the westbound loop of the clover. He avoided looking at the skid marks, the newly replaced guardrail the state had made Mick's parents pay for and said, "I wish Mick were alive."

He popped the Ramones out of the tape deck and finished driving the loop in dead silence, all the way around back to eastbound exit 53.

He drove the clover again, and then a third time, waiting for Mick to appear.

Sean made fists of his hands and pounded them on the steering wheel. He shouted, "What am I doing wrong?"

A thought niggled in the back of his mind: *did you really expect Mick to appear like magic?*

He banished it as quickly as it came.

Maybe I'm wishing for too much, he thought. Perhaps I need to start small...or, maybe the conditions aren't right.

He started the Ramones CD again, turned it up loud like Mick used to like it. Joey screamed for sedation as the car approached the west bound Exit 53 ramp. Sean accelerated into the turn, then punched off the stereo, just as Mick had done before Sean made the wish.

The blaze of the setting sun burned his eyes as he spoke the words aloud: "I wish Mick weren't dead and buried in his grave."

The glare in his eyes cheered him. The sun had been blinding the day Mick had died. The glare now was another part of recreating the circumstances of the first wish: every little bit helped, he thought.

The temperature in the car dropped ten degrees. A shiver ran up his spine, the hair on the back of his neck standing on end. His hands started shaking on the wheel. Yet, there was no sign of Mick.

He drove the clover circuit twice more, waiting, but nothing happened. And the minor elation he felt faded faster than the dipping sun.

Sean took a deep breath through his mouth, exhaled with an audible sigh as he weighed his options. He could continue, keep trying with different variations on the wish. Or he could cut his losses and return home now.

The latter option appealed to him. He was tired. He was hungry. And he was disappointed. But he had to give it one more shot.

Mick had been smoking, Sean remembered. But he'd ditched the cigarette just before the accident occurred. Sean lit up a Camel and started the CD again, turning it up loud. He sucked hard on the cigarette, blew smoke in the direction of the passenger seat, then laid his arm on the edge of the window like Mick had, letting the wind blow the ash off the cherry.

He tossed the Camel out the window just as he drove the car onto the east bound ramp and punched the stereo knob to off just where the clover's turn was the sharpest.

"I wish Mick were alive," he said, sticking with the simplest version of the wish. The last brilliant rays of the setting sun seared his eyes as he crossed the top of the curve.

He finished up the loop and there was no sign of Mick. He felt no different, felt no sense of any accomplishment. Nothing indicated that anything of import had occurred.

What had he been thinking? Clovers. Wishes. Mick had just

lost control. His wish hadn't caused anything and another wish couldn't undo it. Stupid, lunatic idea anyway.

Sean exited the clover and headed for home.

§

Thursday night used to be freak night at the used record shop, Sean thought. Whatever happened to the denim and leather crowd? He missed hanging out.

Rap music blasted from the speakers placed at the end of each aisle, and the teen-star wannabees gyrated to the pounding bass beat stolen from some 80's top-10 song he couldn't remember the name of. *No originality*, he thought.

Sean tuned it out, wishing the store would play something more to his taste. He plucked a Smithereens CD off the shelf and turned it over to review the cover art.

A figure in the corner of the cover art caught his attention.

Mick? Impossible.

He dropped the CD onto the shelf as if it had burned him. Then, looking up, he saw Mick hurry down the aisle on the other side of the CD bins.

"Mick!" he called, but he Mick continued down the aisle as if he hadn't heard.

Sean hurried down the aisle, bum leg preventing him from sprinting around the corner after Mick.

Mick? Or a guy that looked a lot like Mick?

He'd missed the funeral, his mother said, so doped from pain from his shattered left leg that he couldn't leave the hospital. Five days of his life gone that he'd never get back.

Getting past Mick's death had been mighty hard when he had no tangible rituals to prove Mick had actually died. A tombstone and fresh-turned earth didn't feel real enough.

Mick's parents had given Mick's CD collection to him. Big deal. Maybe Mick just lightened his load and moved away. Having Mick's records didn't mean he was really dead.

Sean paused at the end of the row and looked left, then right.

Where did Mick go? Sean could swear he saw him go this way. He searched down a few more aisles.

Sean left the store and headed for his car, pulling his cellphone from his pocket and hitting the speed dial for Mick. After a moment, he heard the three-tone intro and the monotone announcement that the number had been disconnected.

§

Sean pulled into his driveway and pushed the gearshift into park. The car ran by automatic transmission; no more shifting his own gears, thanks to Mick. He struggled with the parking brake, his left leg shaking with the effort of lifting it high enough to press the pedal.

He laid his head back and closed his eyes, listening to the Smithereens blast out of the speakers. New speakers, no buzz, unlike Mick's old rattletrap. Sean pounded his good thigh with a clenched fist. When would his mind stop making the comparisons? All roads led to Mick, it seemed.

He clicked off the radio, threw open the door and pushed himself up from the seat. No more low-riding cars either, he thought, struggling to stand on his weak leg. Eighteen years old and half broken, like an old man.

At least he was alive.

Sean looked up at the front porch and his heart began a wild beat, thumping in his chest like a fist against his breastbone.

Mick sat on the front steps of the house, smoking a cigarette.

Sean felt himself trembling. The short walk across the lawn took him longer than usual. He stopped in front of Mick. Dried blood streaked his blond hair brown and splattered over his left shoulder, nearly obliterating the Ramones logo on his t-shirt. Did he smell a tinge of decay beneath the acrid scent of cigarettes?

Sean tried to keep the quaver from his voice. "Mick, what are you doing here? You look like hell." The purple bruise straddling Mick's forehead appeared vivid, almost fresh, while his own injuries were fading. "That's quite a shiner you've got there. Who'd you piss off this time?"

"I'm here to collect." Mick sucked on the end of the cigarette, the tip burning bright scarlet in the shade of the porch awning.

"Collect what?" Sean limped closer, pocketed his keys. "They told me you were dead."

Mick's smiled. "Do I look dead? Just a little banged up." He pointed at Sean with the cigarette. "That was some stunt you pulled, driving us into the sun like that."

"You're not blaming the accident on me."

"But I am, Sean," Mick said, putting the Camel to his lips.

"You were driving too fast."

"You forced me to take the ramp, then you wished me blind. Of course the accident was all your fault."

Sean felt anger building. Lately, he'd been making peace with the idea that he'd lost Mick, and now he shows up here out of the blue.

Sean felt a twinge of pain behind his forehead. He lifted his right hand and rubbed, sliding three fingers up the center and down the bridge of his nose.

He ought to be glad Mick is alive, not angry that he'd wasted so much time trying to get over him. Worse, that he'd spent so much time trying to get past the guilt of being glad Mick was dead and the guilt of feeling grateful that Mick's death proved a cleaner break than having to end a friendship they'd had since grade school.

Sean shook his head. Released the breath he realized he'd been holding. "Get lost, Mick. I'm not up for this right now."

Mick stood, took a last drag from the cigarette and tossed the butt at Sean's feet. Sean stomped it out, then struggled up the steps to the porch.

"Sure thing," Mick said, "but don't get used to the idea. I'll be back."

Sean opened the door and took a step into the house, then turned to watch Mick go. But Mick had vanished. Sean stepped out onto the porch to look up and down the street, but Mick was nowhere to be seen.

In the aftermath of Mick's departure, silence pervaded the neighborhood. No sound of birds, no shushing of leaves in the breeze, no road noise coming off Holabird Avenue.

A slow dread chilled him, filling the ache around his heart with fear. He stepped into the house and locked the door.

§

A squeak from the open window in his bedroom woke Sean. A shiver ran down his spine.

He scanned the room, his eyes looking for anything out of the ordinary, and then he saw the red-hot glow of a cigarette hovering over the chair near his desk.

In the moments it took for his eyes to adjust, Sean watched Mick materialize out of the darkness, the macabre lips of his Cheshire grin clasping the lit cigarette.

"What are you doing here?" Sean said.

"Making sure I collect," Mick said. "I told you I intend to."

"I don't see how your being here at—" Sean glanced at the digital clock, "three-twenty-two in the morning is aiding your cause. And put out that cigarette. The last think I need is for my mother to smell it in the room in the morning."

Mick grinned. "She'll never know. Now, about what you owe me."

"But it's your own fault the accident happened. Any poor choice of words on my part doesn't make me the bad guy."

Mick stood and walked toward the open window. Faint moonlight illuminated a semi-circle patch of carpet just beyond the drapes. He took one last drag on the cigarette and flicked it outside then knelt to examine a box sitting in the puddle of a moonbeam.

"What are you doing with all my CDs?" he asked Sean.

"Your mom gave them to me," Sean said. "They were here when I got out of the hospital."

"You didn't give them back?" Mick asked. He picked up a Black Flag CD. "I could never live without my music."

"Couldn't return them," Sean said. "Your folks moved away before I had the chance."

Mick shook his head, pulled another cigarette from the soft pack in his T-shirt's breast pocket and lit up. "You're just racking up debt, Sean."

"I still don't know how you expect me to pay."

"You'll figure it out," Mick said. "You always were the smarter of us two."

He rose and the Black Flag CD toppled back into the box on the floor. He put one foot up on the sill and grasped the window frame in his hands and turned to face Sean still lying in bed.

Outlined in the moonlight, Sean could see the livid bruise, the blood-stained clothing Mick still wore.

"Dude," Sean said, sitting up, "have you got a place to stay? You need to clean up."

"Don't worry about that," Mick said, running a hand across the bloodstain on his chest. "Don't worry about me. Just remember you have to figure out a way to make us square."

"But—"

"Until next time," Mick said, crawling out the window to the waiting oak.

Sean heard a step on the branch, the rustle of leaves as Mick departed, then he sprang out of bed and bent his head through the open window. He saw nothing, heard nothing. Mick had vanished.

Sean shivered and pulled back into the room, closed the window and crawled back into bed, yanking the covers up over his shoulders. He was nearly asleep when he had a thought: *he hoped his mother wouldn't smell the smoke from Mick's cigarettes.*

Like a jolt of caffeine Sean was wide awake. Mick was right when he said his cigarette smoke wouldn't matter.

Sean never smelled the cigarette himself, didn't detect any odor of it right now. The room smelled as fresh as if his mom had just changed the sheets. He lay there, shaking, wide awake until the sun came up and sleep finally claimed him. His last thought was that Mick said he would pay...and he was. He was paying. The question was, how long would Mick make him pay?

§

He woke to Joey Ramone singing about Sheena the punk rocker. It came from outside, still, the music blared so loud it rattled the window of his bedroom. Why wasn't his mother yelling?

He got out of bed, went to the window and opened it. The music roiled out of the speakers of his car. He didn't know they could play so loud.

Dammit. Any more of that and his brand-new sub-woofers would buzz like Mick's. All four windows gaped open and he could just barely discern a stream of smoke spilling out the passenger window.

Who sat in his car? As if he didn't know.

Sean dressed as fast as he could and limped down the stairs. His mother read the newspaper at the kitchen table, a cup of coffee at her elbow.

"Isn't the music bothering you?" he asked.

"What music?" she said, not looking up from the editorial page of *The Sun*. "Better close the windows of your car," she added, reaching for her coffee. "It looks like rain."

Sean opened the screen door and stepped out on the porch just as it began to pour.

Great, he thought, buzzing speakers and wet upholstery: a winning combination. Add in the ghost of Mick Past and he'd hit the trifecta.

He hurried to the car, clambering into the driver's seat as fast as he could.

"Go. Away," he said to Mick, shoving the key into the ignition and starting the car. He lowered the volume on the radio and closed all the windows.

Mick still wore the clothes he'd been killed in. The bruises and bloody wound on his face glowed in contrast to the pallid whiteness of his dead flesh. He curled a greying lip in a facsimile of smile.

"Not until you pay," he said. "You owe me." He took a last drag on his cigarette and flicked it out the window.

"I've paid," Sean said. "I've paid with my leg, I've paid with my face, I've paid with my peace of mind." He put the car in reverse and backed out of the driveway. Raindrops tattered on the window to the Ramones throbbing beat.

"Where are we going?" Mick asked.

"*I'm* going out for a drive," Sean said. "You, I hope, are going to hell."

"No such luck," Mick said, lighting up another cigarette. "I'm here to stay. At least until you pay up."

Sean could smell his own tang—the fear of sitting in an enclosed space with a dead friend—and the faint, pungent odor of long-extinguished butts in the ashtray. Was Mick in the car with him, or wasn't he? Had he been in the house last week, or not?

Sean hadn't known where he was driving to until that minute.

He made the decision in the split-second he realized he honestly didn't know what reality was. He signaled left and pulled into the turn lane for Interstate 95. *Exit 53 here we come,* he thought.

§

Pouring rain sluiced over the windshield wipers making everything harder to see.

Sean was driving fast. Faster than he usually drove. Fast like Mick. He sucked hard on the Camel, filling the car with smoke. His eyes burned. The east-bound exit 53 ramp loomed in the distance, but it was approaching fast. The Ramones blasted through the speakers.

Mick's hands were on the dashboard, his face white in the dim glow of the dash lights. "What are you doing, man?"

"Fixing something," Sean said, raising a shaking hand to his brow to brush the hair from his eyes. "I'm gonna wish you back to hell."

"Be careful what you wish for," Mick said. "You wish me to hell and you'll find yourself there with me."

Sean accelerated. "I just want peace, Mick."

"That wish won't buy it," Mick said, relaxing back against the seat. "You send me to hell, and you'll regret it every day for the rest of your life, and then some."

"What do you want, Mick?"

Mick took a long drag off his cigarette, tapped the ash off into the ashtray and pursed his lips. After a moment, he said, "Admit it's your fault I'm dead."

Sean shook his head. "You always were a jerk, Mick."

Mick just smiled.

"Saying the accident was my fault and believing it are two different things."

"Sure," Mick said. "But admitting it puts you on the road to redemption, so to speak."

"Right," Sean said. "If I admit I killed you, it will make me feel better."

"No, Mick said," stubbing out the cigarette in the ashtray. "If you admit you killed me, you'll recognize that you owe me. You fouled up, you pay up. Them's the rules."

"And where does that get us?" Sean said. He put his own Camel to his lips and drew deep, exhaling while Mick spoke.

"Once you realize it's your fault, you have no choice but to use the last wish for me...not yourself."

Sean gave him an incredulous stare. "You want me to own up to killing you, then waste my peace of mind on an apparition? You always were selfish."

Mick laughed. "That never seemed to bother you before." He winked at Sean, then pulled another Camel from the soft-pack with his teeth.

Sean started laughing, then shaking his head.

Exit 53 approached. Sean signaled right, then eased the speeding car onto the ramp.

He pressed the button on the driver's door to lower the driver's window, then took a long draw on his cigarette and tossed it out the window. He turned off the radio with a jab of his finger, and turned his head to face Mick, his countenance solemn.

Mick looked scared. "Do the right thing, Dude," he said.

"I will," Sean said, looking Mick right in the eyes, "Wishing you dead will bring me the peace I covet."

He accelerated into the turn and punched the brakes hard.

"No!" yelled Mick, his face showing astonishment.

At almost the last second, Sean said, smiling, "I wish you peace, Mick."

Tires squealed on the wet pavement, the front tires hit the curve first, sending the car end over end through the guardrail and down the embankment into oncoming traffic.

It was worth it, thought Sean, *just to see that look on Mick's face.* And then he heard, "I wish you life," just before the car settled to a stop in the middle of an intersection.

A speeding car, horn blaring, skidded across the street, shearing the bumper off Sean's car, spinning it around on the wet surface. Before he passed out, Sean thought he heard the click of a lighter and the crumple of a cellophane wrapper hitting the floor. The aroma of fresh-lit tobacco assailed him, a red spot danced across his vision, and then it was gone.

Snowbroth

Vonnie Winslow Crist

*T*he moon sliced the sky like a sickle as Clark scooped a pail full of early snow from a nearby rise in the ground. Next, he set the pail on a flat rock near his campfire. After that, he reached inside his knapsack for two packets of dehydrated soup, a jar of peanut butter, box of crackers, mug, spoon, fork, and knife. Finally, he said a quick prayer for the forgotten dead who might sleep uneasy beneath his campsite.

If Muriel had insisted on coming, she would never have allowed him to pitch his tent next to the churchyard. She'd have been complaining about the heathens and ne'er-do-wells buried underfoot in this unsanctified ground. With arms crossed, she would have pointed out the blessed grave sites were located inside the churchyard fence, leaving this clearing at the edge of the treeline for the unidentified or impoverished dead. Of course, that is only one of the things she'd have found to complain about.

Even in the woods, Muriel insisted on food nicely presented and a well-groomed abode. Under her watchful eyes, he would have been placing tidy packets of foil-wrapped chicken, potatoes, and assorted veggies among the coals while she set a folding table with tablecloth, plates, napkins, and matching utensils. A two-person tent would not have been enough. There would be a big pop-up tent with an awning and bug net—even in winter, blow-up mattresses under the sleeping bags, folding camp stools, battery operated lanterns, and a boatload of other odds and ends to make her camping experience more civilized.

And civilized was just what Clark did not want to be on this camping trip. For a few hours, he wanted to remember what camping, and life, had been like before Muriel. He needed to find himself again.

Suddenly, he stopped opening the cracker box, tilted his head, then reached into his boot and slipped out a hunting knife. It had been years since he camped out in the open, alone, but his rusty wilderness skills awoke at the sound of soft footfalls in the nearby woods. Without looking, he knew someone approached his campsite.

A young man, hardly more than a boy, appeared at the edge of the clearing. Dressed in a raggedy plaid shirt and jeans, the teen was hatless and barefoot.

Jeeze, that kid is under-dressed. He has got to be freezing, he thought. Out loud, Clark said, "Whatcha doing out here without a coat and shoes?"

The boy stared at the crackling campfire, but failed to respond.

He is so far gone, he can't talk anymore. I have got to help. Clark stood, motioned for the young man to come closer. "Get yourself over next to the fire and warm up. I'm melting some snow for soup and coffee. Nothing fancy, but I have plenty to share."

Raising his eyes from the flames to Clark's face, the kid nodded, then shuffled over.

Though he didn't say anything to the boy about the smell, Clark coughed and covered his nose with his hand. *Lordy, the kid needed a good scrubbing, haircut, and some clean clothes.* Silently cursing himself for being such a soft touch, Clark reached behind the log he was sitting on and pulled an extra sweater, pair of socks, and his tennis shoes out of his pack. He could imagine Muriel screeching at him, telling him not to give away his things to a druggie—for she would certainly think the worse of the pitiful teen in front of him. But the old Clark who made up his own mind before Muriel arrived on the scene would have chosen kindness.

"You are gonna catch your death in this weather without more on than a shirt and pants," he said. Suppressing thoughts of his wife from his mind, he tossed the boy the clothes. The clothing hit the kid in the chest, then fell to the ground. Figuring the boy must be slow-witted or something, he climbed to his feet, walked over, picked up the sweater, socks, and shoes, and held them out.

Looking first at the proffered clothing, then at Clark, and then at the clothing again, the kid finally reached up and took the stuff. Moving in a slow, deliberate manner, the boy pulled the sweater on, sat on a log by the fire, and slipped his feet into the socks.

"What's your name?" Clark tried to be friendly without prying into the boy's life. He figured the kid was probably a runaway, and suspicious of strangers with lots of questions.

Before the teen could answer, a scrawny dog wandered out of the woods. It lowered its tail, hesitated a few seconds, then looked pitifully at Clark.

Muriel would have insisted he chase the stray away. In fact, she'd have demanded he tell the runaway boy to leave, too. But she wasn't here, so he intended to do what was right, not what his wife demanded of him. In fact, when he went home tomorrow or the next day or, what the heck, the day after that, he was going to stand up to Muriel about a lot of things. This camping trip was about finding Clark again, and maybe that's just what was happening. At least, he hoped so.

"It's okay, girl. I've got half a sandwich in here somewhere," Clark said as he reached next to his right leg, pulled open a garbage bag, and began to sift through the food he had discarded. Sure enough, there was a slightly mangled ham and cheese sandwich in the bag. He pulled it out, tore the bread, meat, and cheese into chunks, got up, walked a few steps into the darkness, and placed them on the ground about six feet from the fire.

The dog crept over to the food like she expected to be beaten at any minute. When she got close enough to eat the scraps, she glanced at his face. His heart melted; the poor creature's rib bones stuck out and her eyes were filmy. She was likely near blind.

"I'd like to meet the fellow who treated you so bad. Teach him a lesson, I would," he said. But even as he spoke, he speculated that

Muriel would have no problem throwing rocks at the dog to scare it off. She'd just want the creature gone.

Momentarily lost in thought, he flinched as the teenager, now shod and wearing a sweater, touched his arm, then pointed at the metal pail at Clark's feet. Not only had the snow melted, but the liquid was simmering.

Clark smiled at the kid.

"All righty!" He said as he tossed a couple more handfuls of snow into the pail for good measure. Now that he needed soup for two, not to mention leftovers for the dog, he had to increase the amount of snowbroth he was making.

After he scooped one last fistful of snow into the soup pot, he emptied several cup-sized dried chicken noodle soup packets into the pail. Then, he did a quick search through his knapsack looking for more ingredients. He located two more instant soup packets and a can of concentrated vegetable, barley, and beef soup. It didn't matter to him that he was mixing soup flavors. He doubted it mattered to the starving dog and scrawny kid. But it sure would have mattered to Muriel. Good grief, she'd have thrown a hissy fit at the thought of mixing soups.

Squelching thoughts of his mean-spirited wife, he tore open the soup packets and popped the lid on the soup can and emptied their contents into the simmering snowbroth. "That ought to do it," he said. Raising up his mug and the empty soup can, he added, "And now we have a soup mug for you, too."

The boy lifted his hand and gave a slow-motion thumbs up.

"Let's see about that coffee. Let me go over to my truck and get some more gear. I'm thinking I have a tin pot and two old thermos cups stowed in there we can use."

He strode over to his pickup, yanked open the passenger's side door, and rummaged through a canvas dufflebag. The black truck looked much like the one his Uncle Wink had driven ten years ago when he and his buddy, Gilbert, took Clark on a camping trip in these very woods.

Of course, Wink wasn't his uncle's real name. It was Winston, and he was Clark's Aunt Jetty's second husband. After only a year of marriage, Aunt Jetty had divorced Wink. He'd never been told the details, Clark just knew Wink was uninvited to every family event from then on. Nowadays, Wink lived alone in a cabin on the hillside above this church. Which was why, Clark suspected, thoughts of Uncle Wink, Gilbert, the black truck, and the long ago camping trip entered his mind.

As he filled the tin pot with snow from an untouched snowbank and returned to the campfire, Clark felt the eyes of the boy and dog follow his every movement. Poor things, they were probably hungrier and colder than he had ever been in his life. A quick glance in the direction of the pair seemed to confirm that.

"It won't take more than a few minutes to make that coffee," he said as he moved the snowbroth soup pot off of the warming rock and placed the pail of fresh-dug snow for coffee on it instead. "In the meantime, we can have ourselves some supper."

Using the metal spoon from his knapsack, he ladled the steaming liquid into the mug and soup can. He placed the can of snowbroth on the ground near the teen's feet, then dug a second fork from his knapsack and offered it to the kid. After slowly raising his arm, the boy paused, turned over his hand, and unclenched his fist. Clark laid the utensil on the kid's palm, then folded the boy's fingers over the handle. He imagined Muriel berating him for sharing camping utensils with the teen, much less for touching the kid's unclean hand.

"You are cold as a corpse! Maybe we had better forget camping, and drive you somewhere warmer. My wife won't let you in our house—she barely tolerates me, but I've got a cot in the garage with lots of blankets."

He did not add that he used it many nights when Muriel was on a rampage. Some days, their five-year marriage seemed like fifteen. But Jetty's divorce had upset Ma so much, Clark remained married to his wife for his mother's sake. He knew now, if he wanted to reclaim himself, that would have to change.

He studied the shivering dog. "And there's room for a pup there, too."

"Ain't none of you driving anywheres," a voice behind Clark said. The statement was followed by the sound of a trigger being cocked.

Hells bells, he thought. He had been so concerned for the teenager and the dog, he'd forgotten to be aware of his surroundings. Slowly, so as not to startle the speaker, Clark turned around.

"Wink? Uncle Wink?" he said to the man who stood pointing the gun at him. "It's Jetty's boy, Clark."

"I know who you are. In fact, I've been watching you since you first got outta your pick-up." Wink wiped his mouth with the back of his sleeve. "Your wife sent me down here to put an end to your miserable life."

"Muriel?" The woman was ill-tempered, but Clark never thought she wanted him dead. "I can't believe..."

"Believe it," Wink licked his lips. "Muriel upped your life insurance, and paid me $3,000 to make this camping trip your last."

"He shot me."

Clark was so focused on his former uncle, that he forgot about the raggedy teen and stray dog until the boy spoke.

The kid raised his hand, pointed at the dog, then at Wink, and said, "He and another man shot us both."

"If Gilbert and me shot you and your mutt, you'd be rotting beneath these weeds." Wink smiled and kicked at the ground. "I done it enough times to know when you bury a boy, he stays buried. 'Course it's too bad you're here tonight, because I don't leave dangling strings. Tonight, I *am* gonna shoot you and that flea-bitten..."

Whatever Wink was going to say next was lost in a shout. Hands pushed their way through the snow covered, but still unfrozen ground, and grabbed him around his ankles.

As Clark watched, several boys crawled out of the earth and joined the plaid-shirted teen and his dog by the fire. During the commotion, he had the sense to grab the gun from Wink before the man shot anyone. Now, he wasn't sure whom he should point it at.

The boys barely acknowledged Clark and the gun. Instead, they knocked Wink flat on his back and pushed him into the earth. More hands reached from beneath Wink and locked on his struggling body. Within five minutes, nothing remained of Aunt Jetty's ex-husband but a slight indent in the sod.

Fear, not the low temperature, held Clark frozen in place. Though the sod beneath his feet seemed solid, he could not be certain he wasn't about to meet the same horrible fate as his late uncle-by-marriage. Though he held Uncle Wink's gun, he knew he didn't have the stomach to pull the trigger and shoot a bunch of kids.

I'm a goner, he thought as he scanned the gang of dead, but not dead teens. Their exposed skin was bruised and torn. Some of their arms and legs were bent in unnatural positions. And the smell was worse than week-old road kill on a summer's afternoon.

In unison, the undead boys turned what remained of their eyes towards Clark.

"They shot us," said the teen to whom he had given the clothes as he gestured towards each of the undead. "And more. You woke us with your prayer."

"Prayer?" Then, he recollected the words he had uttered earlier in the evening when preparing his snowbroth. "Look, I'm sorry if I..."

"Thank you."

A chorus of thank-you's rose from the undead boys. Even the dog, whom Clark figured was an undead creature, too, whined and wagged its tail.

"We'll share snowbroth with you, then sleep," explained the plaid-shirted teen.

The undead pulled several more logs around the campfire. They sat down, raised their hands toward the warmth of Clark's fire, and passed around the soup can and mug of snowbroth. Each boy took a sip, closed his eyes, and seemed to enjoy the hot liquid sliding down his throat. Instead of sipping snowbroth when the mug or can was passed to him, Clark refilled the containers with more of the tasty soup until about a cup remained.

"For the dog," he said, and sat the mug down on the ground. The undead canine lapped up his portion of the snowbroth, looked at Clark with milky eyes, and woofed.

"Coffee?" he asked the undead. "I know it's only instant, but it will warm you up a bit more."

The boys shook their heads. Each then raised a hand in farewell and warned, "Be careful," before sinking into the ground.

At last, only the raggedy teen and his dog remained. "You are kind," he explained. "So we allow you to go home." Almost as an afterthought, he asked, "Your clothes and shoes? Do you want them back?"

"Keep them." Clark wished there was something else he could do for the lost boys. "Is there anything..."

"Leave the gun. Go home," said the teen. "And remember us," he called over his shoulder when he and his dog walked into the woods.

Clark broke up camp and loaded his gear into the truck, but he didn't extinguish the campfire with the water he'd boiled for coffee. He thought of the undead boys and dog. Come spring, when all traces of his presence at the campsite were gone, he decided he would send an anonymous note to the police about seeing Wink take a boy into these woods. He'd put it together with newspaper clippings, always wearing gloves when handling the note and envelope, and mail it in another town at a drop-box with no camera.

The families of these boys deserved to get their children's bodies back so they could be buried by loving hands and remembered. He sat in the front seat of his truck and thought about what the boys had said about Gilbert. He suspected on that long ago camping trip with Uncle Wink, the two men had considered killing him, but knew Aunt Jetty and the rest of the family would have realized their involvement—so they had spared Clark. He was not going to be so generous.

Clark was pretty good at reading people, and he imagined Wink's old buddy could be easily manipulated. All he needed to do was get Gilbert out to this patch of ground, say a prayer, and let the undead boys mete out justice. With Gilbert still alive, he doubted the murdered teens and dog would find peace even if they were returned to their families.

Phone reception was unreliable here, but nevertheless he flipped through his old-fashioned address book, located Gilbert's phone number, and punched it into his cell phone. After three rings someone picked up.

"Hello."

"Hey, is this Uncle Wink's friend, Gilbert?" Clark asked. It wasn't a very original approach, but it was straight-forward.

"Yeah. Who's this?"

"It's Clark, Wink's nephew."

"What the hell do you want?"

Well, Gilbert hadn't changed—still surly. "Uncle Wink asked me to call you and have you meet us for a few drinks around a campfire at the foot of the hill below his place. You know, near the old church. We're here now, if you want to drive over."

There was a long pause. *I hope I haven't spooked him*, thought Clark.

"You two providing the booze?"

"Yup. You'll see my truck if you come. It's black."

Another long pause.

"What the hell. I'll pull on a coat and be over in about ten minutes," said Gilbert.

"See you then," Clark managed to say before Gilbert hung up.

He gazed over at the campfire. As soon as Clark saw Gilbert coming up the church's drive, he would go over to the fire and summon the undead boys. At least one of the teens needed to be sitting on a log opposite Clark with his back to the road so Gilbert would think Uncle Wink was waiting. After waving Gilbert over, Clark would let the undead have their way with the other murderer. Once the boys were finished, he'd put out the fire with the melted snow in the coffee pail and leave. Since he would have helped the teens extract their final revenge, Clark expected them to again allow him depart unharmed.

While he waited for Gilbert, he considered his life. Starting tonight, he was fixing his own food, only drinking bottled water, and sleeping in the garage with a knife under the pillow. He had found the old Clark, and he didn't intend to let Muriel bury him.

Of course, there were details like lawyers, judges, property dispersal, and divorce degrees to sort out, but he intended to begin to live *his* life again.

When Clark spotted headlights coming up the church's drive in his rearview mirror, he climbed out of the truck, walked to the campfire, and started to pray.

Blood Born

Meriah L. Crawford

*M**ost people who experiment with calling demons don't* survive that tricky learning period. If you don't do it quite right, the demon can't come all the way through. Demons apparently find this quite annoying, so they tend to eat you and return to where they came from, usually leaving no sign they were ever there.

And when the raising is successful? Carnage.

By the time I was four blocks from the construction site that morning, I could tell that this demon raising had worked. If it hadn't, the road wouldn't be blocked off, helicopters wouldn't be hovering overhead, there wouldn't be a dozen emergency vehicles with flashing lights parked in the road and on the sidewalks, and the scent of blood and death wouldn't be hanging like a haze over the whole area.

I considered turning around and driving off, but the officer directing traffic pointed at me and gestured toward the curb. As I pulled over, he held up a finger and spoke into a radio, then stood waiting, looking nervously back at the site.

My client on this job was a developer building a ninety-six-unit apartment complex in a sketchy area that the city was trying to revitalize. For the last couple of weeks, they'd been having trouble with vandalism at the site. At first, it looked like basic bored-kid stuff: discarded cans and bottles, small fires, candles, some torn clothing. But then I found a mound of disturbed earth and, buried a couple feet down, the bodies of three ferrets and a guinea pig. The next day, one of the workers was cleaning debris from a spot where one of the fires was set, and he found symbols marked on the concrete slab. The marks were faint, but they'd actually left depressions in the surface. Not much would etch concrete like that, and certainly nothing kids should have access to.

The officer finally headed over and I lowered my window. The faint scent of blood and viscera entered the car. From that distance, all I could tell for sure was that there was more than one body, and it was bad.

The officer leaned down, his right hand resting on the butt of his Glock. "You Ella Farriss?"

"Yeah."

"Detective'll be over in a minute."

"How did you—"

He put up his hand to stop me and went back to directing traffic. Typical. Dealing with the police is definitely not the most fulfilling part of my job.

Until I became a vampire two years ago, I'd been planning to get my teacher's license and become a high school English teacher. But by the time the wounds had healed and I was well enough to start back at school, I'd lost all interest. In truth, my enthusiasm had started to wane even before that, but the aggression and adrenaline surges that vampirism brought made teaching children a very bad idea. Before long, I'd started doing what my mother liked to refer to as "odd jobs." The people who hired me, finding me through word of mouth, called me a "fixer." This time, it was looking like they'd waited too long before calling me in.

After a few minutes of waiting for the detective, I pulled my cell phone out and scrolled through the photos of the symbols again. The foreman had described them in a voicemail he left for me that morning, a little before sunrise. I'd been sleeping "like the dead," as my roommate often joked, so I hadn't heard the phone ring. Fortunately, the foreman followed up the call with an e-mail that included pictures of the marks, so I was able do some research before driving to the building site. I'd learned that the symbols were traditionally used in demon raising—a very bad sign—but they were drawn crudely. I had hoped that meant whoever created them either failed, or succeeded only well enough to die in the process. So much for that.

Finally, I saw the detective in charge of the scene coming toward my car, and it was good news. Alessandra Pira was a tall, powerful blonde in her thirties. We'd bumped into each other twice before on jobs I'd done and she regarded me with some suspicion, but also treated me with respect. I'd have preferred blind trust, but she was a good cop— maybe even a great one—and I knew she'd be willing to work with me.

I climbed out of my car as she came near and started to say hi, but I didn't get far.

"Ella," she said, cutting me off, "explain to me why your number is the last one the foreman called before he died."

I grimaced. I barely knew him, but he'd seemed like a decent guy, and I knew he had kids. "Damn," I said.

"What was he to you?" she said angrily. "Why did he call?"

"Okay, Okay, hang on." I explained about the job and showed her the photos on my cell.

She stared at them for a bit, then shrugged and said, "They must not have really been etched into the concrete, because there aren't any marks there now. In fact, that whole area is clean."

I raised my eyebrows, and her cheeks turned pink. The photos were pretty clear, but people are quick to bring on the disbelief and denial when it suits their understanding of the world.

I shook my head and said, "If I could take a look?"

"I shouldn't let you into that area, since it's part of an active investigation."

As soon as I heard "shouldn't" I knew she would, and with just a little bit of coaxing, she did. After clearing me past the police barricades, she told me that the foreman, who had died on the scene, had apparently lived only a few minutes after sending me the images from his cell phone. The other three dead were workers who'd also arrived shortly before dawn. No one else had died since then and there was no trail of blood or destruction, so I was guessing the demon was still there, but dormant in daylight. Thank the gods for that.

As we headed around one skeletal building—a three-story framed cube with no walls yet—she asked what the symbols meant.

"Oh, I'm not exactly sure. Some kind of devil worship nonsense, I think."

She gave me a mildly suspicious look, but let it go. "Any ideas yet who's been vandalizing the site?"

"Nope. I've only been on the case for a couple of days, so I'm really still getting started. Have your people been able to gather—" and I stopped there, stopped everything, because we'd come around a corner to where one of the men had been killed.

The body had been shredded. I couldn't even tell if it was the foreman. It was just a spray of blood and flesh, with bits of clothing and half a boot mixed in. The scent of spoiling meat flooded my nose, and it smelled...wrong. There were parts missing. A leg and some organs, at least. I caught myself as I started to try to smell exactly which parts were gone; the cops and crime lab personnel would hardly forget the sight of a woman taking deep breaths at a crime scene, trying to figure out where the gall bladder was.

And then I realized the detective was staring at me, studying me, and that I should have expressed some horror by then. It was too late to fake it with any believability, so I shook my head and said, "It doesn't even look real."

She nodded, seeming to file my reaction away as interesting information, and we walked past, entering one of the buildings that had some sheathing up. I started to go back to my question about evidence when I smacked hard into a wall of magic, and staggered back.

Pira stared at me. "What the hell was that?"

I reached my hand out and pressed it against the wall, and it was like an angry, humming shield of energy. I pushed harder, but I simply could not pass through it. And that scared me. I moved to where Pira had entered it, and it was solid there too. "It's...magic."

"Uh-huh," she said. "Right. Looks like mime to me."

She reached out, grabbed my arm, and dragged me forward. I slammed into the wall, hard, yelping. Pira's eyes widened, but she tried again, more gently, to pull my arm through. No dice—and she could tell I wasn't faking it. There just wasn't any way.

Pira reached for her radio, and I said, "You sure you want to do that?"

"Why wouldn't I?"

"Because no one will believe it. Even the ones who see it with their own eyes will stop believing it in a couple of days. All they'll be left with is the memory of you telling them magic kept me out of a room."

She shook her head, pulled the radio out, and held it to her mouth before the truth of it sank in. "Damn."

"Yeah."

"So, what now?"

I stood thinking for a moment, trying to decide how much I could safely tell her. "How long will you have people here? When will you clear the scene?"

She shrugged. "We have three teams out here collecting evidence, walking the area, but it will still be hours. And it will be days before we clear the scene for construction to start up again. Wait—why can I go through but you can't?"

"No idea."

"Ella—"

"Look," I said, stepping away from the magic, which was starting to get very uncomfortable, "I'm really not positive, and it's not that important, anyway. What is important is you need to have your people out of here before dark—long before dark—and the sooner the better."

"Why?"

I just gave her a look and hoped she'd go along, but it wasn't enough. And then I tried to tell her the invisible wall was dangerous and unstable, but that wasn't quite enough either. This was her job— their job—and not mine. I didn't really have a place here at all, if you went by the book. But she'd known it wasn't that simple, even before I ran into that wall of magic.

Twenty minutes later, when she learned that one of the victims was a retired Navy Seal and another had a third-degree black belt in

Judo, and that the forensic team had no idea what kind of animals shredded the men, but they were all scared witless, she finally agreed to close the scene overnight. She was far from certain that I could handle it, but she was pretty sure that she and her team weren't equipped.

Of course, they didn't simply leave and go home. Officially and in front of witnesses, she ordered me out. Quietly and alone, she asked me how much space I needed, and said she would position cars and undercover officers on foot about two blocks away. We picked a time, and I left to get supplies and information and to prepare.

By 5:20 p.m., when the sun was nearly touching the horizon, I was back and ready to go. My cousin Kylie had given me an *athame*—a ritual knife—that she thought would let me cut through the magic, and I had a *szabla*—a Ukrainian sword like a short sabre—and magical protections that I hoped would do the job. I'd fought two demons before, but they'd been easy because they were already weak. One had been wounded in a fight with another demon, and the other had simply stayed in our world too long without taking blood. This one would be fresh and boiling with energy after four kills. Not to mention, I had no idea what kind of demon I was dealing with.

As I stood facing the buzzing wall, I slid the *athame* free of its sheath. It squealed and twisted slightly, reacting to the magic just inches away. Not for the first time, it occurred to me that I should have asked for help—from some of the mages I knew, or from the police. A mix of pride and fear of exposure had kept me silent. *Stupid*, I thought, and stabbed the wall. A wave of hot, foul air threw me off my feet onto the concrete floor.

After that, finding the demon wasn't hard. With the wall of magic down, I could see the screen he had raised to keep hidden until dark—and he knew it.

Down came the screen. Out came the demon. The battle was on.

He didn't bother with weapons. Instead, the seven-foot-tall, horned, green demon rushed me. He moved with an impossible speed for his size, but I moved a tiny bit faster. Still, he caught my side, ripping gashes along my ribs.

The demon stumbled past me, unprepared for my dodge, and I slashed at him with my szabla. The blade tore a deep wound in his side. Both of us were hurt, but he was losing blood far faster. The enchantment that had been worked on the sword called to blood, drawing it out in rivers.

We both moved back and sized each other up for a moment before he came at me again. It was a head-on rush that turned into a dodge left, then a dive, and he slashed at me with his feet, which also had wicked claws. I could have dodged it, but knew it was as much an opportunity as a danger. The demon connected with a glancing blow, tearing into my leg as I hacked his foot clean off.

Up until then, our fight had been all but silent, but as he collapsed with a floor-shaking thud, he let out a howl that echoed off the walls and swelled into the late afternoon air above us. I hoped Pira could keep the cavalry from rushing in. Surely, the sound would be enough to argue patience.

The demon was down, but far from done, and I was bleeding heavily from my own wounds. The pain hadn't reached me yet, and wouldn't while the adrenaline coursed through me, but I knew I needed a quick victory. Getting close enough without getting killed would be the hard part.

And then I felt the nauseating, itchy sensation I get when someone's getting ready to do powerful magic, and there was no more time. To his surprise, and even a little bit to mine, I lunged, jumped, grabbed a bare ceiling joist, and launched myself at him, sword first, aiming for his neck. He slashed at me, but too quickly, missing, and the szabla sliced cleanly through his neck as I crashed to the floor beside him. His massive head tipped back and thunked to the floor as I rolled away.

A blinding, stabbing light flared explosively, filling the room, followed by a groaning-screeching-roaring noise that overwhelmed all thought. It lasted for maybe a minute, maybe two. And then, silence.

The demon and all his parts were gone. The floor was clear. The sun was setting with a red glow, and a gentle breeze rustled some trash in a pile in one corner. I felt a moment of disbelief, followed by relief, and then a sickening wash of gut-churning pain that curled me into a ball.

I'd asked Pira to give me at least three hours before she came in with her people, thinking it would be enough time for me to clean up after eliminating the demon. If she kept her promise, there was more than enough time for me to lie there and recover—and it would be a lot less painful if I could avoid moving—but I knew her better. I would never have waited, not after hearing the noise we'd made, and I didn't expect her to either. I hauled myself up, actually sobbing from the pain, staggered a block and a half away to a dank, narrow alley I thought they'd ignore, and collapsed behind a derelict trash bin.

It wasn't until maybe an hour later, after the worst of the pain was past and I'd partly healed, that I noticed the thick, blue-tinged blood on my shirt. I was in trouble.

From that moment, my priorities changed. I listened carefully, and could hear that Pira and her people were back on the site. None were near me, so I slid out, dragged myself upright, and headed for home.

Once there, I cleaned myself up, picked the debris from my halfway healed wounds, and stowed my weapons while sucking down a pint from the fridge. And then, I drove straight to my bank. It was past five, but I knew Miroslav would still be in his office, and he would know what to do. He always did.

Miros had been a family friend since before I was born, and a treasured adviser to my father. As a child, I'd thought of him as a *niceoldguy*, and largely dismissed him. It wasn't until a few months after I became a vampire that I discovered he was a wizard—and one of the best. Since then, Miros had become my treasured adviser, too—and sometimes a sort of therapist.

I found myself tensing as I knocked on his office door, and entered at his invitation. After his warm greeting I wished we could content ourselves with the usual small talk, but I knew this wasn't a problem that I could safely ignore. After a few minutes, I asked what he could tell me about the effect of getting demon blood in wounds.

"That would be bad," he said. "Extremely bad. You'd want to avoid blood-to-blood contact with demons at all costs."

"And if it does happen?"

He let out a harsh laugh. "Trust me—you don't want to know."

"But I...but what if I do? I mean, what if I already have?"

Miroslav froze for a moment, and then he groaned. "Ella," he said, rubbing his face. "Ella...you were such a sweet child. You know, I remember when you were six, and you had this red wagon with wooden panels on the sides—do you remember it?"

"Miros?"

"Yes?"

"Demon blood? In open wounds?"

"Yes." He sighed. "Yes, Okay. So. Type?"

"Type?"

"Type of *demon*," Miroslav said, frowning at me like an impatient school teacher.

"Hell if I know."

He rolled his eyes, then walked over to a mahogany-paneled section of wall, reached right through it, and pulled out a huge leather-bound book. It still freaked me out when he did that. And then, I'd think "cool," and wish I had just a hair of magical ability.

Mom was a corporate witch, and Dad was a financial wizard—in both senses. But me? So far, nothing. That owl from Hogwarts would never have brought me a letter. With two magical parents, I'd had a 93 percent chance of being born with magical ability. Instead, I was a seven-percenter: not even a smidge of mage. Rare and special, that's me. Just not in a good way.

Miroslav had set the book on his oval conference table and was flipping pages with a fierce look on his face. He found what he was looking for and waved me over. "Corporeal? Obviously." He turned a few more pages. "Winged?"

"No."

He continued turning pages, and my vision blurred. The book seemed to be vibrating, and when the pages went by, the air moved more than it should. Magical books always gave me the creeping willies. Goose bumps raised on my arms, and I edged away slightly. Miroslav, of course, noticed and frowned at me. He'd demanded a lot of me in the year and a half I'd been meeting with him, but he seemed harsher than usual, and very, very disappointed. I wanted to apologize, but I wasn't even sure why. Fighting the demon had been unavoidable—and if I hadn't made it bleed, I wouldn't still be around to talk about it.

"Height?"

"Sevenish."

He looked questioningly at me, and I said "Feet." I still knew damn little about demons and all the rest of the mystical world I'd suddenly found myself a part of two years earlier—I'd always tried to ignore that part of my parents' lives, since I couldn't really take part myself, but I did know that a seven-inch demon could be just as deadly as a seven foot one, and I also knew they could be as tall as seven yards. Or seven stories, for that matter. Seven miles? Maybe. But I probably wouldn't have lived to talk about that.

"Horns?"

"Two." Trying to anticipate the questions, I added, "On either side of its head. Curling." I gently pressed the edges of the wounds that ran along my ribs, and wondered if I'd start growing horns myself—maybe from my side. That would be attractive.

"Fire?" Miros asked.

"Um..."

"From its nose or mouth, or even its..."

"Nope. No fire from any orifice."

"Huh. Boring," he said, as he flipped through more pages. "Tentacles?"

Miroslav went through almost a dozen other characteristics, including color, sounds, ooze, weapons or magical items, and magical skills, before he turned the book toward me to show me some pictures.

He was turning the pages himself because we'd discovered previously that the magical books didn't like me. The first time I touched one, it actually tried to bite me. Miros said he'd never heard of it happening before, and tested me on three other books before I refused to play that game. The first one gave me an electrical shock; the second—a thick, heavy book about potion mixing—jumped onto my foot and tried to hide under a desk; and the third screamed so loudly that the neighbors (we were at Miros' home that time) actually called the police. He'd decided the books must be reacting that way because I'm a vampire, but he hadn't had an opportunity to put it to the test with another vamp. In the meantime, I wasn't getting any closer to them than I had to.

Miros had gone through eleven pages before I spotted the demon I'd killed. It was called a Narrabeen Queller Demon, and it was the butt-ugliest thing I'd ever seen, aside only from the one I'd met in person. Bumpy, slimy, oozing skin, extra-long fingers that ended in claws, and an odd assortment of eyes on all sides of its head. I looked at the description but, naturally, I couldn't read a word.

"Looks like gibberish," I said.

"No, it's demo-mageic." At my enquiring look, he added, "A cross between demonic and an ancient mage language. No one really speaks demonic or mageic, or ever did. They're really a sort of Esperanto for each group, to allow at least basic communication. The authors used a blend of the two to make sure only demons and mages—witches— could read it. They had to do both because the demons would only cooperate with their research if they wrote it that way."

"Huh. Okay." I wondered vaguely why the demons would cooperate regardless, but that was a subject for another day. "So, what does it say?"

"Well," he said, scanning the page, "there's some fairly useless stuff about the Queller's habitat, culture, dining preferences and the like. It's got only basic magical abilities, like shooting low-wattage fireballs and moving small objects. Parlor tricks, really. As demons go, it's a pretty pathetic one."

I let out a harsh laugh, and he looked up.

"That pathetic demon nearly kicked my ass."

He studied me briefly. "You look fine. A bit tired and rumpled perhaps, but—"

I took my jacket off so he could see my arms, then pulled my shirt up far enough to expose the slashes over my ribcage. The deep claw marks were healing well—my vamp blood gives me amazing healing abilities—but they were still ugly and red. A norm would have bled out before an ambulance arrived. Easily.

Miros knew it, and his concern showed in his face, but all he said was, "You need training."

"Yup," I said, and nodded. "Yeah. I do." It was a topic we'd discussed often. I'd always dismissed the idea, because I could easily kick the ass of any non-magical man or woman alive, but I'd never faced anything like this before. If this was the low end of the demon ranks, I needed some serious training, and soon.

He smiled, finally looking pleased at something, then turned back to the book. After a couple minutes he said, "Ah, Okay, here we go." He placed his finger on a section of the text that was written in larger, darker letters. "Oh dear. 'Warning, avoid contact with Queller Demon blood. Results are unpredictable, but usually fatal within forty-eight hours.'"

"*Fatal?*" I glared at the wounds on my arm. "Stupid damn demon. What does it say I can do about it?"

He scanned a couple pages. "It doesn't." He shook his head. "That's all it says."

"Well, that's bloody useless."

He smiled grimly. "Yes, quite. But then, it would be anyway, wouldn't it? None of this stuff applies to vampires, my dear. You're new territory, aren't you?"

"Yay. Such an adventure. How utterly fascinating. But what do I do, then?"

"How long has it been?"

"Maybe three hours."

He closed the book rather harder than he needed to. "Why didn't you come to me immediately?"

"Well, I thought it might concern the bank employees if I strolled in covered in blood and muck, my clothes hanging off me in tatters. Not to mention, I was too weak to even get myself home for well over an hour. I had to crawl into a dank alley to stay out of sight."

His scowl finally softened. "I'm sorry, my dear. Of course." He slipped the book back through the wall, and we both sat in big, comfy leather chairs near the windows looking out onto the park. "Are you feeling anything...unusual since receiving the injuries?"

I waited before answering, taking a moment to be very aware of how I felt, and what my senses could tell me. I could hear Miros' secretary on the phone, explaining to a very important client that Miros was in a meeting with auditors and simply couldn't be disturbed, but would call the instant he was free. I wondered not for the first time how much she knew, but let my senses wander further. I realized there was an odd sort of buzzing sensation around the wounds. There'd been too much pain earlier to give it much notice, but the buzzing was becoming more distinct. I could almost hear it. Almost taste it. I tried to explain, but Miros just frowned at me. Again.

"All right, let me think," he said, and he slipped into an odd meditative state that I'd learned not to interfere with. His eyes unfocused and his body stilled as he turned his whole attention inward. Miros might come up from the depths with the perfect answer in a minute or two—or an hour, or a day—but I thought it was just as likely he'd come up empty. And what then? Wait and see, probably. Never my favorite choice, but one I'd had to settle for on more than a few occasions. The interaction of vamps with magic, demons, fairies, zombies, doctors, and the criminal justice system was dangerous and unpredictable, and no matter how badly I wanted to, I couldn't know the outcome before it got here.

§

Now, sitting in Miros' office, I somehow felt safe. He might not be able to solve this, and I might even die in the end, but I was tired and sore, and I knew he would do everything in his power to protect me. So, while Miroslav pondered, I set up my laptop and got to work. If nothing else, I could report my success to my client. Twenty minutes of typing later, I finished my message to the developer, explaining in very cryptic terms that the immediate problem was resolved, but the people who caused it were still unknown and should be considered dangerous, and shut the computer down. Miros was still meditating, so I closed my eyes and, almost instantly, I slept. My dreams, as usual, were filled with chasing, fighting, magic, and the sweet-copper taste of blood.

Sometime later, I awoke to the scent of burning sage and hibiscus flowers, and was alarmed to find myself lying on the floor of Miroslav's office, surrounded by seven chanting witches wearing flowing purple robes. Miros stood beside me reading from a small green book that looked like it had fangs.

"How—" I said, but Miros glared at me, and I was silent. Fine, but he had some serious questions to answer later—not the least of which was, how the hell do I protect myself if I don't wake up when someone picks me up and carries me across the room? I tried to shift so I could see the room better, but found I was unable to move. I recognized the feel of the magic: it was a restraint spell, and an incredibly powerful one. I couldn't even twitch a finger, though I could still turn my head and snarl.

And then, one of the witches—my Aunt Clair, in fact—added a handful of something that smelled like a cross between a swamp and a big-city subway station to the fire, which was burning in a small brazier. The witches, their backs turned to me, raised their arms together and spoke the words of what I knew was a protection spell, and I felt the instant ear-popping isolation of a tight, well-constructed circle.

Usually, the circle was meant to protect the people inside it from outside interference or danger during a ritual. But this time, after a moment of staring in confusion at the oddly wavering images of the witches surrounding me, I realized I was the only one inside the circle. They had raised it to protect themselves from *me*. I'd obviously missed some interesting conversations, yet again, and I felt the familiar petulance of my youth.

So many things went on around me that, because I wasn't magical, simply couldn't involve me. God, I hated it. And even now, when I *was* magical, when I was the center of attention, I was still left out. And it made me mad—so, so mad. Twisting with bitterness. And then their chant changed, and the pressure of their magic increased four-fold, and I felt the rage moving like a force inside me in response. And then I realized: It wasn't just an overgrown tantrum coming on, it was the demon's blood in me, coming to life. Fear struggled for a foothold, tried to pull me back from the abyss of fury, but it was no match for it. None at all.

The air around me bent and churned, my muscles writhed, and a scream ripped out of me. Miros and the witches flinched at the sound, swayed at the force of the energy I'd released against the circle without even trying, and I felt a vicious thrill. I could stop them all. I could brush them aside like dolls. At last. I let the rage and the power build inside me, holding it close until I thought I would explode. The sounds of their chanting rose higher and higher, but their magic couldn't reach me. Not now—and not ever again.

At last, I was ready: I let loose the demon.

A wave of crimson rolled out of me and crashed against the circle, obliterating it. Miros and the witches were thrown to the ground; the windows were blown out. A cacophony of screeching and howling filled the air. It was coming from me.

Oh, oh, *the pain*. Too much. It was too much. E*scape, window, escape*. I ran to the nearest one, stumbling, clawing for the ledge. I couldn't get through. I was too big. But it was a huge window. It didn't make sense. I looked over my shoulder and saw what was catching on the window frame. *Wings*. Yes. Good.

I tucked them in, tipped through the window, and propelled myself forward, falling. The air rushed against me, and it was exquisite. I stretched my wings and arched my back, and my plummet turned into a glide. I tipped them gently, knowing somehow what to do, and swept down the street, then beat the wings, climbing higher. The air cooled them, cooled me, and the rage ebbed.

I swooped, glided, soared, feeling new muscles, new power. I could sense people below me, feel emotions bubbling from them: fear, anger, loneliness, bliss. Inside myself, at last, I felt a calm that I hadn't known since I was a child. Born from rage, I'd finally found my peace.

And then I remembered Miros, Aunt Clair, and the other witches. I discovered I could turn almost instantly, even at high speed, and aimed myself back toward the bank. I struggled so hard to fly faster that I slowed terribly, nearly lurching into a building, before I relaxed into it again. I let my body fly, the calm returned, and I moved through the air with breathtaking speed.

When I got back to the building, I latched on to the brick outside the shattered windows with my claws. Claws? I took a moment and made note of my red skin and the wicked two-inch talons on my fingers before peering in the window. One witch, a woman I didn't know, was leaving supported by two of the other witches. It looked like an ankle problem, so they could heal her easily enough. Probably would have done it already if they'd had enough magical energy left after trying to restrain me. The thought made me smile again. It was juvenile, but at least I knew I'd be taken seriously from now on.

Most importantly, Miros seemed fine as he went around the office righting tipped chairs and collecting papers from the floor. Good. I wanted to see him, speak to him, but there was one thing I had to do first; one bit of business I needed to take care of. The men who called that demon: they still had to be stopped.

The fact that stopping them was my priority told me I was still Ella inside, no matter what I looked like. My new attributes would just make it easier to take care of the demon raisers—and much easier to find them. I just had to hope that my new form wasn't permanent—or at least not a full-time thing. But that was a problem for another day.

Beneath the buzzing of the people, machines, animals, and buildings that I could feel all around me, there was a single, singing thread linking me with the demon callers. The thread led me west toward the mountains. Moving—they were moving. Fleeing. Smart.

Smart, but futile. I laughed a deep, harsh laugh and dropped away from the building, spreading my wings and gliding into a powerful, sweeping beat toward two doomed men running through the dark. The vampire that still lived in me was hungry, and she would feed well that night.

Reanimated

Nicole Givens Kurtz

M_urder is murder," Tanisha Moore said around a wad of_ stale, pink gum. Her mass of dark coiled curls waved in the waning, afternoon breeze. Yellow caution tape roped off the adobe and stucco house. She peered through her sunglasses at the slob of a man standing across from her. Roger hunched inside his tattered tee-shirt.

"Sometimes there's nuthin' under the skin, 'cept blood and bile." Roger tossed Ashley, his four-year-old daughter, into the air with his hairy arms swinging her up and catching her as she fell. She giggled infectiously.

"That's my point." Tanisha popped her gum.

Roger pressed his beefy lips into a slash of annoyance. With his eyebrows huddled together in confusion, he pulled Ashley to his chest. As he did so, her face wrinkled up and bordered on releasing a cry that would send her angst sailing across the well-arranged yards of the Truth or Consequences' residential neighborhood.

"My point," Roger said tightly, "is that Sherri got what she deserved."

"So, you confessing?" Tanisha quirked an eyebrow.

No one deserved to be stabbed twenty-seven times no matter what she might have done. Uniformed police had been to the Cross home many times over the years for domestic disturbances. Sherri refused to file charges. Roger had a temper. Sherri had bruises.

But Tanisha wasn't here to argue with Roger. She had come to investigate a murder.

Roger gently dumped little Ashley to the ground, and she tumbled out like an apple from a basket, fresh and cherry-cheeked.

"No, but…"

"But you think she had it comin.'"

"Well, yeah. Yeah, I guess you can say she did." His green-eyed gaze followed Ashley as she stood and walked around the yard, tripping on gravel and sidestepping cacti. The New Mexican sun sparkled brightly in a crisp blue day.

"She was your wife." She didn't like Roger's air of apathy.

"Yeah, Tanisha. She's little Ashley's mother," he mumbled with another quick downward glance at his daughter who now snaked through his parted legs.

Ashley giggled as she looked up at Tanisha, her cheeks chubby and the mop of strawberry-blonde curls bounced in the breeze.

Tanisha gave him a deadpan look before nodding. She ignored Ashley's attempts to be picked up and hugged. With a flick of her thumb, Tanisha clicked her pen and walked down the steps to her cruiser.

"Be talkin' to you," she called over her shoulder.

As the dirt-encrusted leather seat crinkled under her weight, she pushed her sunglasses into her hair. With a short glance into the rearview mirror, she noted that Roger Cross stared after her, little Ashley between his legs, as her cruiser pulled away. Something strange had happened in the Cross family house.

Something foul.

For years Tanisha had performed her police officer duties with disinterest and apathy. Cop burn-out threatened to overtake her. It seemed that as soon as she put one vile, vicious criminal behind bars, two more—murderers, thieves, and rapists—would crop up in their place. Disenchanted with the system, she'd fallen into a routine. It was a rut from which nothing seemed able to rescue her. To a point, she was simply going through the paces…but her heart, hell, her entire mind wasn't in it.

This attitude of indifference had infected all aspects of her life including driving, eating, and even living. She'd once had an incredible thirst for life, and now felt as if it had been slowly suctioned off.

Her radio exploded with static.

"Tanisha, this is Piper, pick up, over." Piper Peterson's voice squeaked over the radio.

Tanisha cringed. Piper's voice always seemed as if it had been cleaned with bleach and waxed to perfection.

"What do you want now, Piper?" She couldn't keep the solemn loathing out of her tone.

"There's an urgent report on your desk from Max."

Tanisha sighed. Max, the medical doctor, who doubled as the county's coroner, always dropped reports on her desk. That wasn't strange.

"Soooo…"

"Max said to call it in to you and tell you 'cause it's important." Piper's voice escalated an octave into a full-fledged whine. "It's about the Cross body."

Tanisha wondered how quickly Sherri Cross went from being neighborhood friend to being "the Cross body."

This close community hadn't had a murder in a few months, except for the strange piles of human corpses found at the cemetery, a few months back. They'd been totally unearthed from their coffins and just left there. Now, *that* had been something to call her about.

At the time, she had thought those were the works of teenagers horse-playing around and pranking the cemetery's manager.

"Fine." Tanisha gripped the steering wheel in annoyance. "I'll be right there."

Tanisha's heartbeat continued its steady *thump-thump-thump* pace. Nothing much ever excited her to the point where she could say her blood raced anymore.

§

The light's glare off the paper reflected against Tanisha's reading glasses. Piper, her long, dark brown, braids brushing her desk, leaned over her shoulder—her eyes wide with wonder.

"What is it?" she asked for the third time in two minutes. Medical speak was as foreign as French to Piper.

The words seemed to muddle on the page before Tanisha's eyes. She removed her glasses and rubbed her tired orbs. "A lot of gobbledy-gook."

Piper's smooth forehead wrinkled. "So, what was the emergency?"

Just then Max appeared at the door that led from the morgue to the police office. Seeing them, he marched directly to Tanisha's desk.

"Max." Tanisha nodded in his direction.

Max's bushy beard quivered and his huge face blotted out the overhead lights, casting her into temporary shadow.

"Why don't you come down to the morgue? Now." A slight wheeze followed, and his sweaty and bloated face seemed pale. His apron was splattered with bluish streaks and some brownish-red stuff that was probably dried blood. It also contained stray hairs. Sweating profusely, Max swallowed hard. Tanisha couldn't remember a time in her six years on the force that Max's face wasn't red and perspiring. He reeked of old sweat and spoiled beer.

"Why?" She gazed up at his sunken eyes. "I read the report."

"You gotta *see* this. Reading it isn't enough. Not." *Wheeze.* "Nearly." *Wheeze.* "Enough."

"All right."

Tanisha got up, leaving Piper behind, staring at them in puzzlement, and followed him down the cracked stone steps, past the holding tanks and the janitors' closets to the basement, which was outfitted to be a morgue. It took up three-quarters of one extremely large room.

Sherri Cross stared unseeingly up at Max's bright, exposing lamp.

"Max, her eyes are open," Tanisha pointed out with a small, chill slipping up her spine. She knew for a fact that Max had closed them when he got to the crime scene. Her stomach clutched in warning.

"They keep doing that!" He gently closed her eyes once again. "Damn things won't stay closed!"

"Does she have, you know, one of those things?" Tanisha crossed her arms to quell the warning in her gut.

The strong odor of death and decomposition filled the morgue along with faint hints of ammonia and soap. Max removed the tarp over Sherri's body and pointed at the diagonal "Y" incision. He pulled back the skin and most of the muscle around her uterus to point out what Tanisha could only guess was an ovary.

"See here," he pointed with a gloved hand.

"Yeah Tanisha's eyes watered against the stench. She unwrapped a piece of gum and stuck it in her mouth. Her nose burned from the odor, but she didn't move away.

"This ain't human," he said with a wheeze. "This ain't *right*."

She peered at the metal object protruding from Sherri's ovary. It blinked in a slow beat. *What was that? Some modern IUD?*

Or was it one of those devices?

"Is it some sort of birth control?"

"I checked to be sure some new trials weren't be conducted around here. No, no, Tanisha. This ain't right."

"No, that ain't right."

She chewed her gum silently with her lips closed. Her eyes remained on Max's damp face as he covered the body up again. When he stood up, he noticed Sherri's eyes.

"Damn it!" He closed them again.

"Well?" Tanisha leaned against the wall.

"You gotta do something about this. It seems those damn crazies had it right." With a hurried look over his shoulder to the body on the table, he grunted and shook his head.

"Yeah." She agreed. It would appear the rumors had been true. As she walked to the morgue's exit door, her heartbeat increased and the first small quiver of anticipation rushed along her spine.

§

On the third day after Sherri Cross's murder, Tanisha dropped by Roger's house again. The placed looked deserted. The front windows, somber and vacant, stared back at her with cool, cheerless indifference. She stepped onto the porch and rang the bell. Even from this distance she could hear it ringing throughout house. A hollow echo ricocheted through the closed-up space.

Tanisha leisurely made her way back to the cruiser. As soon as she closed the driver's side door, heavy splats of raindrops splattered against her window.

"Tanisha, pick up!" Piper squawked from the radio.

"What now, Piper?"

"Tanisha, Max said to tell you that Sherri's body is gone!"

"Ten-four."

Gone.

Three days. Sherri could be anywhere.

Tanisha blew out a slow, steady breath. Bodies that have been reanimated had a way of losing control and becoming violent, especially those who had suffered a violent death. Of all the emotions, the rage remained.

Roger hadn't turned up either.

They needed to find Sherri Cross before she hurt someone.

Unlike the bodies piled in the cemetery, Sherri Cross's disappearance hinted of the other cases she'd read about occurring all over the southwest. Some of the native people reported herds of, what could only be deemed *reanimated*, people roaming down from the Santa Fe area. Rumbling on the Internet, pushed as more "alien" garbage out of Roswell, the information had bled into urban legend and myth. Rumored to have originated from rogue lab rats outside of Los Alamos, scientists had created a device to effectively reanimate human beings.

Tanisha had stored it all away as general knowledge. She'd never dream she could actually get her first one. That secret knowledge gave her thrill and she suppressed a tiny smile. She touched her lips—it felt odd—smiling. Her muscles weren't used to it.

According to the blogs and websites she'd read, the people didn't even know that they were dead. Violent attacks, such as the one Sherri endured, sometimes forced them to come back from the dead— just out of pure, unadulterated stubbornness. Some other sites claimed the damn device had been activated by the hypothalamus.

Funny. A tiny, elongated metal device, it had smooth rounded edges that appeared to be implanted into Sherri's ovaries. The device, always described as the same, ended up in different human body parts.

"Piper, put out a BOLO for Sherri Cross, a white female, mid-forties with angel blonde hair." Tanisha started the cruiser, and drove down the street a bit. "Suspect is possibly nude, but may have stolen some clothes."

Who had killed Sherri Cross? Where was Roger?

Tanisha pondered these questions as she drove around the block, circling the Cross home. The fluttering in her stomach returned, bringing with it shots of adrenaline that pumped through her veins. Something smelled funny about Roger's statements right from the beginning. That's the thing about stabbings—they were almost always personal.

If Sherri's body refused to stay dead, then it had to be because she wasn't ready to leave this good Earth.

As Tanisha made a right to circle the block for a fourth time, a pale flash of blonde hair scurried out across the street in front of her. The rain intensified and came down in sheets.

"What the…?" Tanisha threw the cruiser into park and got out. Immediately drenched from the rain, she raced, with her heart in her throat, after the nude woman who was nearly down to the next street's crosswalk.

Her heart racing, and stomach flip-flopping, she ran. The cold rain spattering on her face, the plastering of her clothes against her body, the energizing odor of rain, the trace hints of garbage uncollected and…the smell of death—she felt it all and more.

"Halt! Police!"

The fleeting figure, hunched over and sporting an obvious autopsy "Y" down her front, twisted once to see Tanisha running toward her. Screeching, she increased her speed. As she fled, Tanisha thought she spotted something in her arms.

"Stop! Sherri!" Tanisha slipped on the sidewalk, tripped, but rolled to a squatting position in the street. The stinging of the scrapes didn't immediately set in. By the time she'd regained her balance Sherri Cross had vanished.

"Darn it!"

For the first time in a very long while, Tanisha got angry. She trudged back to her cruiser, jerked opened the door, and plopped down into the seat. Slamming the door closed, she snatched up the receiver and barked, "Piper, pick up!"

"Piper here." Her scrubbed clean voice only served to irritate Tanisha more.

"I just saw Sherri Cross heading west on Peach Court. She is nude and barefoot. She's also carrying something, so tell the boys to be careful."

"Roger that. Oh, speaking of the Cross family. Max just got called to a crime scene over on Knuckles, two blocks from Elm. It's another homicide."

Tanisha flicked on the heat as she headed to Knuckles, only one block over from Cross family home on Yucca Drive. She could make out the lights of another squad car and the meat wagon. Yellow caution tape sagged in the rain, sectioning off the scene.

A gray rain slicker covered Max's broad body, and an umbrella held by Officer Yazzie protected his head from the pelting rain. He leaned down over the battered and bloodied body.

She stepped over the crime scene tape and approached the two men.

With one glance she knew to whom the pulp of brains and blood that lay at her feet belonged.

"Roger Cross."

Max nodded. "Yeppers."

"I just saw Sherri Cross. Now, I know what she had in her hands—their daughter."

Officer Yazzie 's eyes widened in surprise. "Naked?"

"Yeah. And barefoot."

"With the kid?" Yazzie shook his head.

"Well, scoop him up guys and take him back to the morgue." Max turned to Tanisha. "Somebody killed him good. Could hardly recognize him."

"It's so violent. It had to be Sherri." Officer Yazzie moved the umbrella to Max's new position.

"Murder is murder." Tanisha took out a new piece of gum.

§

Two more days went by with no sign of Sherri Cross. Tanisha and Max got into a heated debate about whether or not Sherri should still be classified as a homicide because she was obviously well enough to run around the streets.

Lacking any real clues, Tanisha returned to the first murder scene at the Cross family home. She could find no trace of an intruder or break-in. Just like Roger's murder, Sherri's had been overkill and extremely violent. Blood was everywhere, in the bed, spray across the walls and even under the dresser. Roger Cross must have killed Sherri, but the motive for such an act was still sketchy. How had he managed to continue to live there without cleaning up the mess?

Maybe he hadn't. She didn't read the autopsy report on how long Roger had been dead.

Just as Tanisha started down the steps to her cruiser, she heard little Ashley's infectious giggle. It echoed across the neighborhood and Tanisha followed it, drawing out her gun as she did so. She raced down Yucca, heading south. Again, the effects of adrenaline and exhilaration pumped into her bloodstream, increasing her heart rate and forcing her senses to sharpen. Sensory delight made everything crisp, and each sense nearly overwhelmed her in intensity. Every inch of her skin tingled with the turn of the corner. *Closer.* Just a few feet more to finding Sherri Cross and solving this case!

Her heightened awareness opened her to the smell of wet trees and grass, sounds of cars and the Cross girl's laughter, and above all she could *feel*... Her heart thundered with power and galloped in her chest as if it meant to leap out.

The clouds were currently withholding the rest of the rain, but the soggy ground caused Tanisha's feet to slap noisily against the sidewalk. As she made a right onto Desert Rose Avenue, she saw little Ashley fly into the air, right beside the monkey bars that stood in an empty, wet, playground. The air cold and chilly skated across Tanisha's still damp skin. She raised her gun and stepped closer.

A grayish shape shot up in the air and snatched Ashley close to its chest. Its limp hair was streaked with dirt and Little Ashley's hair was also wet and muddy—as if they'd been living under a tree or in the caverns outside the city.

The rotting corpse of Sherri Cross now stood rooted to the spot. It gripped Ashley, who squirmed and fought in vain to get down. Sherri's skin had sloughed off in places, but her eyes were still clear and firm. And defiant.

Tanisha took a quick sip of air; her finger on the trigger of her gun felt like it weighed a ton. Bustling with life, Tanisha thought of how crisp the sky's grayness seemed. She could smell the juniper from the playground's surrounding gardens and she could finally hear the squealing of tires on the still damp pavement.

"Now, Sherri, I know that Roger murdered you, and that's not right, but you're dead now." Tanisha's gun pointed at a space right above Sherri's eyes. One of the blogs, she'd read said the kill switch came right between the eyes. The device could send signals to the brain, but the bullet would keep the brain from working.

The stab wounds had proved fatal to Sherri when she was human, but there was still no cure for a bullet to the brain.

Tanisha released a steadying breath. She had no idea who had caused the reanimations, and the blogs had all sorts of possible options—the CDC, the folks at Area 51, and on to the Los Alamos labs in Santa Fe.

One thing was certain. Sherri Cross had been killed by her husband, Roger. She'd been reanimated, by some device, and she wanted her daughter. Something triggered that device—it could've been death.

Tanisha chose to believe it was Sherri Cross's love for her daughter.

"Come on, Sherri."

Sherri's blonde head shook and bits of hair and scalp drifted to the ground.

"Yeah, you're dead and now that you've killed Roger, little Ashley has no one to care for her."

Tanisha silently prayed over her gun. Sherri deserved peace. The Lord needed to take her in. The prayer felt strange on Tanisha's lips for she had never done anything like this. She'd never even felt like this before…so vibrant, so *real*.

Sherri's eyes flashed with anger and she pointed at herself. Her lips had fallen off sometime over the last two days. Vocal chords too probably. She couldn't form words.

"No, you can't do it. You're *dead*. Now, put her down so she can come over here to me."

Furious, Sherri wrapped both arms around little Ashley, pulling the child into her decaying flesh.

Ashley whimpered.

"I'll give you to three. Then I'm going to shoot." Tanisha's heart sped up its thump, thump with each indication that she might have to fire her gun.

Would her prayer be enough to send Sherri back to the grave? If the bullet short circuited Sherri's brain would that be enough to stop her? Did Sherri's brain even still work?

Sherri's eyes grew wider and she mouthed the word, *NO!*

"One… two…"

Sherri retreated back, her daughter still in her arms. She glanced at Ashley and her clear, intelligent eyes, misted over, as if with tears. With a drooping nose, she nudged Ashley affectionately.

"Three! Four! Sherri, I will shoot. Move away from the child!"

At this, Ashley kicked out and tumbled onto the ground.

Tanisha fired.

The shot landed dead center in Sherri Cross's brain. She collapsed to the wet ground.

Tanisha raced over to the twice dead Sherri and picked up Ashley.

"Murder is a murder."

Ashley growled, and Tanisha held the little girl tightly. For the first time in years, Tanisha could feel tears on her face. Sherri Cross only wanted to protect and care for her daughter. She had experienced firsthand the fury and destruction of her husband while alive.

Driven by her protective nature, she'd fought death to find her daughter.

Moments later a shock of pain shot through Tanisha as Ashley bit into her shoulder. Staggering from the surprising force of the bite, Tanisha dropped the little girl. It was only then she noticed the girl's decaying flesh and the stench of death. Eyes round with hunger and mouth wide with need, Ashley snarled as she took another leap at Tanisha.

Uncle Sharlevoix's Epidermis

Gregory L. Norris

*T*he big old house on Charrington Road was always dusty, but lately certain rooms had developed a skin, which lay in a film over the walls like on the pudding Aunt Cassandra served when rare guests visited. Uncle Sharlevoix was gone, planted in the ground for just over three years. I was one of the infrequent guests whose callings grew rarer after the funeral due to the demands of my life.

"Auntie," I said, seated at the oblong dinner table with its scratched rosewood veneer—unintentional tattoos from so many past family dinner gatherings and dropped forks.

"Yes, Cedric?" she answered from over the top of her porcelain teacup, now stained a severe shade of plum-purple from her lipstick.

"Have you noticed anything odd in the house?"

"Odd?" she parroted and then considered.

Fretting, her eyes wandered out of the dining room, past the faded though still elegant Japanese patterned paper. I tracked her gaze to the length of wall running behind my back and the imagined direction of my late uncle's laboratory rooms, where a thin coating of living tissue had appeared among the cobwebs and neglected objects d'art; especially in Uncle Sharl's private study, where glass jars filled with cloudy liquid and expired things and his other scientific hobbies lurked, abandoned by a hobbyist who wouldn't return.

"You mean...?"

"The skin," I said.

"Skin? I suppose that it is."

"So, you've noticed it along the chair rail and the wainscoting? Over the wedding cake molding and cornices? Pale pink and pulsating, as though the walls are growing their own epidermis?"

The flesh above Aunt Cassandra's left eye ticked from nerves. "Not that I go back there much anymore. This house, big as it is, keeps me occupied."

I drew in a deep breath. Aunt Cassandra's perfume had lost its light floral prettiness and, for a terrible moment, all I could smell was the one foul component included in every brand of ladies' scent designed to accentuate its fragrance.

"Skin," I repeated. "Cells dividing, multiplying, growing thicker and more elastic. Across the walls, ceilings, and floorboards."

To which, my aunt responded, "Well, dear, as your late uncle was fond of reminding us, matter never truly dies—it just changes its form."

Uncle Sharlevoix was dead. Part of him, however, had transformed and was growing in scabrous pink patches in the darkest and most mysterious rooms of the big old house.

§

My uncle was, as you can imagine, a strange man. Some would say eccentric, though I prefer the former. Over the course of his life, Sharlevoix Beauregard Smythe worked as a tree farmer, a tree surgeon, a consultant for the state, the state university and, later, a delver into the mysteries of the Universe, both small and vast, unlocking the secrets of microbiology, one of his favorite passions and pastimes. Some of the trees he planted around the Smythe Family estate as saplings are now elder giants with half a century's worth of added rings. At least one of his experiments crawls through the halls and over the walls of the big old house on Charrington Road.

Uncle Sharl and Aunt Cassandra were married forty-two years before a tiny vessel in his brilliant brain exploded, and blood formed bruises, and more of the conduits in his grey matter shattered in sequence, causing the catastrophic breakdown that led to my late autumn morning in the dining room with my elderly aunt.

"Tea, dear?" she asked.

"Don't switch the subject, Aunty," I chastised. "And you know I don't drink tea. I prefer coffee."

"Your uncle loved his tea. A nice, robust Darjeeling with a splash of lemon was his favorite. He claimed it helped him to think."

"I think," I said, "that the house is too big for one person."

And there it was, that other oddity spoken of for the first time since my return following the funeral.

"It may be too big for *two*. Have you thought about selling the estate?"

Aunt Cassandra finished her tea and avoided my scrutiny. "Please do not go there again, Cedric. You'd have to drag me out of this house by my stockings."

"I have no intention of doing that, Aunty, though I wish you'd at least consider the notion. In any event, I'll stick around long enough to help you put things in some sort of order. Clean the place up. Scrape the walls."

My aunt's eyes shot open like old shades drawn too quickly. Her mascara magnified whites and pupils alike. "Oh no, dear, no," she said. "Not about joining me for a time—you know how much I enjoy the company. But Cedric, you mustn't do anything to the skin on the walls."

"Why not?"

"Because…" she said, but then fell silent and raised the teacup to her lips, stemming further discussion.

§

The house on Charrington Road was a cryptic old place. I summered there as a boy, and maintain there are rooms I remember playing in, like the Pink Parlor, only those rooms no longer exist. Or I've not been able to find them, despite many attempts to map the estate's layout and catalog contents. The house's cells, I imagine, have multiplied, divided, and regrown new limbs in the form of rooms and whole new wings.

After my morning coffee, I walked outside the back portico and wandered the dead gardens. It was, perhaps, the year's last good morning. A bright, warm November day unfolded, and on a pleasant breeze were reminders of summer: grass and leaves, a hint of floral perfume from October's asters. The wild tangles of overgrown reeds and shrubbery spilled over the stonewalls delineating the gardens from walking paths. In the summers of my youth, Uncle Sharl tended the flora with strict geometry, imposing shape, order, and science on the vast green spaces he so loved. Now, all was chaos.

I picked my way through brambles and briars, past the sundial with its sad smile, and the granite bench upon whose seat was carved a single word: *Resurgam*.

"'I will rise again,'" I whispered, and remembered my batty old aunt's cryptic behavior over breakfast.

Uncle Sharlevoix was brilliant, if batty, too. My late uncle, through his research into the unknown properties of the Greater Universe and the microscopic galaxy spirals contained within our genes, was convinced he would discover a way to beat the grave. If he had unlocked such forbidden knowledge before his death, the *Eureka!* moment clearly hadn't struck in the ancient greenhouse wherein the plants that populated the summer gardens were cultivated. Seasons of abandonment had shattered three of the glass panes. Dead leaves cluttered an environment where, in my memory, only green things flourished.

I tried the door. It resisted. I pushed harder and the old wood croaked open. Inside on a corner table stood two clay pots that contained misshapen growths rising up from desiccated soil; thick, gnarled stalks, each having put forth five digits. To my horror, the lifeless plants resembled human wrists and hands, the fingers capped in cracked gray nails frozen in a pose suggesting they'd suffocated while grabbing at thin air.

Vines and shoots, thorns and stamens, everything within the greenhouse was dead.

§

Not so in Uncle Sharl's laboratory. Yes, it was true that the glass jars filled with formaldehyde and biological remnants were canopic in nature. I lifted one from the credenza upon which it and several dozen others sat. The organ inside, something gray and crenulated, vanished in a snowstorm of liquid dust. Dead things, things pinned to boards and splayed open, insects and arachnids and ugly, expired horrors stored neatly in rolling cabinet drawers or hung on walls behind glass, but...

On the window shelves, the flora abandoned by Uncle Sharlevoix bloomed lushly in the light of that last resplendent November afternoon. I wondered how the plants could subsist here, let alone flourish, until I heard the buzzing of flies and caught darting, dark afterimages near the windows, smelled the cloying sweetness from the waxy throats of fat flower blossoms, and made the connection. A small ecosystem had formed in a forgotten corner of the house, like the pale pink skin stretched thin over the wall in another part of the room.

Mastering courage, I turned away from the flesh-eating blossoms and willed my feet toward the patch of epidermis, similar to others growing elsewhere in the house on Charrington Road. Perhaps the segments were expanding their reaches, linking up, swelling in layers in an attempt to become whole.

As I neared the section of wall, a shiver teased the nape of my neck. I fought it, failed. The room fazed out of focus as it tumbled. When the world again stabilized, I identified the source: eyes, somewhere in the room—I was being watched!

I caught a reflection in one of those glass cases behind which bugs and beasts were impaled to boards. Eyes, one pair, bright red, leered at me from somewhere in the laboratory. I spun around. The eyes manifested there, close to the window.

The eyes were really flowers, but the sensation of being studied persisted and crawled across my skin, conjuring gooseflesh. Eyes, red and unblinking, drew me into their hypnotic pull. In some disconnected way, I understood that I had fallen into a trance state. My eyes burned from not blinking. At the periphery, the buzz of flies formed a sort of music, itchy on the ear. In counterpoint, individual notes shorted out abruptly as the makers of the melody vanished into tiny pools of deadly nectar in the throats of flowers.

Blink, a voice in my thoughts commanded. My eyes resisted.

It took the slithery sound of the skin moving close behind me to force my muscles out of their paralysis. I sucked in a deep breath, jolted out of my stance, and turned in time to see the skin on the wall reach down toward me, like a serpent in the branches.

The skin put forth a rudimentary limb with one wiggling finger. I gasped a rosary of expletives and stepped clear of its clutches. The skin stretched out, grabbed at open air formerly occupied by my right shoulder, and lost its grip on the cracked ceiling plaster. Gravity launched the skin-snake out of the canopy and flattened it on the dusty floor. The loud, squelching *splat* as it struck hardwood exorcised the last trace of the flower's spell.

Revulsion seized hold of me at the horrifying vision of the skin, wriggling in death-throes; writhing worm-like at both ends as it expanded and contracted. An elastic, agonizing peal rippled up through its layers of skin cells. Several long, tense seconds later, the patch of epidermis ceased pulsing and, before my eyes, went gray and lifeless.

§

A stiff wind sent in storm clouds later that same day. By dusk, rain fell in torrents and hammered the old house.

Aunt Cassandra fixed one of her usual succulent dinners—roasted chicken, the skin golden and salty; red potatoes crusted with rosemary from her kitchen herb garden; baby peas and pearl onions; and the old-fashioned chocolate pudding with its filmy top layer for which she became famous among family and friends, with dollops of fresh whipped cream on top.

I stabbed at the skin with my spoon. The thin crust split. The matter beneath was damp and pillow-soft.

"Aunty?"

Aunt Cassandra glanced up from her dessert. She had dressed for dinner in her finest black silk-satins and an ostentatious broach with a glittering opal at the center. "Is everything satisfactory?"

"Above and beyond, dear," I said. "You are, as has so often been said, a culinary genius."

"Thank you," Aunt Cassandra said. She then scooped a huge spoonful of pudding out of her bowl and savored the experience through rolled eyes and a soft moan.

"Aunty, about the skin…"

My aunt's euphoria shorted out. She faced me directly, her eyes narrowed, her lips pursed. "Yes, Cedric?"

"The skin on the walls."

"Yes?"

"What exactly was my late uncle working on when, you know… when the tragedy struck?"

Her mouth twisted into a smile. "The mysteries of life. The conquest of death. Hybridization and cytoplasm, photosynthesis and grafting."

"Grafting?" I asked.

"Yes, dear—the skilled application of one species' branch to another's roots. There are, I fear, things out there still skittering about on the grounds that got loose from his laboratory before he fully understood that which he created. I've seen this one abomination… with the loveliest blue tentacles and a face one could almost believe was human, like a child's…"

Her voice trailed to a whisper. Then, as though grasping that she had revealed too much, Aunt Cassandra ground her teeth, stemming further discussion on the subject.

"A nice cup of tea, dear?" she asked.

I reminded her that I drank coffee and offered to clear the plates.

"No, Cedric, why don't you call it an early night."

I returned to my room. The rain beat a somber staccato against the roof and outer walls of the old house. And the skin divided and multiplied in certain dark rooms around me.

The wind howled. Limbs from the surrounding trees crept closer toward the house, driven into undulation by the storm. The effect created in my room mirrored that of black and white stop-motion photography, projected through the windows onto the walls and ceiling.

I lie on my spine and pondered the things I'd seen and heard during the daylight hours. Wooden wrists and fingers, sinister petal-eyes, slithering patches of skin, and obscenities with tentacles and child faces jumped out of my imagination and superimposed over the flickers. My pulse galloped. The urge to switch on the lamp at bedside possessed me, but fear held me rigid.

Between shutter-clicks, a shape formed, grotesquely human, a caricature. I heard it as it completed crawling in from the base of the door and across the floor, its movements wet and sticky. On suction cup fingers, it pulled itself closer, closer yet. My heart jumped into my throat, lodged in my windpipe. Suddenly, I couldn't breathe.

Closer.

Mustering all of my energy, I bolted upright, reached for the lamp, and turned the switch. Light drove shadows back into corners, and the primitive horror attempting to stand upright, waving jelly limbs that had no skeletal structure, bent backward in panic and wriggled away, making what sounded to my ears like a scream.

§

The rain fell. A cold November rain, one week later and the world beyond the windows of the old house on Charrington Road would be blanketed in white instead of gray.

When I arrived to the Smythe Family estate, a palace few visited, my main concern was for an elderly aunt living alone in an endless succession of rooms set on a vast, remote plot. My motives were mostly noble in nature, though I admit there was another reason for my visit.

The house was filled with decades of acquired treasures in the art, the silver, the furniture, and objects sharing space with so much dust and, in certain rooms, skin. As one of the sole surviving Smythes, I was due my legacy. I didn't think this as being entirely selfish; it felt practical.

But I soon came to the realization that there was something far more valuable there than original Impressionist paintings and Revere silver. Around the house, in the laboratory rooms, and loose on the grounds were manifestations of my late uncle's scientific genius.

Twice, the pale pink flesh growing, dying, stretching out, had attempted to communicate with me.

"Aunty?" I asked.

"Yes?" said Aunt Cassandra over vibrant eggs that glowed with their sunny sides up, beside ham steaks with seared scarlet flesh and hot buttered toast served on her favorite antique Royal Doulton plates.

"Uncle Sharlevoix…did he write down his ideas?"

"Why yes, he did. Your late uncle kept an extensive journal regarding his scientific experiments and interests."

I picked up a slice of toast and aimed the point at an egg yolk. The tiny sun went nova. Hot liquid poured past the fine layer of skin holding all intact. "Where did Uncle Sharl keep his journal? I've been through his laboratory twice and didn't find it."

"You didn't?" Aunt Cassandra answered. And though she said no more on the subject and, instead, raised her teacup to her lips, I sensed she knew far more than she chose to share.

§

I followed fresh tracks wound through the dust on the floor and again entered Uncle Sharlevoix's laboratory.

The skin on the wall quivered, pink and gelatinous, inspiring comparisons to jellyfish and juicy fruits and whole galaxies held together by the skin of energy particles. It *was* alive, after a fashion. A life form born of dust and debris cursed by the will to endure against nature's version of planned obsolescence.

Dust is mostly made of shed human skin cells. Like leaves dropped in the autumn, which nourish new plants in the spring, Uncle Sharlevoix's epidermis had birthed something *other*.

I approached the skin and whispered, "Uncle Sharl?"

A muffled sob drifted out of the flesh in counterpoint to the rain's elegy.

I extended my hand, brushed the backs of my knuckles over the quivery mass. Heat and electricity crackled over my flesh. It cooed like a pet, folded its primitive digit around my wrist. Then its grip tightened and all pleasantness evaporated. Pain flared. I pulled away. The skin held on. When it refused to release me, I aimed pointer and middle fingers at its mass and dug.

The skin popped. The gelatinous layer beneath came rushing out in liquid spindles. Wetness sprayed my face. A foul, coppery taste blossomed on my tongue. Energy raced down my throat, tugged at my eyeballs, jabbed oily fingers into both ears. My next desperate gasp for breath came through a fleshy filter.

The room plunged into darkness. Hours later—or it could have been days—I woke to find myself seated in the chair at the big dining room table, my head resting on wrists. I attempted to swallow, only to discover that my mouth was miserably dry. Water...I had never been thirstier.

Sunlight streamed through the windows. I stretched. The effulgence rained over the skin of my bruised arm. The pain was gone, however. My entire body felt reborn.

In glided Cassandra, who looked radiant in the golden glare. She carried a big book with a worn cover under one arm.

"Finally, you're awake," she said.

"Yes."

Cassandra set the book on the desk. "The journal of fantastic secrets, dear. May I bring you anything else?"

I opened the book to the last page with writing. "Yes, water. And coffee."

"Coffee?"

My eyes fell into the words on the pages; sentences and spells that referenced photosynthesis and resurrection.

"Make it tea, dear," I said, and began to read.

Gas

James Dorr

Behind me," Mike Peterson had told his tour group not *twelve* hours before, "is the Science Building." He'd gestured upward to take in the huge limestone arch of its entrance. "We'll be entering the original part first—most of the students call it the Old Quad—built in 1898. But, as you'll see, other sections were added on later as interest in science brought new endowments. In the late 1920s, for instance, then during the war years of the 40s, then, finally, during the post-Sputnik boom of the early '60s when the Olbers Memorial Annex was completed. We'll end our tour there."

"What about libraries," someone asked. An elderly woman, as he remembered. "Yeah," another voice piped in—this one an overweight middle-aged man's. "And what about the laboratories? You know, where the *real* science is done."

"Yes," Mike said. "The library is in the wing I just mentioned— mostly it's just called the New Annex now, even though it's nearly forty years old in its own right. As for the labs, you'll visit one of the teaching labs toward the end of the tour, although the main labs—the ones the faculty use for research—are still mostly down in the Old Quad basement."

Mike started up the steps to the entrance, then paused at the top to open the doors. "Be sure and stay together," he cautioned as the tour group—parents, mostly, of prospective students, but mixed with a smattering of older alumni—trooped into the building. "Even with endowment money, the college often built newer additions to follow the contours of the hillside. They saved on construction costs that way, but, as a result, the corridors inside will often join at crazy angles. In other words, this is an easy place to get lost in."

§

How many times, Mike wondered now, had he gotten lost in the building himself? And he was a graduate student in chemistry, nearing the end of his second year. In fact, it was rumored that even professors were known to take wrong turns and get lost themselves, at least in the basement where he was now, finishing up the equipment inventory Professor Mosely had asked him for. Even old hands like Professor Harkins.

He picked up a beaker, fingerprinted, with two or three milliliters of some half-solidified mass in the bottom. He dumped it—with Mosely, whatever the substance was, it wasn't likely to be dangerous—and rinsed it out, then held it up as he polished the outside, wincing at the distorted reflection he saw of his face. He thought the lights flickered, which didn't surprise him. He'd noticed a storm coming up when he'd checked in.

Then he laughed, remembering the tour. One of the younger parents *had* gotten lost, despite his warnings, and it had taken ten minutes to find her. If she'd been down here, where tunnels had been cut between some labs, where others dead-ended, where ventilation and service ducts were sometimes so wide they could be confused for small hallways themselves…

He shrugged and got back to checking glassware off on his clipboard. Such was the life of a graduate student, working his way to a hoped-for doctorate. Leading tour groups and answering questions on Saturday mornings to help pay tuition. Washing out test tubes most every night—they still used test tubes, even in cutting-edge biochemistry. Even if old man Mosely wasn't exactly the cutting edge himself.

But Mosely and Harkins shared equipment, and working for Mosely in the catacombs of the chem section at least got him closer.

He laughed again, his laugh turning bitter, remembering the middle-aged man on the tour—the one who had asked about labs before. He remembered the way the man's over-bright print shirt had stretched over his belly.

"Harkins still here?" the man had asked.

Mike had nodded. "Oh, yes," he said. "In fact, he may even be in the building—he often works weekends—although he'd be in his lab downstairs. Were you one of his students?"

"Nah," the man said. "I was just wondering. I thought maybe he'd gotten fired. Wasn't there a scandal of some kind about five years back? About military funding or something?"

"Sort of," Mike answered. "Actually, it was more like eight years ago—I was in high school at the time. And it wasn't really a scandal. Professor Harkins had had a Defense Department grant, but then, after the Cold War thawed out, the college went through a divestiture period, trying to cut military ties. Doctor Harkins was caught in the middle and…"

"I seem to remember something about students picketing—wasn't it this building?"

Mike nodded. "Yes." He remembered reading the newspapers too, and clipping the pieces about Harkins out to put in his scrapbook. Because his family didn't have money, he'd had no choice but to go to the state university for his undergraduate degree, but, when it was time to study further, he had known even then that he'd find some way to come here. "Yes," he said again, "but you know students. The 'peacenik' contingent. Anyhow, it was all cleared up. Most of the funding was given back, but some—at the government's own request—was funneled into civilian research. In fact, the main project he's working on now is funded by an insurance company—it's all quite up front. It involves basic medical research in life expectancy."

"In other words," the overweight man asked, laughing, "eight years ago, Harkins was trying to find better ways of killing people, but now he's trying to make 'em live longer?"

Mike took a deep breath to keep his anger from reaching the surface. "Yes," he had answered.

§

There was no doubt the lights flickered this time. Mike glanced at the clock on the wall to his left. It was practically ten, almost time to call it a night in any event. He listened—he couldn't hear any thunder. Maybe the storm was ending, he thought, as he took off his lab coat and started to hang it up, then reconsidered.

Maybe, he thought, if it was still raining, he ought to wear it home to his apartment. Not that the nights weren't warm in the summer, but why get any more wet than he had to?

He put the coat back on as he turned off the lights in the laboratory, then made sure the main door was locked behind him. He started to walk to the nearest stairway, a walk that would take him down dim, narrow corridors past Harkins' lab, when the lights brightened, then flickered a third time. And this time there was a sound, not of thunder, but a kind of popping noise followed by a soft hissing.

He stopped. *A hissing?* From the direction of Harkins' lab? The noise quickly faded to nothing—*was* probably nothing—but still he remembered the interview he had had with Harkins, that got him the job he had now with Mosely. The job he understood would be a sort of apprenticeship until Harkins' next grant came through.

"You want to work with me?" Harkins had asked, his blue, owl-like eyes peering up at Mike from behind thick glasses. "You know I sometimes use dangerous chemicals?"

"Nerve gas, wasn't it?" Mike had answered. "During the '80s? I know the newspapers never quite said it at the time, but when I was at State I did some research…"

Harkins had chuckled. "Then you know what I've been doing since then. The religious groups…?"

Mike nodded. "Yes. Though the newspapers never quite said *that* either."

§

The hissing had stopped. It *had* been nothing. But now Mike thought he heard a sound of tinkling glass. To be on the safe side, he retraced his steps. The nerve gas was gone—he knew that its return to the Army had been what had ended the students' protesting—but more recent substances Harkins worked with could be just as lethal. In any event, there were other staircases out of the basement.

He passed the locked door to Mosely's lab and turned right at the next intersecting hallway, then left at an angle where the floor began to slope upward. On either side, paint peeled from otherwise featureless walls while, over his head, the dusty, bare light bulbs hung between pipes that often met with the walls at their own bizarre angles. The lights flickered again and he hurried his steps, realizing he'd entered—which wing was it? The one built in 1923, for biology classrooms. The one with the steam tunnels—tunnels as big as the hallway he strode through—that cut back in vast bow-like curves to the older section.

He took another turn to his right. A stairway should be just ahead, he thought—or was it off the hall to the left? This wasn't a part of the building he walked through very often, at least in the basement.

He thought once more of his earlier tour group, trying to remember the way the hallways joined on the floor above him. Wasn't it there where the woman had gotten lost? Lagging behind to look at a display case, then, when she'd realized the group had gone on, not having the sense to stay where she was?

"I'm sorry, Mr. Peterson," she had said after he'd found her. She'd wandered into one of the teaching labs and screamed when she saw what was apparently her first dissected cat, its abdomen slit open and its organs floating around it in its formaldehyde-filled display jar.

"Mike," he'd corrected. He'd taken her hand and led her out, threading their way through the relatively simple plan of the upstairs classroom floor until they reached where the others were waiting.

He tried to remember now—had he and the woman gone this far? He remembered they *had* passed a stairwell. Perhaps to the left. He tried to remember.

He thought he felt something brush his shoulder, just like he'd touched the woman's shoulder when he'd first found her, her eyes glazed over, staring at the corpse of the cat. But when he looked up, there was nothing there. Just crumbling water pipes, half lost in shadow.

Then, when he lowered his eyes again, he found himself facing the crumbling bricks of a dead-end wall.

§

He nearly panicked. The lights were dimming. He smelled a faint, sour smell in the air. But then his mind went back to his undergraduate days, to Ms. Fitzholland's Basic Psychology lecture course. To the subsequent lab course. Rats in mazes.

It hadn't been his favorite subject, but now he remembered the "right hand rule." The rule that said that if *you* were ever put in a maze, the way to get out was by always taking your turns to the right, just reversing direction when you reached a dead end, until you'd traversed every possible path.

Why not? he thought. The staircase was *somewhere*. He half closed his eyes, reaching his hand out to brush against the wall as he turned, walking slowly, taking always the rightward path.

He remembered the human corpses just as the lights flickered one more time and left him in darkness. He listened and thought he heard hissing again, but this time he retained his composure. He thought instead—he knew where he was now. He thought back, barely a month before, when he and Mosely had been unloading the long, heavy masses under Professor Harkins' supervision.

"Peterson," the professor had said when they'd gotten the last of the body bags stacked on the gurney, "you said you knew that not all the protests had been anti-war. Do you remember what the religious groups—the ones that came later—had been upset over?"

Mike had nodded. "What you'd been doing before, with the nerve gas, wasn't just finding more powerful poisons, but also discovering antidotes for them. Then, when the first insurance grant came, you said you thought you could find a way of bringing back people who'd died of diseases. Not really died, of course, but…"

"No, that's what I said," Harkins corrected him. "People who'd died. The church groups said I was trying to play God. But dying is just a chemical function and, with the proper reagents, there shouldn't be any reason why, if it's caught in time, it can't be reversed."

"You mean you've succeeded?" Mike had whispered. He knew exactly where he'd been standing, the sharp upward angle the floor had taken—that he and Mosely had just pushed the gurney up—and how the cement had been cracked at the point it once more became level. More important, now that the lights were gone, he remembered the *feel* of the floor underneath his sneakers.

"No," Professor Harkins had said. He remembered how disappointed he'd been, too. "No, but I think I *have* made a break-through. The reason I'm bringing it up now, though, is I think I may have money for an assistant this fall. That is, if it's okay with you, Mosely. But, if I do, I want to make sure you understand, Peterson, what kind of flack you may be getting into."

Mike had said he understood. In fact, he thought now, it was the very *power* of science, and Harkins' research, that had attracted him here in the first place. Not genius, exactly. Not Harkins so much as an individual who could teach him, but rather the sheer power that the professor represented. The power to, as the fat alumnus had put it that morning, to find ways to kill people *and* make them live longer—both at the same time.

But the important thing right now was that he *had* remembered the corpses. He knew the path he and Mosely had taken, wheeling the gurney into the lab, and, more to the point, he remembered the path they had taken back, out to the loading dock off the New Annex. He wondered exactly how long he'd been walking, taking his always right-turning path through the maze of corridors that had brought him back to where he was now, approaching Professor Harkins' lab—and Mosely's lab, too—from the opposite side of where he had started.

It didn't matter. Somehow, he had managed to circle the entire Old Quad, but, if he kept going, he knew the way out. He didn't mind that the smell was stronger—the unpleasant sour smell he'd noticed before, mixed now with a kind of overlay odor of almost-sweetness. He didn't mind that he heard, once again, the faint popping noise, and the sound of glass breaking somewhere in the distance. That, once again, something touched his shoulder.

It wasn't a corpse sneaking up behind him—that much he at least knew. He laughed out loud, thinking of the horror movie he'd watched on TV when he'd gotten off work the previous Saturday. Unlike the movie hero, though, he had been allowed to watch Harkins on subsequent nights as the professor had anatomized the corpses, testing each part for electrical impulses before preserving them for further study. Just like the cat that had frightened the woman upstairs that morning.

Rats, on the other hand…Harkins did animal experiments, too. Mike wheeled around, thought he saw a shadow, and wondered if maybe the professor was closer to success then he'd let on to being. But then he realized that basements held ordinary rats as well. Especially in buildings as old as this one.

And then he realized one more thing. He *had* seen a shadow. *A shadow in darkness.*

He stared at the wall, and then at the fingers he'd brushed along it in his right-turning journey. The light was faint, but both were glowing.

§

He thought of the first day he'd been on campus, two years before, at the end of the summer. The sun had been bright, but many parts of the campus were wooded, including the hillside the multi-winged Science Building brooded over. He'd found the sight beautiful—light and shadow, sparkling through greenery. That's when he had first seen Professor Harkins in the flesh.

He'd started to run to greet the man he had recognized instantly from his pictures, but then a voice, much like his own, had called him back. "Stick with the group," the voice had said—the voice was that of a graduate tour guide. "All of you, stay together with me, especially once you're inside the building. It's an easy place to get lost in."

Mike laughed. Yes. Easy to get lost in. And even professors, the rumors went, could get lost in the basement.

But now he knew, even without the strengthening phosphorescent glow that coated the walls, that a final turn would take him to where the Annex angled off from the Old Quad. And then, to his left, he would find the ramp that would take him up to the outside air.

A final turn. And then, ahead of him, he saw the gas.

It had come from Professor Harkins' lab, not the long way as he had come, but through the ductwork that cut between corridors. It swirled down the hallway toward him, glowing so fiercely it hurt his eyes.

Within the gas, he saw shadowy figures, not of corpses, but *parts* of corpses.

Of hands and arms. Of torsos and heads, their flesh falling off in advanced putrescence. Twitching, inching their ways independently through the swirling.

"No!" Mike shouted. He turned—he'd find another way upstairs—but behind him, in the distance, he saw the glow brightening, too.

"No," he said again, this time more calmly. He estimated the width of the cloud between him and the Annex.

It wasn't as though he hadn't already been breathing the stuff, it occurred to him. Even if in small doses, which let out nerve gas. Ruled out other poisons as well. Whatever it was, it hadn't killed him. He took a deep breath, then took off his lab coat and wrapped it around his nose and mouth. He ran directly into the glow.

He felt his flesh tingle where…*things*…grabbed at it. He ignored the feeling—as well as the stench.

The stench he kept with him.

§

Outside, the air was warm, if still damp. The storm had ended. Mike left the Annex wishing almost that it were still raining, but, at the same time, he was glad to see the moon starting to peer through the rapidly diminishing clouds. He took one look back at the building he'd just left, then wadded up his now filthy lab coat and thrust it into a nearby dumpster.

As for himself, as soon as he reached home he'd get in the shower and, under a stinging spray of hot water, he'd do his best to put the events of the night behind him.

He walked tiredly down the hill, drinking in the fresh, moist air, feeling its cleanness against his skin. He wondered exactly what time it was—the campus seemed to be nearly deserted, even though it was Saturday night. He did see one couple, in front of the Overseas Studies Building. He thought a moment, then left the path he was walking on and crossed the puddled grass to approach them.

"Excuse me," he called out. "I don't have a watch. Do you have the time?"

The woman looked up. Her face froze in a scream, while the boy who was with her whirled, then grabbed her arm, pushing her back. He stood between her and Mike, backing slowly, pushing her with him as he retreated.

"Hey," Mike shouted. He took another step, just as the moon came out completely from behind the clouds. He felt his shoe slide on the edge of a puddle.

He looked down to see a face—

—*one that was rotting, its flesh peeling off even as he stared, like the paint of the basement walls—*

—a face that looked up at him, already showing the death-gray of bone, and yet with just enough shape in its features that he had no doubt the reflection was his.

Under Two Moons
Jonathan Shipley

I *leaned into the window as the security shuttle descended* into the endless warehouse district just as night descended on the city. From the air, the district held the aspect of a giant checkerboard, blocky buildings stretching in all directions to embrace the spaceport on three sides. An extra-ocular scan revealed the warehouses filled with timber and unprocessed nuggets of metal. That fit with the Meggothi people being primarily exporters of raw materials. But how did it fit with murder?

I knew little about general Meggothi culture. The bulk of my information was highly political in nature—all the pre-conference briefings had been heavily slanted toward government policies and personalities. I was part of the Imperial diplomatic team negotiating a border dispute with the neighboring system. This murder investigation was complete improvisation. But when a Meggothi warlord interrupts interstellar negotiations to request Imperial help with a local murder, that's a strong indicator of desperation. The Excellenza Trejhin, who represented the Will of the All-Highest Emperor at this conference, saw the request as an opportunity. So, she sent me to investigate. "Go, Darryd," she had said without one bit of instruction how to handle this. It had all happened quickly.

There were ironies all over the place. I was just a provincial adjutant beginning a career with the Diplomatic Corps. I had never even been to Throneworld, which in Imperial circles made me very provincial indeed. I had rejoiced that I had been assigned as support staff for a regional conference moderated by one of the Emperor's elite Excellenzi. I was rejoicing less now. It was no mystery why I had been assigned this investigative task. I was a lower functionary, completely extraneous to the substance of the negotiations. The problem was that lower functionaries weren't trained to handle individual missions like this in the name of the Empire. At least I was competent with fieldwork. My only hope was that my data-linked implants could find answers where the Meggothi had failed.

As the shuttle settled onto one of the cargo ways that crisscrossed the district like an astrogational grid, I continued accessing cultural details, letting the data visuals stream down the edge of my peripheral vision. Meggoth was an old humanoid world with colonies on three other worlds within its system and rudimentary interstellar travel. But not terribly advanced socially. There was a violent undertow running all through its history, and the succession of warlord to warlord was always bloody. The fact that they had opted for Imperial mediation instead of outright war with their neighbors was atypical. Trejhin called it an "event window" with the potential of becoming a turning point in their cultural awareness. An Excellenza would know those things; I would not.

"The body is this way, Excellenz," the port guard said, cutting the shuttle engines and beckoning me out of the craft toward an alley mouth.

My mouth quirked. I was a long way down the command chain from an Excellenz. But he was playing it safe. For all this local knew, I could have arrived with Trejhin from Throneworld where I regularly basked in the Presence of the All-Highest. Nonsense, of course, but it gave me a whiff of what one day might be. Only the very best were selected as Excellenzi. I was a fool even to hope.

The cargo way was striped with the vari-colored light of the two moons that hung high in the sky as we walked the half block to an intersecting alley. The corpse lay sprawled halfway back from the alley mouth. I winked on my ocular enhancer as we approached to take in the fine details of the crime. As the scan data began flowing, I knew something was wrong. The Meggothi were humanoid, divergent, but not far removed from Imperial genotype. There was no physiological reason that death should leave the body drained of all fluids.

"This body looks almost mummified," I observed. "Are you sure this man has been dead only a matter of minutes." He even smelled long dead, which was to say no sweetish odor of on-going decay, even with enhancement.

The guard nodded grimly. "He reported in less than an hour ago. But there have been others just the same—a whole string of them. One minute they're fine; the next, they're nothing but dry husks. We don't know what to do."

I digested his fear as much as his words, reminding myself that this was a culture where murder was common. To my semi-trained eye, there seemed to be an attitudinal disconnect. "Is there any pattern to the victims or the locations?"

"All of them happened pretty close to here, if that's a pattern."

"Oh." I was processing the fact that this was the most recent murder in a series that all took place in the immediate area. It was unsettling, because I hadn't come armed. The guard had an energy pistol of some sort, but Meggothi weaponry didn't seem to impress this attacker. I had energy deflectors built in my uniform, but it wasn't battle armor.

"Do you know what the victim was doing here?" I asked.

My companion shifted uneasily. "Investigating the murder from this morning," he said. "He was one of us—port security. He knew he wasn't supposed to be here alone but thought his weapons would protect him. Said he believed in guns more than any old superstition."

My eyes cut to the pair of pistols still holstered at the corpse's waist. Internal sensors informed me neither had been fired recently. "Whatever did this," I said slowly, "must have been very fast. He didn't even have a chance to draw his weapons."

"Or maybe he did…but was too scared to think straight." He gave a shudder and patted his own weapon for reassurance.

But there was something else. "What old superstition was the deceased referring to?"

The guard grimaced. "Shouldn't have said that. No point in reaching out to the Empire if the Imperials just think we're superstitious primitives."

Diplomatic Corps dealt with this attitude a lot as we contacted less advanced cultures, particularly humanoid cultures. As a species-cluster, we seem to have a penchant for posturing. "Superstitions are often just a different slant on factual occurrences," I said, giving the standard response. "Please share what you know."

He hesitated, then pointed up toward the moons. "Double full moons—only happens once every couple generations. Supposed to be a time of death and danger. Our ancestors used to offer blood sacrifices to hold all that at bay, but now we want a new start, not the old ways. And whatever it is, Imperial tech can handle it…right?"

I kept my expression neutral, but behind the façade, I was becoming more unsettled. It looked very much as though the Diplomatic Corps had just been played, if not in the conference itself, then at least in the timing of it. The Meggothi wanted Imperial tech on planet to deal with a known local danger. If they'd been open about their intentions, Throneworld could have sent in squads of Stedren warriors and all would have been fine. Instead they got me.

"Exactly what are we dealing with—supposedly?" I demanded.

"Demon," the guard shrugged. "Lives in some unnatural place and can come through only when the pull of the moons is strongest. Supposedly."

A demon. I let myself relax a little. If there was anything a star-faring empire knew, it was that demons by one definition were merely vastly different sentients races by another. What was needed was applied xeno-diplomacy, not blood sacrifice. Still a couple of Stedren would have been good leverage for that conversation.

"Hate to ask, Excellenz," the guard muttered nervously, "but would you mind if I waited back in the shuttle. Starting to feel a little queasy."

"That will be fine," I nodded, glad for the privacy. I needed to report in for instructions. As soon as he disappeared around the corner, I tapped my earstud. "Excellenza, there are complications. I think these murders may be the warlord's ulterior motive for inviting us here for a conference."

I waited for a response. *The Excellenza Trejhin is engaged at present*, a neutral voice in my head informed me. *Your message will be relayed at first opportunity.*

I frowned. The conference must be at a critical juncture for her not to accepting background messages. All trained diplomats could routinely follow two or three conversations at once. I sighed and turned back to examining the corpse.

Leaning closer, I tried to read an expression on the desiccated face. Terror, maybe. A check of hormonal levels would have answered that, but there were no bodily fluids to analyze. I ran the databank on possible causes of desiccation. If this guard had fallen in a vat of brine and pickled himself over a period of time, that might come closer to explaining his state of body, but it was obviously not that.

The whir of a passing cargo sled caught my attention. There was intermittent traffic down the cargo ways from warehouse to port, but it was all stevedroid. Nothing living. I shrugged off the feeling of being very much alone to continue my task.

I let the data flow. Though there were many ways to do violence to a humanoid body, a physical attack in the open could be narrowed down to blunt instrument, incision with an edged object, biochemical reaction, or energy weapon discharge. And though this bore a superficial resemblance to a biochemical attack, there was no trace of reactive process. I refined my query to focus on non-hom life forms that fed on humanoid body fluids. Probably something insectoidal.

A voice sounded in my head: *What have you discovered, Darryd?*

Trejhin. Perhaps the conference was in recess. A moment later that was confirmed as the alleyway was overlaid with a ghostly representation of one of the warlord's reception chambers, small clusters of conversations in progress in all the corners. Trejihn stood in resplendent silver uniform at one side of my field of vision. If she had been accepting a reciprocal visual overlay of the alley, she would have been positioned center, eyes in me, but her visual focus was on events at her end. She wanted an auditory report only.

"Odd circumstances, Excellenza. Concerning the murder itself, the life essence has been completely sucked from the body. It is the second murder today in a series, all occurring in this warehouse district."

What sort of psychic death signature?

My mouth tightened. "That's beyond my training, Excellenza."

Then put your hand in the forehead and relax into extended interlock mode. I may be able to sense something through you.

I did what she instructed and felt a low-level jolt run through me. It wasn't a pleasant sensation, but I tried to hold myself steady and open. Finally, it stopped.

The psychic death signature is horrific. Trejhin sounded less assured this time. *I'll handle things. Leave immediately.*

Her serene expression never wavered, but I caught all sorts of subtext from her voice inflection. Trejhin wanted me out of here because I wasn't safe. I backed up, breaking into a run as I turned. I spared a very brief thought for the negative image of an Imperial officer running in fear, but it was swallowed up in the echo of Trejhin's command: *Leave immediately.*

Racing around the corner, I pulled up short. Another corpse lay sprawled in front of me, desiccated like the other. Not breathing, I stepped closer. Yes, it was my Meggothi companion. He hadn't made it back to the shuttle. I lifted my eyes to the craft, not half a block away, and saw something occupying the cockpit, writhing like smoke in the wind.

I tried. I began telling myself this was just a xeno-sentient of some unknown species…then panic took me. I dashed the opposite direction, not daring to look behind me. "Darryd to Trejhin," I broadcast frantically. "Emergency! No transport!" Though she was physically distant, I had been raised to believe that Imperial Excellenzi could deal with anything. I desperately hoped it was true.

You're still there? Trejhin's disembodied voice sounded unnerved. *I'm overriding local control to send the nearest ground transport your way. You're in extreme danger.*

I didn't need an Excellenza to tell me that. I kept running. Was it really a demon? Random images from primitive belief systems were bubbling up from my subconscious, but that was just fear. This didn't make sense.

A stevedroid came up behind me, beeping to warn out of the way. My ride, I realized. I slowed, forcing the automated sled to slow as well, then grasping its control column, I swung myself up on the long platform piled with timber.

As the stevedroid picked up speed toward the port, I summoned the courage to look behind. A cloud of smoke followed, carrying with it the stench of a charnel house. I superimposed a dozen filters, finally picking up more shape at the infrared end of the spectrum. I was shortening the light band even more when filtering became redundant. The smoke itself coalesced into a huge, three-legged creature loping not far behind, its head horned and serpentine, its body covered with tentacles. Three red eyes fastened onto me and I felt my will falter. My body turned leaden as though hit with a stasis beam. If I had been moving under my own power, I would have been doomed, but demon or no, the indifferent stevedroid kept its pace, whisking me past lifeless warehouses.

As I lay unable to move, eyes locked on the horrific thing behind me, a cold realization seeped into my brain: this was no xeno-species in any normal sense. Its physiology violated several laws of bio development and the way it morphed between smoke and substance was not possible for any known species or species-cluster. This was not a "natural" creature. And once I arrived at "unnatural" creature, it was only a short step to "demon" and back to local superstitions. A greater horror welled up inside of me: Imperial tech wasn't intended to deal with demons. The thought of my Empire helpless appalled me as nothing else could. There had to be something—mental if not physical. Though I was not psi trained, I knew the principle of focus and release as practiced by the Excellenzi. I dredged from within myself the will to attempt a psionic blast. It was beyond my skill, but I had nothing left to lose.

I focused as well as I could, drawing auxiliary power from the implants, then released my intent as a perceived beam of energy aimed at my pursuer. It was a child's attempt, but unbelievably the demon reacted, hissing at me balefully as it suddenly fell back. A moment later it disintegrated into shadowy smoke as though tired of holding physical form. I felt a tingle in my extremities as my body returned to life. I could scarcely believe I was still alive. I had no illusions that I had defeated the demon. It was still out there, waiting for another victim before again coalescing.

The cargo sled reached the port on route to a freighter on the far side. I held my position on top, not quite trusting my legs to support me nor death to have released me.

Darryd?

"I seem to have survived, Excellenza," I said shakily. "But I must apprise you that the creature we are dealing with is a supernatural demon not of this physical reality."

No, you mean a xeno-sentient antithetical to humanoid life.

"I mean a demon." I transmitted a replay of the creature morphing impossibly from smoke to solid substance.

A long silence followed. As it stretched into minutes, I wondered if Trejhin had returned her attention to the conference, or was ordering a psi-evaluation for me, or what? Finally, quietly she spoke again.

I have forwarded your evidence on to Throneworld. Expect drastic consequences.

I gave a sigh. "Meaning I will be declared unfit for duty. Well, perhaps I am unfit for duty after what I've—"

I meant consequences for Meggoth. Contrary to all official positions, we do run into deadly supernatural entities at times. They are regarded as a threat of the First Magnitude at the highest quarters. She paused again. *Throneworld is going to nova the sun of this system. That is one solution that works where others do not.*

I felt a surge of belief in the Empire. Yes, we did have a way to deal with demons. The danger of the double full moons would be gone with the moons themselves. Then I shuddered as the full meaning of that sank in. A whole system destroyed; a people destroyed. This was horror of a whole different sort. A training phrase floated through my head: "The Empire is not cruel but will not hesitate to act on necessity." I had never envisioned a necessity this harsh.

There remains the question of what to do with you, Trejhin's voice continued. *You've seen too much to continue at your present grade...perhaps a promotion.*

"I have done nothing except flee on command," I pointed out. "And condemned a world to death," I added under my breath.

You have endured an attack by a demon and more importantly, have seen how bitter reality can truly be. I could hear a grimness in her inflection that indicated she understood the moment well. Maybe dealing with bitter realities was the gist of being an Excellenz.

"The conference?" I said hesitantly.

No longer relevant in the face of a nova. I thought Trejhin had dropped out of link with those very final words, but a moment later she added thoughtfully, *You're weathering all this better than most, Darryd...I think you just might survive the court on Throneworld.*

Moonset

Steven R. Southard

***I**will kill everyone in this room," the monster said.*
As a rule, Patrol Officer Kendra Monroe didn't think of suspects as monsters, but as she looked at this guy she thought that rule was due for a change.

A young Latino, shorter than average, the man didn't strike her as physically intimidating. Still, his eyes stared at her with a shark's cold indifference. Despite being shackled in heavy-duty handcuffs and double leg irons, he somehow conveyed an aura of a predator calculating weaknesses.

Her boss, Santo Herrera, laughed. "Do I look scared?"

To Monroe, he didn't. Massive and well-muscled, Santo had long seemed to her to portray the ideal cop.

"Any of you boys scared?" Herrera looked around the room. Four burly male police officers stood watching the suspect, two armed with Tasers, and two with rifles.

All of them shook their heads, but Monroe considered the extra precautions taken for one man represented a sign, if not of fear, then at least of respect for what this suspect might do. Respect only went so far, though. Before the interrogation, she'd asked Herrera for a weapon, but he'd denied her, saying, "You're an analyst, not a street detective."

"I'm only here out of curiosity," the suspect said in unaccented English. "Still, I promise you, none of you will leave this room alive."

Before her boss could overreact, Monroe began the interrogation. "You're here because you're a person of interest in connection with six murders. I am Officer Monroe and this is Lieutenant Herrera, lead detective of this precinct's night shift. I'll remind you once again of your right to legal representation. If you don't have your own lawyer—"

He smirked. "As I said before, I waive that right. Lawyers are irrelevant."

She blinked. In her experience, all suspects wanted lawyers. "All right. What is your full name?"

"I am Dismas Maria da Cunha Ribeiro."

Even his identity had been cloaked in mystery. His fingerprints matched nothing on file. As the criminalistics expert on the graveyard shift, Monroe had scoured databases but found no record of his existence. She'd analyzed his DNA, and it categorized him as being from western Spain or Portugal, with no hint of any Mexican or Central American background.

"All right, Mr. Ribeiro." Monroe found it impossible to meet his gaze for long. His eyes glared like twin black portals to another place, a realm darker, colder, and far more ancient than the Southern Precinct of the El Paso Police Department. "Do you recognize any of the people in these photographs?"

A small computer screen faced each seat at the interrogation table, and she caused six images to appear on the screen in front of Ribeiro.

"Of course," he said, after a fleeting look. "These are the six most recent people I killed."

A confession. Just like that. Monroe gaped at him, then recovered. "Why did you kill them, Mr. Ribeiro?"

His straight lips slowly formed a cruel, sneering smile. "Four were on my list, and two," he shrugged, "got in my way. What *I* want to know is why policemen were already there at the home of my last target."

Herrera leaned toward him. "In an interrogation, *we* ask the questions."

After a slight lift of the eyebrows and a twitch of the head, Ribeiro turned to look at Monroe. Those eyes froze her soul. "It was *you*, wasn't it? The pretty lady with the computer. You figured it out."

It had been her, and her computer. Kendra Monroe had detected his pattern, identified the killer's next victim, and recommended the stakeout. Though trained in forensic science and criminalistics, she'd also developed a fascination with data analysis, search algorithms, and pattern recognition. As one of very few black women in a police force dominated by Hispanic men, she'd needed to develop a standout skill. Months before, Herrera had chided her, saying "That damn computer is your crutch, Ken. You're letting it think for you. Up here," he'd tapped his temple, "is all the computer a policeman needs. Someday that computer of yours will fail you, and you'll be lost without it."

But it hadn't failed her. She'd been right, picking the right address and the right night.

Not that it had saved the victim, or one of the cops. And no computer could have predicted the sick and bizarre videos taken from the body cams.

"It *was* you," Ribeiro repeated, nodding at her. "As a reward for your ingenuity, I shall kill you last, and without pain."

She fought for self-control as a cold, liquid fear seeped through her gut. She glanced away, seeking relief from his murderous eyes. Four pictures hung on the cinderblock walls of the room, each picture featuring butterflies. The department's psychologist had recommended colorful, cheerful butterflies, believing such images would calm the accused. It may have worked for *her*, a little, bolstering her composure.

"Noted, Mr. Ribeiro. We've added verbal threats against police officers to the tally of your lesser charges. Earlier, you mentioned a list of targets. How did you come up with this list?"

"That's a long story."

"We have time."

He regarded all six officers, his sneer increasing its curl. "Very well. Why not? To begin with, I must tell you about something that happened in the year 1635. In that year, Portuguese *bandeirantes* marched through the forests of Brazil, seeking gold and native slaves. These were—"

"What the hell is this?" Herrera asked. "What crap are you feeding us now?"

"Patience, Lieutenant. The lady asked how I developed my list." With his hands cuffed behind the chair, he shrugged. "This trip through history is necessary, first."

Herrera snorted and leaned back in his chair.

"These *bandeirantes* were despicable and barbaric men," Ribeiro went on. "Not only did they capture male slaves, but they raped and killed women, slaughtered children, and destroyed villages. One man among them became sickened by their brutality and snuck away from the slaver band. He walked a long distance through dense forests, then came upon a tribe of *Guaraní* natives. He befriended them and stayed among them for months. He learned their customs, their religion, and their language. The more he learned, the more he realized his own people were the real savages. Their lust for gold and slaves had turned them evil."

He paused and shut his eyes, as if steeling himself before going on. "Then his former companions found him. They considered him a traitor and arranged a special punishment. They forced him to watch as they executed the entire *Guaraní* tribe and burned their village. Next, they slashed gouges in his skin with their daggers, and threw him in the river." He stopped and looked around the room. "You know about piraña, of course, but have you heard of the *cañero*, the vampire fish?"

"Is this gruesome fairy tale going somewhere?" Herrera asked. "Wake me up when he gets to something relevant."

"Go on, Mr. Ribeiro." Monroe didn't want to undercut her boss, but the bodies of the six murder victims had been so oddly mutilated, she could tolerate a meandering historical tangent if it would lead to the truth.

Ribeiro focused on her as he continued. "A *cañero* is a small, slender fish of the Amazon Basin. It is so narrow, it slips into any available crevice or orifice in its prey, latches in place with spiked barbs so it cannot be extracted, and drains its prey's blood. And, yes, gentlemen," he looked around the room with a smile, "the *cañero* is small enough to enter the male sexual organ, where its spines dig in—"

"All right, you sicko, that's enough of that," Herrera snapped. Two of the standing officers winced, and one stifled a gasp.

Monroe thought of the victims she'd examined. Each had suffered a Class IV hemorrhage, losing more than two liters of blood, and had sustained lethal interior lacerations—in various internal... *organs*. The strangeness of these murders had baffled the entire department, causing many to wonder what sort of peculiar tool the depraved killer had used, and why.

Then they'd seen the videos taken by officers earlier this very night. On her first viewing, Monroe had thrown up.

"No more about the cañero, I promise." Ribeiro smiled. "After being pushed into the river, this man—certain his life was over—invoked a final curse upon his torturers. He called upon two *Guaraní* spirit-deities, *Mbói Tu'ĩ*, the god of fishes, and *Abaanguí*, the moon god. These two gods must have taken mercy on the man and...intervened. They altered him in certain ways."

Monroe's cellphone buzzed. Flushing with embarrassment, she fumbled for it. Her teenage son had texted her saying he couldn't find anything to eat for breakfast. *God, that boy is always hungry.* She sheepishly looked at her boss. "Sorry, Santo." Then she turned to the suspect. "Go on, Mr. Ribeiro."

He gave a wicked smile. "Thank you. By now you've guessed that this doomed man, the man in the river, was me."

Monroe blinked and shook her head. "What? I thought you said all this stuff happened in 16-something or other."

"1635, yes."

"That was hundreds of years ago."

"Yes. One of the gifts bestowed by the *Guaraní* gods was eternal life."

Monroe gaped, half-believing this man. With his jet-black hair, flat stomach, and smooth skin, he looked no more than twenty years old. Only his eyes hinted at a far greater age. Their liquid depths reflected a ceaseless malevolence, an unending disdain for people and for time itself.

Her database searches had revealed nearly a hundred cases of unexplained deaths with similar characteristics in dozens of countries going back at least two centuries. She'd dismissed those data as irrelevant, except for one odd connection linking most of them. Had this one man been responsible for all those murders, too?

"Did I say eternal life?" Ribeiro smirked. "I meant *half*-life. I'm a sort of vampire."

"A vampire." Herrera grunted.

"More specifically," Ribeiro said, "a vampire *fish*. A *cañero*. I shape-shift into a man-sized *cañero* at the time of every moonset, and become human again at moonrise, courtesy of the gods of fish and moon."

"That's it." Herrera put both palms on the table. "He's making up garbage now. We're done here. Take him to his cell."

"Santo," Monroe said, "I'd like him to tell us why he's killing people from a list."

"I don't care, Ken." Herrera kept his voice even, but the undertone told her not to contradict him. "We have his confession; we got video of him murdering two people. He's just spouting nonsense now, setting up his insanity defense."

"You already know about my list," Ribeiro told her with a sly smile, "don't you, pretty lady? Your computer told you how the people are linked. They're all descendants of my *bandeirante* cadre. I killed the original group, and as many of their wives and children as I could track down. Through the centuries, they kept breeding and I kept killing. In recent years, the Internet, that marvelous tool, has helped me hunt them down. I'm nearly done. Only three more to go."

"In Providence," she whispered.

"Oh, you *are* good. Yes, I leave for Rhode Island on a red-eye tomorrow night."

She glared at him. "I've already warned their PD about you."

"Warned them, did you?" He threw back his head and laughed. His hilarity died to a few chuckles, and finally a smile. "Warned them, like you warned your own department earlier tonight? How effective was that?"

Not effective at all. Body camera footage showed him confronting the officer guarding the victim's front door. He picked the man up by his belt and hurled him impossibly high into the air. The man landed on street pavement two blocks away, dead on impact. As Ribeiro broke through the door, the backup officers sprang from hiding and followed him in. They got to the bedroom in time to see Ribeiro's finger plunge into the mouth of poor Rita Crespo. She tensed, but her shock didn't last long before she succumbed to the loss of blood.

The officers had fired twenty-six rounds at him from their Glock 22 pistols, but to no effect. Watching the video, Monroe had zoomed in the view and seen bullets enter his body, then excrete out and drop from holes that sealed and left unblemished skin. In the video, Ribeiro turned to face the policemen, tilted his head, and asked, "How did you know I'd be here?" He grinned and held his hands up. "Arrest me. Take me in."

Rather than answer Ribeiro's question, Monroe pursued a different course. "When I asked why you killed people from a list, I already knew your list. I want to know why you kill at all. What's in it for you?"

"Ah, that." He flashed another grin. "As angry as I was with my old *bandeirante* pals, the gods *Mbói Tu'ĩ* and *Abaangui* were furious with them. After all, the slavers had killed an entire tribe of worshippers. While I have nothing against *bandeirante* descendants myself, it seems gods think in rather longer terms. In exchange for killing those descendants, I don't age, I have super-strength, and I'm invulnerable in both my human and *cañero* forms. After I've killed the last three targets, tomorrow night, I'll get to live in *Ywy Mará-Ey*, the *Guaraní* land-without-evil, their version of Heaven."

"I said, we're done here." Herrera stood. "No more of your horror fantasies. None of us believes you, anyway."

"Really, Lieutenant?" Ribeiro tilted his head. "Your officers' camera videos weren't convincing enough? Very well, I'll demonstrate."

Monroe saw his shoulders twitch and she heard a metallic snap. Ribeiro brought his hands up to the table, with manacles and broken chain still attached. He pointed his index finger at Herrera. To Monroe's astonishment, the digit lengthened and narrowed until a pencil-thin finger protruded a foot past his knuckle. From a point just behind the fingernail, six blade-like spines sprang out, each angled back toward him.

Everyone else in the room flinched at the sudden snapping of the barbs. A spasm of dread clutched at Monroe's core. She hyperventilated, transfixed by the monster's murderous finger. She believed now, and knew Ribeiro could do what he said.

"This has been a fun little chat," Ribeiro said, looking at Herrera and Monroe, "but the moon will set soon and I'll become a *cañero* again. It's time I kept my promise to you."

Using bare hands alone, he bent and fractured the high-strength, steel handcuffs, removed them from his wrists, and cast them aside. Monroe gaped in wonder and fear as Ribeiro did the same with his heavy-duty leg irons.

"Now, then." He looked around the room. "Who's first?"

"Tase him," Herrera said, drawing his pistol.

The two officers armed with electric weapons fired. Electrode darts struck Ribeiro's short-sleeved orange detention shirt. Power that should have shocked him to unconsciousness had no effect.

Ribeiro grabbed the taser wires and yanked the electrodes free. He stood and walked toward the standing officers. "I told you, I'm invincible. Perhaps that word is too long for you. It means your weapons can't hurt me."

"Stay back, or we'll shoot," one of the rifle-toting men said.

Herrera didn't wait. He fired, shooting to wound. Rounds tore into each of Ribeiro's thighs.

Unarmed, Monroe felt an intense tide of terror rising. She stayed out of the way, edging toward the door as the men aimed their firearms. She pressed a button beneath the table to sound an alarm at the front desk, summoning additional officers.

The shots to Ribeiro's legs didn't slow him down. He drew near one of the taser-armed men. That officer swung a fist at Ribeiro, striking his chin. The man gave a yelp of pain and clutched his mangled knuckles. Ribeiro extended a finger and jabbed it in the man's ear. The officer spasmed, then slumped to the floor.

Monroe gasped.

"Let him have it," Herrera ordered.

Both Colt M4 carbines let loose with a deadly salvo, deafening in the small room. Unable to look away, Monroe saw again what she'd witnessed in the video. Bullets penetrated Ribeiro's skin, only to be ejected by his body while skin reclosed around the holes.

One rifleman reached in his shirt and pulled out a silver crucifix on a chain. He held it out in front of him, facing Ribeiro.

"A nice try, but that won't work." The attacker shook his head. "I'm a vampire by *Guaraní* curse, not by some Christian burial problem. He seized the man's rifle in both hands and pushed it horizontally against and through the policeman's waist into the cinderblock wall, severing him in two and knocking two of the butterfly pictures off the wall.

Herrera and his remaining officers continued to shoot while Monroe worked her way to the room's only door. Overwhelmed by panic, she wondered when more help would arrive. She knew now that Ribeiro would kill everyone in the room.

Ribeiro dispatched the other two guarding officers, one by slamming his head into the table, and the other by throwing him across the room into the wall.

"Ah, Lieutenant Herrera," the murderer turned to Monroe's boss. "Do you believe me now?"

Santo Herrera reached under the corner of the interrogation table with both hands and snapped off a table leg. The table slanted; coffee cups slid off and shattered on the floor. Holding the splintered end of his wooden shaft, the biggest cop on the graveyard shift yelled and charged toward Ribeiro.

Ramming his makeshift stake into Ribeiro, Herrera forced him against the wall. He drove the wooden spike all the way through the man's chest. Nose to nose with the killer, Herrera snarled. "I believe this—you're dead."

Ribeiro looked down at his punctured torso, then back up at Herrera. "Stake through the heart. Clever. But I'm afraid that's another vampire myth we've debunked tonight. He reached an index finger into Herrera's mouth. "Don't struggle," he whispered.

Monroe heard the snap of Ribeiro's finger barbs. The eyes of her powerful boss went wide for a moment, and then the spark vanished from them. Ribeiro withdrew his finger and let the giant man fall.

The killer pulled the table leg from his chest, and the hole sealed up behind it. Ribeiro's teeth gleamed as he faced her. "As promised, I've saved you for last, pretty lady."

She jerked open the door and saw three officers in the hallway with pistols drawn, aimed low.

"Run! Don't try to stop him," Monroe yelled, and ran. There was no point in opposing Ribeiro. What could anyone do against a super-strong, invincible monster, except maybe escape?

After rounding a corner, she heard someone yell, "Hey, you!" followed by a series of thuds, crashes, and more shouting.

Monroe didn't stop as she fled out the station's front door. Adrenalin-charged, she had no plan other than to try to get away. Without thinking, she ran to the right, rounded the corner of the red brick police building, and peeked back. The early morning summer sun started a trickle of sweat down her neck.

From her vantage, she watched the front door of the Central Regional Command headquarters, her heart pounding. In seconds, Ribeiro ran out, still wearing his orange detention outfit. He glanced in all directions, then smiled and faced her. "I can smell you!" he shouted.

She ran down East Overland Avenue, trying to think of options. Behind her, Ribeiro sped like a twenty-year-old track star, despite being clad in prison slippers. Monroe, at age thirty-five, lacked super muscles, but had kept in good shape and knew the area. She ran through alleys and parking lots, hurdled trash cans, scaled low walls, and dodged among the cars of the city's morning traffic.

He stayed with her, still in pursuit, and gaining.

Desperate for ideas, she tried to focus. *Where should I go? How can I get away?* She thought of pulling out her smartphone and asking…what? How to outrun a speeding monster? How to defeat an invulnerable enemy?

The words of her late boss came to mind: "That damn computer is your crutch, Ken. You're letting it think for you. Someday that computer will fail you, and you'll be lost without it."

He'd been right. She was lost. About to be killed by a shape-shifting part-man, part-vampire fish.

Fish…fish…he's supposed to turn into a fish at moonset. When he'd mentioned that during the interrogation, she'd idly checked the time of moonset on the computer—8:09 AM. Glancing at her watch, she saw 8:06.

Too much time. He'd get to her long before his shape-shifting time. She was already tired from running, gasping for breath, her leg muscles throbbing with pain. Police sirens wailed in the distance. They'd arrive too late to help her, too.

Behind her, she heard the relentless rhythm of his pounding footsteps. Closer…closer. He wouldn't tire, wouldn't stop to catch his breath. Maybe he didn't even *need* to breathe.

He did have needs, though. He needed to get to water soon, so he could swim after he became a fish. *Damn,* she cursed herself. She'd been running south-east, *toward* the Rio Grande, exactly the wrong direction.

Monroe jinked left and scrambled up a chain-link fence, dropping down on the other side just as he reached it. He didn't bother climbing, and instead ripped it with his hands and ran through.

She'd come to the old train yard, filled with east-west train tracks and rusty, graffiti-covered railroad cars. She hoped to elude him among the cars, maybe just long enough for the moon to set and bring on his man-to-fish change.

Change…change. There's something about change. I can't remember.

Monroe rounded the back of a tank car, climbed up through the open door of a boxcar and dropped down the other side, then scaled the linkages between two others, listening for him between her own gasping breaths, her eyes scanning everywhere. *Have I lost him?*

"Hello, pretty lady." Fingers of iron clamped around her wrist. He spun her around to face him.

The eyes held her, too. She could not look away from eyes of such dark depths, twin abyssal ponds that, in their blackness, led back through centuries to the Amazon River of 1635. Each of Ribeiro's eyes merged a cool, human intellect with the blank and indifferent stare of a fish.

"You've impressed me." He smiled, and it looked genuine for once. "In almost four hundred years, you're the first person who figured out my patterns and anticipated my moves. Congratulations." He bent in a slight bow, though his hands remained locked around her wrists.

Struggling against the power of his grip did her no good. The man she'd caught had caught her, and wasn't letting go.

"I promised you a painless death, didn't I?" He looked up and frowned, as if the idea of sparing his prey from pain disturbed him. Then came that smile. "In my considerable experience, I've learned when I enter the ear, my victims die quickest, often without making a sound. Yes, I'll go through the ear."

One hand released one of her wrists, but she'd only begun to jerk away from him when that hand seized her around the back of her neck, bracing her head in position.

With her newly freed hand, she grabbed his arm, but it felt like holding a steel bar.

Ribeiro released her other hand and held his finger before her eyes. It lengthened and narrowed until it resembled a flesh-colored pencil. "This won't take long," he said, "and you won't feel a thing."

He turned her head for the insertion, and she now faced west. The train tracks all led that way, coming to a stop a hundred yards away.

End of the line...for me, too.

Her life didn't flash before her eyes. Instead, tears filled them and she thought of Tyrell. Her son would have to grow up without his mom, too. *Who'd be the one to feed that kid?*

Food. That was part of what she couldn't remember earlier. It came in an eye-blink now. Change requires energy. A kid changing to an adult needs sleep and food. Butterflies, like the ones in those stupid pictures, need time in a cocoon to change out of their caterpillar phase.

The pencil-finger touched her right ear and pushed in.

It takes energy to change form. That leaves an animal vulnerable. Maybe this *is Ribeiro's only vulnerable moment.*

With buildings in the way, she couldn't see the final segment of the Moon descending but sensed a softening in Ribeiro's grip on her neck.

Monroe balled her fists together and struck low and upward, in a place men wished they weren't so tender. His finger whipped out of her ear. His body shuddered and he bent forward with a grunt of agony, both hands cupping his groin.

Her police training took over and she had him unconscious and prone in seconds. Beneath her, the transformation continued, his arms becoming fin-like, his legs morphing into a tail, and his skin turning smooth and clammy.

Other police officers rushed up. "Are you okay, Ken?"

"Give me your gun, Manuel," she ordered. "He's going invincible again."

Wearing a puzzled expression, the nearest man handed her his pistol, the grip facing her.

Monroe thumbed off the safety and used a two-handed grip to empty the magazine into all areas where brains and hearts reside in people and fish. This time, blood came out and bullets stayed in. "That's for Santo," she whispered.

Manuel gaped in surprise. "Hope you know what you're doing, Ken. You just shot an unarmed ma—what the...?"

Dark blotches appeared on the body, grew, merged, and gave off a putrid odor.

"Aw, that's rank," Manuel said and held his nose. Another officer wretched.

"Thanks for the gun." Monroe ejected the Glock 22's magazine, verified an empty chamber, and handed the weapon back. "I guess Ribeiro had four centuries of decaying to catch up on."

"There are six dead back at the station." Manuel holstered his pistol. "What happened here?"

She stared down at the rancid, black blob that had been Ribeiro. *I must have killed him midway through his transition.*

"You could say," Monroe shrugged, "it's one fish that didn't get away."

By Her Hand, She Draws You Down
Douglas Smith

By her hand, she draws you down.
With her mouth, she breathes you in.
Hope and dreams and soul devoured.
Lost to you, what might have been.

By her hand, she draws you down...

Joe swore when he saw Cath doing a kid. He had left her for just a minute, to get a beer from the booth on the pier before it closed for the night. Walking back now, he could see Cath on her stool, sketchpad on a knee, ocean breeze blowing her pale hair. A small girl sat on another stool facing her, a man and a woman, parents he guessed, beside the child.

Kid's not more than seven, he thought. *Cath promised me no kids. She promised.*

The sun was long set, and the air had turned cool, but people still filled the boardwalk. Joe wove through the crowd as fast as he could without attracting attention. Cath had set up farther from the beach tonight, at the bottom of a grassy slope that ran up to the highway where their old grey Ford waited.

"Last night tonight," Cath had said when they had parked the car earlier. "*It* wants to move on. I can feel the change."

Joe had swallowed and turned off the ignition. He was never comfortable talking about it. "Where's it headed?"

Cath had just shaken her head, grinning. "Dunno. That's part of the fun, isn't it? Not knowing where we're going next? That's fun, isn't it, Joe?"

Yeah, loads of fun, he thought now as he approached Cath and her customers. It *had* been fun once, when they'd met, before he learned what Cath did, what she had to do. When his love for her wasn't all mixed up with fear of what she would do to someone.

Or to him.

The child's parents looked up as Joe came to stand beside Cath. The father frowned. Joe smiled, trying to hide the dread digging like cold fingers into his gut. Turning his back to them, he bent to whisper in Cath's ear. That flowery scent she had switched to recently rose warm and sweet in his face. *Funeral parlors*, he thought. *She smells like a* goddam *funeral parlor.*

"Cath, she's just a kid," he rasped in her ear.

Cath shook her head. Her eyes flitted from the girl to her pad. "Bad night. I'm hungry," she muttered, ignoring Joe.

Joe looked at the drawing. It was good. But they were always good. Cath had real talent, more than Joe ever had. She would set up each night where people strolled, her sketches beside her like trophies from a hunt. People would stop to look, sometimes moving on, sometimes sitting for a portrait.

Eventually Joe and Cath would move on, too. When the town was empty, Cath said. When the thing inside her wanted to move on. They had spent this week at a little New England vacation spot. At least they were heading south lately. Summer was dying, and Joe longed to winter in the sun. Sleep for Joe was rare enough since he'd met Cath. Winters up north meant long nights in bars. Things closed in then, closed in around him. On those nights, he would lie awake in their motel bed, feeling Cath's eyes on him, feeling her hunger.

He looked at the sketch, at the child captured there, perfect except for the emptiness that spoke from the eyes, from any eyes that Cath drew. And the mouth.

Where the mouth should have been, empty paper gaped. Cath left the mouth until the end. The portraits always bothered Joe when they looked like that. To him, the pictures weren't waiting to be completed, waiting for a last piece to be added. To Joe, something vital had been ripped from what had once been whole, leaving behind a void that threatened to suck in the world around it. An empty thing but insatiable. Waiting to suck him in, too.

"Cath," he whispered. "You promised."

She ignored him again. Joe wrapped his fingers around the thin wrist of her hand that held the sketchpad. "You promised."

Cath snapped her head around to glare up at him. Joe caught his breath as anger met hunger in her grey eyes, becoming something alive, something that leapt for him.

The father cleared his throat, and the thing in Cath's eyes retreated. Cath turned to the parents. "Sorry, can't get her right. You can have this." Tearing the sketch from her pad, she shoved it at the mother. "We gotta go." Cath stood and folded her stool as the child ran to peek from behind the father's legs. Joe grabbed the other stool and the canvas bag that held Cath's supplies. He put an arm around Cath's waist, leading her away.

The father started to protest. "But you're almost done. You just need to draw in the mouth."

Cath stopped, and Joe swore. He just wanted to get her out of there. She walked back to the man who exchanged glances with his wife. Cath touched a finger to her lips. "Mouths are the hardest part. The most important part," she said. "Everyone—they say, 'the eyes are the windows of the soul.' They say, 'Oh, you got the eyes just right.' They don't know. They don't know it's the mouth you gotta get just right. That's what makes a picture come alive. Like it's gonna just start...breathing."

The father cleared his throat, but the mother tugged at his shirt. Joe grabbed Cath's arm and pulled her away. The man muttered something, but Joe didn't care.

He led Cath to a gravel path that switched back and forth up the steep hill to the highway above. Halfway up, an observation area looked down on the pier and the beach and the boardwalk. Cath twisted away from him there. A low stone wall ran around the area's edge, and two lampposts stood at either end. Putting her stool down under the nearest light, she began setting out her sketches against the wall.

Joe dropped the other stool and sat down. The fatigue that lived with him always now rose to engulf him. He felt dead inside, all used up, like the way Cath's pictures made him feel, waiting to be sucked into the void. "We had a deal," he said.

Cath sat, looking up and down the path. "I'm hungry."

"No kids, remember?" Joe said. "And nobody with a family depending on them." He tried to make his voice sound strong, but his hands were shaking.

She opened her pad. "Kind of cuts down the field, Joe."

"Use one of the sketches you've got put away."

Cath laughed. A bitter, empty sound. Joe imagined the mouths she drew making that kind of sound. Cath looked at him finally. "All gone. Used 'em all."

Joe felt the emptiness again, a void gaping below, drawing him down. He leaned forward, head between his hands, fingers pressing hard on his temples, trying to make his fear go away. "Jeez, Cath. All of them?" He searched her face for some hope.

Cath shrugged. "Girl's gotta eat." She stared past him, and he heard gravel crunching underfoot. Joe turned, his hand slipping by reflex to touch the switchblade inside his boot top.

A fat man in black pants, white shirt, and paisley tie loosened at the neck was struggling down the steep path from the highway, a beach chair in each arm. He walked over to the stone wall and put down the chairs to rest. Nodding at Joe and Cath, he glanced at her sketches. He began to turn away but then looked back. His eyes ran over the portraits lined against the low wall like prisoners before a firing squad. The man whistled.

Joe sighed, from regret and relief. Cath would eat tonight.

§

With her mouth, she breathes you in...

The man's name was Harry. He haggled with Cath over the price then he sat down, and Cath started sketching. Joe glanced at the two chairs that Harry had carried, but he couldn't see a wedding ring, so he kept silent.

Cath worked quickly, her hand slashing at the page, pausing only to switch the color of her pencil. When only the mouth remained unfinished, she put the pad down on her lap.

Harry looked down at the sketch. "There's no mouth."

"Mouths are special, Har," Cath said. She puckered at him, and Harry laughed, a nervous squeaky sound. Cath touched a finger of her drawing hand to Harry's lips. He gave that little laugh again but didn't pull away. Cath ran her fingertips slowly over his lips, tracing each curve and contour. Sitting on the stone wall, Joe thought of her fingers on his own skin at night in bed, tracing the lines of his body. Love and fear and lust—with Cath, they all mixed together, colors in a picture flowing into each other, until you couldn't separate one from another.

She lowered her hand to the paper, her eyes still on Harry's mouth. Picking up a red pencil and dropping her eyes, her hand began to stab at the paper in short urgent strokes. The mouth grew under her fingers as Joe watched. She finished in seconds. Removing the sketch sheet, Cath handed it to Harry. He regarded it for a moment, grunted his approval, and paid her. Portrait under his arm, he picked up his chairs and nodded a good-bye.

After watching Harry labor down the path toward the boardwalk below, Joe walked to where Cath sat cross-legged on the ground, her sketch pad on her lap. She carefully lifted a sheet of carbon paper from the top of the pad. A copy of the sketch she had just rendered of Harry stared up at Joe in black and white. *No color*, thought Joe. *As if all the life's been sucked out of it. No*, he thought. *Not all of it. Not yet.*

From her canvas bag, Cath removed a small rosewood box, its hinged cover carved with letters in a script Joe thought was Arabic. He'd never checked, wanting to know as little as possible about the thing. Cath opened the lid and withdrew what looked like a child's crayon but without any paper covering.

The crayon was as long as Joe's middle finger but thicker, and a red so dark it was almost black. Joe remembered drawing as a kid, the crayons, the names of the colors. Midnight blue, leaf green, sunshine yellow. He knew the name that this one would have carried: blood red. It glinted in the overhead light as if it would be sticky to the touch, but Joe had never touched it, so he didn't know for sure. He didn't want to know.

Hunched over the portrait copy, Cath began to retrace the lines of the mouth with the red crayon, adding color and shading. She worked with almost painful slowness. Joe remembered how once she had made a mistake at this stage, how the fury had burst from her like a wild thing caged too long.

At last, Cath straightened. She gave the mouth one last appraising look then returned the crayon to the rosewood box. Joe walked back to the low stone wall. He knew he would turn back to watch her. He always did.

Below, Harry had reached the boardwalk. The big man put down one chair to wave to someone on the beach. Joe's stomach tightened. A woman waved back at Harry, and a small boy and girl ran to hug him. *Jesus, no*, thought Joe.

He turned back. Cath sat hunched over the portrait of Harry on her lap. Joe rushed to her, praying that it wasn't too late, a prayer that died when he saw the picture. It had started.

The portrait's mouth was moving, fat lips squirming like slick red worms on the paper. A pale vapor rose thin and wispy from those lips. Cath bent her head over the mouth and sucked in that misty thing that Joe never wanted to name.

A scream rose from the beach. A woman's cry, a thing of pain and fear. Between her sobs, Joe could hear children crying.

He walked back to the low stone wall and looked down at the crowd gathered where Harry had fallen. Joe stood there, eyes locked on Harry's still form, feeling the void opening below him again. "Cath, we have to get out of here."

Cath didn't answer him. Joe tore his eyes from the scene below and turned back to her. She was standing now, looking south, down the coastline. "It wants to move on," she said.

§

Hope and dreams and soul devoured...

Joe drove staring at the white lane markers slicing the dark two-lane one after another, like brush strokes by God on a long black canvas. White on black. The negative image of Cath's secret portraits. Black on white, white on black. Just the red missing. Just that blood red.

How long before some cop put it together? A string of deaths, all the victims drawn by a young woman with a male companion. Christ, Harry died with a sketch in his hand.

Cath stirred beside him, and then he felt her eyes on him. He could always feel her gaze, like a physical touch, like a brush dipping into him, drawing something from him. *Is that how you do it, Cath? How you take the thing you take? Capture it in your eyes, then cage it through your fingers onto the page? Have you been feeding on me, too?*

"I'm still hungry," Cath said. Her voice was small, almost child-like in the dark.

He knew what she meant. "We'll hit town soon," he said. But it would be three in the morning when they arrived. No one around. No one to draw. And she had no pictures left. Cath said nothing but looked away. After a while, he figured she was asleep. Then he felt her eyes again.

"I don't *want* to hurt people, Joe."

He swallowed. This was new. She never talked about it, even when he did. He should say something now, something smart, something that would lead them out of this. He should, but he had nothing left to say. He could only nod. "I know, babe."

"It just gets so hungry. I get so hungry."

"I know."

"I can't stop it. It keeps pulling me, making me..."

Joe could feel her pain in those words. And his fear.

"I'm tired," she said. "So tired I wish I could just go to sleep and never wake up. Ever been that tired, Joe?"

He swallowed again. *All the time*, he thought, but he just nodded. Cath looked away, and he took a breath as if he was coming up for air.

"I'm hungry," she said again.

"I know."

Her eyes settled on him again like a beast on his chest.

"I could draw *you*, Joe."

Joe's hands tightened on the wheel. Cath had said it the way a kid told you she could ride a bike or tie her shoe. The lines flashed by in the headlights. White on black, no red.

"Don't even need to see you," she said. "Know you so well."

Joe stared at the road. *Don't look*, he thought.

"Know your face like I know my own," she said.

The burden of her gaze lifted. He looked at her.

Her eyes were shut, and her hand moved in her lap, mimicking drawing motions. "Don't even need light. Could draw you with my eyes closed." Her hand stopped, and she leaned her head back. A few minutes later, Joe could hear her breathing slow and deepen.

So, there it was. He always knew it would come to this. This was why he had stayed, even after he learned what Cath did, what she was. Afraid that when he left, when Cath no longer needed him, she would draw him down. Draw him down onto the page from memory, then drink him in like all the others.

The road lines flew at him like white knives out of the night. White knives and blackness. Just the blood red missing. Taking a hand from the wheel, he felt inside the top of his boot, running his fingers over the bone handle of his switchblade.

A few miles down the road, he found a wide shoulder and pulled over, turning off the engine and the lights.

Cath still slept. Hands shaking, Joe pulled the knife from his boot. *It's self-defense*, he thought. But he just sat holding the knife. It was for the best. How many more would she kill? But he still loved her. Could he do it? He was tired, so tired. He leaned back. He only slept now when Cath did, when he didn't feel her eyes. He closed his eyes. Her breathing brushed his ears, soft and deep, soft and deep, soft...

He awoke to the sound of scratching on paper. He looked over. Framed against the moonlight, Cath sat hunched over her sketchpad, her hand moving in short, sure strokes.

"Kind of late for drawing, isn't it, Cath?" Joe asked. His throat was dry. He fumbled in his lap for the knife.

"Hungry," she said, her voice barely audible.

"Dark, too," he said, blood pounding in his ears.

"Don't need light. Drawin' from memory," she whispered.

Drawing from memory. Drawing him. He knew she was drawing him. "Don't, Cath." His thumb found the blade's button.

"Tired of being hungry." She sat back, eyes on the sketch.

He couldn't see the picture, but he saw the red crayon in her hand. She'd finished the mouth. "Please, don't do it," he said. His cheeks felt cool and wet. He realized he was crying.

Cath lifted the paper to her face. She was crying, too.

"Don't!" Joe screamed. The knife blade clicked open.

"Bye, Joe. Sorry." Cath breathed in through her lips.

Joe saw a pale wisp rise from the paper and move toward her mouth. Saw his hand gripping the knife flash forward. Saw the blade slice her white T-shirt and slide between her ribs.

Saw the red, the blood red, flow over the white of her shirt to blend with the black of the night and the shadows.

Cath spasmed and fell sideways onto him. Surprise mixed with peace in her face. "Thanks...Joe," she whispered. Her eyes closed and her head slumped back. A wisp of mist escaped her lips. *That's me*, Joe thought. Sobbing, he pressed his lips to hers, sucking in the breath and the grey mist from her mouth.

Bitter and sour, the thing burned his throat as he breathed it in. Something was wrong. Joe felt a presence of something dark, something...*hungry.*

His head spinning, Joe flicked on the dome light. Blood soaked into his shirt where Cath slumped against him, the picture still clenched in her hand. Joe stared at the sketch, a scream forming in his mind.

A familiar face stared back at him from the page, a face that Cath knew from memory. The face she knew best of all.

Not Joe's face.

It was Cath.

She hadn't been drawing him. She'd been feeding herself to the thing that had lived in her. Cath had been killing herself.

The emptiness that was the mouth in Cath's pictures gaped beneath him, and Joe felt himself being drawn down.

§

Lost to you, what might have been...

A February evening, St. Pete's Beach. Joe sat on his stool, his back to the beauty of a Gulf sunset. His portraits lay strewn on the sand around him like the dead on a battlefield. A woman and man looked them over while Joe waited. The woman held the hand of a little girl and boy. Twins, Joe guessed. *Couldn't be much more than seven*, he thought. He remembered when that would have meant something to him, before Cath died, before...

The little girl tugged on the mother's hand. "They all look so sad, Mommy." The mother hushed the child while the father haggled with Joe over the price. The day had been slow, so Joe agreed to do both kids for the price of one.

Joe started sketching. His hand leapt over the paper, and the images of the children grew around the emptiness where their mouths should have been. A tear ran down his cheek, but he kept drawing.

He had to. He was hungry.

The Monster Hunter

Gregg Chamberlain

*R**abbi Shulman, can I talk to you?"*

Ezra Shulman looked up from his desk where he was reviewing the accounts for the shul. Moishe Cohen stood at the threshold of the rabbi's office door, one foot stepping forward, the other hanging back. Like Cohen himself, thought the rabbi, always half-in and half-out, one side or the other, but very seldom on the mark.

Rabbi Shulman set a pen down between the pages of the ledger to mark his place and closed the accounts book. "Come in, Moishe," he gestured, sliding the ledger over, out of the way, to one side of the desk. It didn't slide very far. The desk was crowded with an old oversized computer monitor and its tower drive/modem, along with various books and folders and papers, diskettes and flash drives. More of the same, but without the diskettes and drives, sat in piles around the office.

"Find a chair and sit down," the rabbi said to his visitor, and waited, hands folded, for the other to get settled. "So, Moishe, what can I do for you?"

Moishe Cohen sat quiet and fidgeted for a bit. A small man, his neck craned so he could look up past the rabbi at the wall while he gathered his thoughts. A framed reproduction hung there, of an oil landscape of Old Cabbagetown. Cohen then glanced left, then right, then down at his twiddling fingers. Finally, he shrugged his shoulders.

"I need to ask you about something, *Rebbe*, something," he hesitated, "something maybe you might find hard to believe."

"Nu? So, ask." Rabbi Shulman resigned himself to not getting the shul accounts finished tonight. Not unless he took the ledger home with him and reviewed it during commercial breaks while watching the Stanley Cup playoffs. Leafs versus the Habs, just like in the old days. He sighed. It could be a classic, God willing.

Cohen started fidgeting again but forced himself to stop. "It's kind of complicated," he told the rabbi. "I'm not really sure where to start."

"At the beginning is always good," the rabbi suggested. "Is it maybe a personal problem?"

Cohen shook his head. "No, it's nothing personal, not really." He took a deep breath, like a diver preparing to take the plunge. "It's my neighbor."

Rabbi Shulman nodded. "Your neighbor? I see."

The other man nodded. "My next-door neighbor. Irving Nussbaum."

Lips pursed in thought, Rabbi Shulman said, "Nussbaum? I don't recall anyone by that name at temple."

Cohen nodded again, vigorously. "You're right. He doesn't go to temple. I'm sure of it."

"So it goes these days," the rabbi remarked, hands raised upwards in resignation. "Is this a problem for you, Moishe? You're not so regular yourself, you know."

The other man shook his head in fast, short jerks. "That's not it, rabbi. It's part of the problem, but it's not THE problem, y'understand?"

Lips still pursed, Rabbi Shulman slowly shook his own head. "No, I don't, actually." He looked over the rim of his glasses at Moishe Cohen. "Why don't you explain to me what the problem is."

The other man appeared to hesitate again. Another deep breath. Then he plunged ahead.

"I think Irving Nussbaum is a Vampire."

§

The microwave beeped. Rabbi Shulman opened the door and took out two mugs of hot water. Dropping a tea bag into each mug, he carried them across the small office space, handed one over to Moishe Cohen, and set the other down on the little bit of open space on his desk. He took his time sitting down, lifting up his cup, cradling its warmth in his hands, smelling the aroma of the chamomile, then taking a cautious, careful, and slow sip.

Rabbi Shulman sighed. No Stanley Cup series tonight, he knew that for a fact. A whole hour he'd spent listening to Moishe Cohen explain his belief that Nussbaum, his neighbor, was a night-stalking nosferatu.

"His teeth! You should see them!" Moishe had lifted his lip with a finger, exposing one of his own bicuspids. "Like fangs they are!"

The rabbi took another long slow sip of his tea before setting the mug down. On the other side of the desk, Cohen perched on the edge of his chair, mug clutched in both hands, untasted and slowly cooling.

"So, Rabbi, what do you think I should do?"

Rabbi Shulman's mouth opened, then closed. He sighed. Took another long, slow sip of tea. Thought a moment. Drank some more tea.

He could feel Cohen's eyes staring at him from the other side of the desk. Well, he thought, time to finish this *meshuga*. Maybe I can catch the third period.

"Tell me something, Moishe," he began, "you're not on any medications for anything, are you?"

The other man stiffened and stared. His mouth opened and closed like a fish gulping air. "What," he gulped. "What are you saying, Rabbi?"

Rabbi Shulman placed his hands flat on the desk around his mug of now-cold tea. "I'm saying—and don't take this the wrong way—I'm saying, Moishe, that maybe you might be letting your imagination get the better of you. That maybe you should get more sleep. That maybe you could do with a little holiday, like a nice visit out in the country or at the beach, maybe."

Cohen frowned. He set his mug on the desk. "You don't believe me. You think I'm *messhuganah*."

The rabbi sighed, shrugged. "It's a crazy thing you're telling me, Moishe. Be honest, if I'd come to you with this story, what would you say?"

"But, *Rebbe*." Cohen leaned forward, gripping the edge of the desk. "He doesn't go to temple. Heavy curtains cover every window of his house. I've never seen him outside during the day, except maybe when there's a thick fog in the morning, and then only long enough to pick up his paper on the porch. He—"

"Maybe works nights, like lots of people do, so he sleeps during the day."

"There are no mirrors in his house, I swear to God, not one!"

Rabbi Shulman looked over the rim of his glasses at the other man. "And you know this…how?"

Cohen returned the rabbi's quizzical look with a defiant glare. "Maybe I was inside once…and looked around."

The rabbi frowned. "Moishe Cohen, you listen to me now—no, you will be silent and listen! Never mind that you've as good as said you broke into someone's house—I'm a rabbi, not a priest, and this is an office in Beth El shul, not a confessional booth over at St. Vincent's, but I still won't be going telling tales to the police." He held up a hand to silence the other's objection. "Not yet I won't, not unless you force me, and that means you sit and you listen and you think about what I'm saying to you. Moishe, this story you've told me, this cockamamie fantasy about your next-door neighbor is just simply the craziest thing I've ever heard. And I've listened to old Mrs. Klein telling me about how she sees Hitler come 'round to collect her blue box every recycling day Tuesday."

Again, the admonishing hand lifted. "No, Not another word, Moishe. There are no such things as vampires. No ghosts and no ghouls, no dybbuks or doppelgangers. If you're not on medication and you're not drinking more than you should, and if this is not some silly joke, then you maybe need to start seeing someone who's more qualified than me to help you deal with your problem."

Moishe Cohen sat for a long moment and stared at Rabbi Shulman. Then, without a word, he stood up, turned, and stalked out of the office.

The rabbi shook his head and sighed. Sometimes sober and stern was the only best way. The results didn't always show up right off, but in the end, things worked out, more often than not. He hoped this would one of those times.

Sighing again, he reached over and dragged the accounts ledger back in front of him. Fingertips drummed on the cover for a moment. Then Rabbi Shulman flipped open the ledger to the page where he'd left the pen for a marker. A few more pages he promised himself, just so he could go home tonight knowing he'd managed to get something done.

§

Moishe Cohen could not believe it. He left the shul and walked to the bus stop, feeling stunned, feeling disappointed, feeling just, well, not betrayed, but very, very hurt.

The rabbi didn't believe him, didn't believe what he had discovered about Irving Nussbaum. What is a man to do when even his own rabbi won't believe him? Even thinks he may be a little bit, well, crazy?

When the bus arrived, Moishe got on, swiped his fare card, and moved on down the aisle. He found an empty seat by a window near the rear exit doors. He stared out the window, not seeing the passing street scene, and thought to himself, *What do I do now?*

He knew he wasn't crazy, not even a little bit. It would be nice if he was, easier, in fact, if he was insane. But he wasn't, no sir, not at all. He knew what he knew. What he knew was his neighbor was a creature of the night, one of the undead. Nussbaum the vampire.

So, what's to do? He wondered and he pondered. He examined the question from all sides, looked at it up, down and sideways. And, in the end, arrived at the obvious logical answer.

§

Moishe Cohen's house was at the end of a quiet cul-de-sac in a quiet neighborhood not too far from Toronto's Kensington Market. Irving Nussbaum, his nosferatu neighbor, that bloodsucking *shmo*, lived—or maybe unlived was the proper term, maybe? Whatever. That *putz* of a parasite had his house to the left of Moishe's.

It was late in the afternoon when Moishe left the shul. As he arrived home, the sun was more than halfway down the sky, promising a pleasantly warm evening. The first full moon of early spring was also already easy to see above the horizon to the west. A pale round orb that would soon brighten the nighttime sky later.

Not that Nussbaum will see it, Moishe Cohen promised himself. No night-time hunting anymore for his bloodsucking neighbor. Not tonight or any other night ever again.

Inside his house, Moishe looked around for what he needed. But finding something that would serve as a stake wasn't as simple as he'd thought. Who bought much of anything made of wood anymore these days?

Well, there was the dining room table set. That could work. The table legs were nice and thick but they were fixed too solid for him to break off and he didn't have a saw. Moishe Cohen was no Mike Holmes Mr. Fix-It. One of the chairs then. With a bit of effort, and one sore right heel, after stomping repeatedly against one of the chairs he'd propped upside down on the floor, Moishe had a couple of okay-looking stakes to sharpen. He managed that using a kitchen carving knife. The blade was likely pretty dull now but that didn't matter when there was a vampire to deal with.

Now for something to pound the stakes into Nussbaum's undead chest. Moishe considered the dining room table legs again then discarded that idea. He hunted around the house and then finally decided that maybe a kitchen rolling pin would work. Good thing his wife was away, visiting her mother. She'd never understand.

Okay, then, thought Moishe, I've got my rolling pin, I've got—he glanced out the window—still a good hour or more of daylight left. He smiled. Plenty of time before Nussbaum would rise from his coffin in search of unsuspecting virgins.

Moishe frowned in thought. Did vampires still sleep in coffins? And what is it with the virgins anyway? He shook his head. No time to waste pondering the mysterious ways of the undead. Moishe Cohen had vampire slaying to do.

He slipped out the back door. Caution was the watchword now. A man stepping out his front door, carrying a pair of sharpened stakes and a rolling pin might be seen and subjected to delaying, and difficult, questions. Worse still, someone might call the police, and wouldn't Nussbaum just love for that to happen. A vampire rescued from his Van Helsing by Toronto's finest.

Moishe took a quick look around his backyard. No one looking over a neighboring fence, waving a friendly hello. Good. He scuttled to the gate that opened out to the back lane where everyone had their garbage cans and recycling bins set out already for tomorrow morning's pickup. He gave a fast look up and down the lane. No one. Closing his own gate, he skulked along the lane to the gate that led into Nussbaum's backyard.

With a quick look around, he first pressed gently against the gate. Finding it shut fast, he reached over the top to fumble around a bit before locating and lifting the latch. The gate creaked as it opened. A loud creak, or so it seemed to Moishe's ears. He froze. Looked about. No house lights snapped on. No back doors banged open. No shouts of alarm. No "What do you think you're doing there?" Nothing. His hunched shoulders relaxed and Moishe smiled, pushing the gate open wide and entering Nussbaum's back yard.

He scurried across the yard to the backdoor. Which was locked, as he had expected, though he tried the knob just in case. No matter.

He already knew how he was getting inside. Unless Nussbaum had discovered the weakness in his home security, which Moishe doubted.

Around a corner of the house Moishe crept, stopping at a basement window on the side of the house facing his own home. Something was wrong with the catch of this window because it remained unlocked. He'd discovered this one night when he'd gone prowling around Nussbaum's place, certain at the time that his neighbor was away and about a vampire's bloodthirsty business. With luck, the catch was still broken.

It was. Moishe slid the window slowly open and slipped inside Nussbaum's basement. He was a bit awkward about it this time because one hand and arm held the stakes and rolling pin clutched tight to his chest. But he managed in the end.

For a vampire, Moishe thought, Nussbaum had a very ordinary-looking basement. A rumbling oil furnace stood tucked away over in one corner. A couple piles of cardboard boxes sat against the far wall. A dusty workbench ran along another wall. But not a coffin in sight, which had surprised Moishe the first time he'd been inside Nussbaum's house. But then he figured maybe Nussbaum had his resting place tucked up inside some little attic-type space hidden underneath the roof. More private that way. Not to mention secure. Except where a determined vampire hunter like Moishe Cohen was concerned.

Moishe stole cautiously up the basement stairs. The door at the top was closed. He pressed an ear to it and listened. Not a sound. Slowly, he cracked open the door and peeped out.

Nothing but an ordinary kitchen. Fridge, stove, sinks and shelves. The window curtains—not the frilly, see-through ornamental sort, but a heavy cloaking kind—were drawn closed.

Moishe crept through the kitchen quietly and continued on throughout the house. All the rooms were dim because every window had the same heavy cloaking style of curtains drawn fast. He knew, from past outside observations, that all the larger windows also had regular window shades pulled all the way down during the daytime.

Living room, dining room, front hallway. Moishe searched quickly. Downstairs bathroom, back porch mudroom, hall closet., and that little storage room under the stairs like in the Harry Potter movies. Moishe checked everything, swiftly, silently, all over the ground floor. Just to be sure, mind. Not that he expected to find Nussbaum in a recliner chair watching T.V. in the den or having a cup of tea in the kitchen.

He tried to creep up the stairs to the second floor but gave that up. Every step he planted a foot on creaked loud in his ears. Time was wasting anyways, so he trotted up the stairs, stake and rolling pin ready.

§

Moishe was surprised to find Irving Nussbaum in the upstairs master bedroom. The room was dark, both because of the heavy window curtains drawn tightly closed and because it was getting darker outside now. Hardly any daylight glow at all seeped in above the top of the curtains. Moishe didn't have much time.

Nussbaum lay stretched out on top of the bed. His folded hands rested on his stomach. He was fully dressed, from his argyle socks and check slacks to his plaid cardigan. A fashion plate, he ain't, thought Moishe.

Softly, almost on tip-toe, Moishe stole up to the side of the bed. He tried to breathe slowly so as not to make any noise at all. He looked down at his target.

Irving Nussbaum didn't seem like much of a vampire, Moishe had to admit. Never mind his tasteless choice in clothes, Nussbaum just looked so...ordinary. With his pale, receding hairline, the slightly doughy face, and the pudgy physique, Irving Nussbaum more resembled a middle-aged office worker who spent too much time at his cubicle desk than a fearsome bloodsucking night-stalking lord of the undead. He looked more like Dracula's accountant, Nussbaum did.

But Moishe knew better. Not every man looked like an Arnold Schwarzenegger or a Denzel Washington. So why should every vampire look like a Lugosi or that kid in the *Twilight* movies?

No, all the facts fit. Moishe knew what he knew. Even now, he was sure he could see what looked like the pointed tip of a fang jutting out from beneath Nussbaum's upper lip.

He had to do it now, while there was still time. Swiftly, Moishe brought up one of his homemade stakes, positioned its tip just above, but not touching, Nussbaum's chest, and fumbled to get a tighter grip on his rolling pin without dropping it.

Was Nussbaum stirring? Were his twitching fingers looking more like claws? Were his lips showing just a little more fang now? Were those puffy eyelids fluttering just a bit before they would snap open, revealing bloodshot eyes blazing with an unholy light?

Now. It had to be now for Moishe. Now before it was too late. Now while he still had the strength of his conviction. Now!

The rolling pin swung down. Slammed against the top of the stake. The tip of the crudely-sharpened wood pierced the loudly-dyed fabric of the cardigan. Penetrated. Crimson blood spurted.

Irving Nussbaum roared. Moishe Cohen's rolling pin struck again. The stake pushed further down. Nussbaum lurched, deep growls rumbling from his parted lips, as he struggled to rise. Moishe staggered but kept hitting and hitting and hitting, the stake sliding deeper and deeper and deeper. Nussbaum stopped struggling and fell back still and silent now. Moishe kept swinging his rolling pin, hitting and hitting until there was a loud CRACK!

Half of the rolling pin flew away, landing with a muffled thump on the carpet on the opposite side of the bed. Moishe paused, gasping, blinking in surprise. He looked down.

Nussbaum's body lay pinned to the bed. The end of the stake, maybe as long as Moishe's hand, projected up out of the cardigan. A dark stain slowly spread out across the bedspread. There was no sign of life in Irving Nussbaum, not that a vampire was really alive, after all. It was over. Nussbaum the vampire was well and truly dead now. Moishe Cohen had saved the city from an unholy menace.

Moishe staggered back from the bed a step or two. He still held the other half of the rolling pin in his hand. He looked down at it, willed his clenched fingers to open, and watched it fall to a thud on the floor. The other extra stake was still tucked like a sword under his belt. He left it there. Took one step forward, then another, until he stood by the bed again. He bent down for a closer look at the now-completely-dead Irving Nussbaum.

Funny how he still looked so ordinary. A bit fuzzier too in the dim light. And wasn't he supposed to be crumbling away into dust now? Oh, well, Moishe thought, maybe he was a young vampire and his body will now just go back to its natural process of decay.

Still, never hurts to be sure. Moishe had left his carving knife back in the kitchen after making his stakes. It was still likely too dull anyway. He didn't feel like hunting around Nussbaum's place for anything big enough to cut off the ex-vampire's head. But a good strong dose of morning sunlight would do the trick just as well. He strode around to the bedroom window, grabbed hold of the heavy curtain and, after a couple real hard yanks, managed to pull it down with a muffled clatter of the hanging rod. One end of rod tore a hole in the now-exposed window shade. Moishe finished the job. The big glass windowpane looked out upon the dusky skyline. Tomorrow's dawn would provide the finishing touch to Moishe Cohen's heroic deed.

Without a backward glance, Moishe left the bedroom. Down the stairs and through the house he went. To the back door. Not out through the basement window this time. No, a hero did not scuttle away from the scene of his triumph. Though a bit of discretion maybe would not go amiss even now. There was still no need to attract any unwanted official attention to himself. So it was out the backdoor and across Nussbaum's back yard in a few quick strides to the gate, out into the lane and then back inside his own house through his own backdoor. Moishe Cohen stood in his living room, safe and satisfied with his success.

§

"Quit shoving," Moishe mumbled, reaching behind to push away whoever was poking him in the ribs while he waited his chance to exit the bus. The poking continued, more insistent now.

Moishe made a quick grab and felt something hard and wooden in his hand. A splinter jabbed into a finger. He yelped. And woke up.

"Well, it's about time."

Moishe blinked and looked around. He was in the recliner chair in his own living room. Now he remembered. He'd sat down in the chair to take a little rest, as exhaustion took over from the adrenaline rush of his triumphant adventure over at Nussbaum's house.

Nussbaum. That voice he'd heard when he awoke. With a start his head snapped back around. He stared up at Irving Nussbaum glaring down at him.

Irving Nussbaum. Who was supposed to be dead for sure, but didn't look so much dead right now. Even with the hole in the middle of his chest which Moishe could see very clearly, thanks to the dark bloodstain marring the otherwise still-very-loud colors of the cardigan. Nussbaum still looked like an accountant, a very annoyed, even angry, accountant. His face twitched with what Moishe assumed was anger, or maybe outrage, fury, the whole *megilla*. One hand held the butt end of what the surprised vampire-slayer recognized as the homemade stake he'd last seen hammered into Nussbaum's chest. The pointed end of the stake, streaked with dark trails of dried blood, tapped tapped tapped against the open palm of Nussbaum's other hand.

Nussbaum continued to glare down at Moishe's fear-frozen face. "Would you maybe like to explain what you thought you were doing in my house?" The stake stopped tapping, its bloodstained tip rested in Nussbaum's still open hand. "Not that I don't appreciate the wake-up call, but a simple knock on the door and a 'Hey, Nussbaum! Time to get up!' would have been enough."

Moishe lifted a shaking finger. "Y-y-y-you're…you're not dead?"

The stake resumed tapping in Nussbaum's hand. "No, I am not dead," he growled, then smiled, a noticeable tic pulling at one corner of his mouth. "Not that you didn't give it a good…whack, so to speak. Took me a good hour or more to work that damn stake up far enough to clear the mattress so I could sit up." The stake tip shifted away and indicated a point a couple inches away from the hole in the cardigan. "But you missed the heart. Next time you should aim here."

Moishe blinked. "Next time?"

Nussbaum shrugged. "Well, maybe not." He grasped the stake with both hands in front of him, pointing it down towards the floor. "Of course, I have to kill you now." He shrugged again. "Tit for tat. Seems only fair after all. You know you've made me really late for my night watch detail at the mall. You think it's easy these days finding any kind of nighttime solo shift work? I can't afford to get laid off. Mall security pay's not great but it beats collecting UIC. Not sure what kind of excuse I can use. Getting stuck in traffic sure won't wash."

He looked thoughtful. "Maybe if I coughed a little bit, I could call in, claim some sick leave time, just for tonight. That stake of yours nicked a lung. Might make for a decent wheezing sound while the hole heals up."

Moishe wasn't listening. Nussbaum seemed distracted and he was taking advantage. He rolled over and off the recliner. Scrambling to his feet he positioned the recliner between himself and his unwelcome surprise visitor. *Unwelcome?*

"Hey, wait a minute," he exclaimed. "How did *you* get in *my* house? I didn't invite you!"

Nussbaum looked surprised. "Invite me? Oh, I get it now." He shook his head and smiled. "Right, right. The wooden stake, my bedroom window curtains pulled down to let the morning sunlight in. Sure. Now, I understand."

Moishe watched as a hairy hand tossed away the useless wooden stake. He looked up to see a lupine smile spread across Nussbaum's face. Lips now gone black parted in a fang-filled grin.

"Oy," said the werewolf. "Did YOU get the wrong monster!"

Choop
Nancy Springer

No weirder than any of the other men she had met at singles dances, Mandy reminded herself, facing him across the restaurant table. So far there had been the Harley-obsessed motorcyclist with half a head, the seminary professor who wouldn't kiss but phoned at two a.m. to discuss the Kama Sutra, the ex-cop impotent since he'd given back his gun, the guy with a big butt who had turned out to be a transsexual—what the heck; to a woman starting all over again at age fifty the whole world was surreal anyway, so what difference did it make that this date was almost certain to be another doozey? An ectomorphic thirty-something with hairless taupe skin and a pronounced underbite, tucking his napkin into his collar beneath his receding chin as he ordered "tender calves' liver in burgundy sauce" for dinner?

"I forgot you're a vegetarian," he apologized to Mandy as the server departed. "Do you mind?" He spoke with a rather charming accent she could not identify.

"Not at all," Mandy said almost truthfully. "It's mostly because of my job." She worked at A is for Animals, a small non-profit rife with crusading vegans. "I still eat fish and, occasionally, chicken. I figure it's a free country."

"Yes, and that is what I like best about it."

"Are you from somewhere else, Choop?" Mandy knew the slender young man only by that rather peculiar moniker she had seen on his "Disco, Discover" name tag—of course he didn't know her surname either, not yet—and she couldn't place his nationality. All she knew was that he liked to dance, was very good at it, and was therefore almost certainly not from Pennsylvania.

"Oh, yes, quite." He smiled toothily, deliberately teasing her curiosity. "Many places."

"Such as?"

"Bolivia, El Salvador, Michigan, Mexico, Washington D.C, Chile, Brazil, Dominican Republic, Texas, Panama, Puerto Rico, California, Argentina—"

Divorce had bled most nice-girl manners out of Mandy; she interrupted. "Are you an American?" She did not want to get mixed up with an illegal alien.

Choop said, "America, you know, it extends from the southernmost tip of Tierra del Fuego to far north of Hudson Bay." His heavy-lidded coal-dark eyes laughed at her.

Mandy tried again. "I mean, are you a United States citizen?"

"Better. I am an autochthon."

Undoubtedly he was playing mind games, and while she did not particularly resent his making a fool out of her—her ex-husband had already done that to death—she did wonder why this relatively young man was bothering to date her. Mandy had a realistic view of herself; what did this thirty-something want with an overweight, graying woman whose round face, all abloom with menopausal pimples, resembled a pot of geraniums?

But what the hell. It was nice to get dressed up, drape her favorite silk scarf (fuchsia, to complement the zits) around her neck and go out to dinner. As long as the guy didn't treat her like bed meat.

"All right," she said, smiling, "I'll bite: what's an autochthon?"

"An aborigine."

"Oh, that's *so* much better." However, Mandy was able to translate "aborigine," and felt annoyed at herself for not having guessed sooner; she should have known by the almondine fold of his eyelids, by his beardless cheeks, his hawk nose and especially by his hair so intensely black that it seemed to suck color out of his tawny skin, tingeing it gray. "You're Native American?"

"Very native indeed."

Even so, she thought, he still did not look like any other human being she had seen. Definitely not Cherokee. Maybe some exotic vanishing native from, what had he said, Bolivia?

But before she could ask what tribe, or maybe "nation" was the p.c. word, he changed the subject. "Tell me now about yourself and the animals."

"What's to tell? It's just another job, really."

"No, no." He shook his head.

"To me a job is just a job—"

Chatting in the car on the way to dinner, she'd found out he'd been a wholesale mutton products salesman, an Espanol-Ingles translator, an inspector of ornamental trees for plum pox, a time-share "body snatcher," a roadie for a third-rate rock band, altogether a *pate-perro*—"dog foot"—one who wanders.

"—but not to you, not this job. You wear it like a crown wherever you go. Always the creature jewelry looking back at me. The golden collie brooch the first time I saw you. Tonight, the tiger cats most beautiful on your ears."

"Just ordinary tabbies." But she felt herself fingering her expensive intaglio earrings and trying not to blush, much affected by the poetry of his insight. "Thank you."

"I suspect that you wear every day the tee shirt with the picture of the dog or cat on it."

"You suspect right."

"Which do you love better, cats or dogs?"

The word "love," so effortless, impressed her even more than his accent and his exotic lineage. "I—I couldn't say; I think I love just about all animals except maybe garden slugs."

"You have many pets?"

"No, none actually, because I had to move into an apartment after—" She stopped herself; she was able to do that now, keep herself from spilling her guts about the divorce, even though it had torn her wide open. "But then I started to work at the animal shelter, and they're all my pets, my babies." Sixty homeless cats, forty stray or throwaway dogs, most of them as sweet as puppy love. A is for Animals had been her family and her sanity for the past couple of years. "The most adorable Rottweiler came in yesterday, half-starved and so—so—" Trying to think of the right word, Mandy envisioned the drop-off dog's yearning yet stoical dark eyes. "So *noble.* She's been neglected, dumped, but she doesn't hold a grudge at all." Unlike certain people; Mandy hoped she would never be one of those. "It always amazes me how forgiving dogs are, and how—willing, how devoted…" Mandy found herself sidestepping the l-word, love. "But no matter how much Lamb has to offer—"

"The Rottweiler?"

"Yes, that's what we named her, Lamb, to show how gentle she is." All of the dogs and cats had names, photos, casebooks. A is for Animals had been founded by, and was operated by an elderly woman, Betty Calhoun, a.k.a. Loony Calhooney, and proud of it. Her eccentric ideas included: no cages and concrete runs; the cats lived communally in rooms with cushions, climbing apparatus, and screened-in outdoor patios; the dogs in packs according to size, with sofas, blankets, toys, and fenced yards, free from being penned in metal crates so long as they stayed "nice." Lamb was as nice as they came. "She's a total sweetie. But she's going to be very difficult to place."

"Place?"

"Find a home for. Not many people are able to adopt big dogs. Plus, she has hip dysplasia."

"She is crippled? So what will happen to her?"

"We will keep her for as long as she needs us. We're not like those other so-called rescues. Only as a last resort, if an animal doesn't have any quality of life left at all, then we put it down."

"You mean kill it?" At her sad nod, Choop raised his heavy black eyebrows. "But only when it is sick, or old?"

Nodding again, Mandy sighed. Choop leaned toward her over the restaurant table. "It troubles you? But why? It is nature's way, is it not, that the strong shall live and the weak shall die?"

"Um, maybe, but me, I want to save them all, diabetic cats, dogs with parvo, even with distemper. It's a hard decision to let an animal go, and when we do, it's because we love them and don't want them to suffer."

"Do you love wild animals, too?"

"Of course."

"That is to say you, individually?"

"Except garden slugs, like I said before."

"When the panther leaps on the deer, which one do you love, the panther or the deer?"

"I, um—"

"The panther is hungry, she has cubs to feed. But the deer cries out as the fangs break her neck."

"Um—" Something about his steady obsidian gaze shook Mandy, mixed her up like a whiskey sour, so that she felt simultaneously zing and tingle and revulsion. The question, the way he asked it, was not nearly abstract enough, far too intense; she almost felt claws and smelled blood.

The approach of the server saved her from response. "Here comes our dinner."

A few moments earlier she had considered herself hungry, like the mother panther with cubs to feed, but now she found herself picking uncertainly at her "tangy broiled salmon cerise." Taking a bite of liver, Choop said with zest, "I can never get enough organ meat."

Mandy murmured absently, "I must admit I sometimes have a yen for bacon."

"It is hard to find a restaurant that serves good organ meat."

Mandy glanced up to notice in surprise that her dinner date had already devoured most of his large portion of liver. He certainly ate fast, hunched over his plate, but otherwise not lacking in table manners: no slurping or noisy chewing. Indeed, he hardly seemed to masticate at all. The "tender calves' liver in burgundy sauce" must have been tender indeed, for seemingly, like a vacuum cleaner, he sucked it down.

§

"What do you want to do now?" he asked her as they left the restaurant. "See what's playing at the CinemaPlex?"

Usually Mandy liked to go to the movies, so her own answer surprised her. "Nah. I don't feel like sitting around." Something, maybe the cool yet tender night air, maybe some courteous yet feral quality of the "autochthon" by her side, was making her restless.

"Bungee jumping?" Choop suggested.

"I don't think so!" Yet Mandy laughed easily, nothing tight in her chest or her thoughts. She had not yet decided how to feel about this weird guy, but joking around with him was definitely better than sitting home by herself.

"Roller skating?"

"If I were twenty years younger."

"Tell you what." Before they reached the car, Choop stopped and turned to face her. "Would you like to take me to meet Lamb?"

The Rottweiler? He remembered what she was called? Mandy focused on his face, although in the benighted parking lot she could not see him very well. "Do you really care about dogs all that much?" she demanded.

He replied whimsically, "My name backwards, you know, it spells Pooch."

Mandy laughed again, figured it out and said, "Not quite."

"Almost."

"What does your name mean, really?" Aborigines were supposed to have names with meanings.

"Choop Akkabra?" There, he'd told her his last name. "Why should it mean anything? What does 'Mandy' mean?"

166

"I've often wondered."

"It means, maybe, woman with a big heart for animals. Come on, you take me to see your babies, yes?" He handed her the car keys. That impressed her; in her experience of men it was a rare one who would voluntarily occupy the passenger seat.

"Okay," she murmured almost shyly, as if he had given her flowers.

Driving made her feel good. She actually hummed happy tunes to herself as she steered his car along dark country roads to the animal rescue where she worked. Choop was right, she did wear her employment like a crown, would willingly have spent all her time with her babies; there was no place she would rather go on a starry night than the cinder-block building isolated amid farmland so as not to disturb neighbors with stench or noise.

As Mandy pulled up to the gate, a familiar brown fetor greeted her nostrils, and all of the dogs started barking.

The shelter was closed, of course, and there was no one around at this time of night, but it didn't matter; she knew the combination to the padlock.

After they had driven in and parked, she led Choop to a back door with a machine that swallowed her employee ID card, spat it out again, and clicked the latch, admitting her and her guest to a utility room.

"Um, listen," she told him, realizing suddenly that she should brief him, "you don't mind walking into a whole bunch of dogs at once?" She had to stand close to him, almost shouting, to be heard over a bedlam of barking from just beyond the utility room's several doors. "Let them sniff you, but the more you ignore them at first, the less they'll bother you. If you don't want them to jump on you, just shove them away and otherwise, don't respond. Don't yell or sweet talk. Just stand there like nothing's happening. Don't stare any of them in the eyes; that's a challenge. After a few minutes they'll settle down, and then you can make friends with them."

His toothy, overshot grin flashed in the shadows. "Not to worry. I like dogs."

"Okay." Briefly she considered whether she should take him into the small-dog area first, but dismissed the thought; there was no danger, really—none of her babies had ever bitten anybody that she knew of—and moreover, all of a sudden Choop sounded a bit cocky. Something in his tone repelled her, making her hope he might step in dog doo or otherwise embarrass himself. She found herself turning away from him and telling herself that, after all, it was the Rottweiler, Lamb, they had come to see, and Lamb was of course in the room with the large-dog pack. Might as well take him on in.

The dogs' excited clamor crescendoed as she turned the doorknob. Reaching in to switch on the overhead light, Mandy called cheerfully, "Shut up, guys!" as she stepped into the canine maelstrom.

Her greeting was automatic and rhetorical; the dogs would not shut up. German shepherds, Labs, Dobermans, Goldies and mutts indefinable would leap in ecstatic greeting while continuing to bark, bark, bark—

Not so.

They gave all at once a canine cry, yelp, yip, as if hit by cars—or clubs—that yowl wrenched Mandy's heart. "What's the matter?" she exclaimed, standing open-mouthed inside the doorway, as Great Danes, Pit Bulls and all her other big babies scattered with their tails between their legs to hide behind the furniture, cowering against the farthest walls of the large, open room. Sixteen sizeable dogs crouched against white enamel paint, shivering and mute. So profound was the silence that it sucked down surrounding noise, quieting the yapping of the beagles and terriers next door. "Lamb, sweetie, what's the problem?" Not yet comprehending the weird hush, not yet afraid, Mandy stepped toward the trembling Rottweiler.

Lamb whimpered.

The chupacabra leapt past Mandy on four long-fingered paws, flipped Lamb as if the big dog were a stuffed toy, and with its fangs sliced into her belly; all in the same swift and preternaturally strong motion it sucked, emptying its prey of life and innards simultaneously. There was not much blood. Lamb only screamed once, at the same time as Mandy did. The—she did not yet know the name of it—the gray-skinned, nakedly hairless creature—never before had she seen anything like it—slender like a small deer, bony of ribs and ridgy of spine, with long hind legs like a rabbit, the invader looked far too frail to be so fearsome. To be a predator, a killer.

But as Lamb's shrunken body lapsed to the floor, as the creature looked up and scanned for its next prey, Mandy saw how its delicate, pointed head culminated in white razor fangs and the undershot jaw of a shark. And against all reason she recognized, realized what she had done.

I come from many places.

I am an autochthon.

I can never seem to get enough organ meat.

"No!" she shrieked as it leaped again. "Choop, no!"

I like dogs.

Raw and slippery, the way some people liked oysters, evidently.

The chupacabra's prey seemed immobilized by the force of its stare or its strangeness. Fifteen big dogs made no sound, no attempt to flee. With its front paws, their claws as long as its fangs, the creature grabbed for its next victim.

Mandy did not wait to see which dog her date was going to disembowel now. She got moving. She was the mom, she was the pack leader, the past few years had broken her so badly that crazy-glued together again she was strong enough to face anything, and she was running—not as fast as she would have liked, overweight, too damn old, short of breath—grabbing for the emergency equipment in the corner, a device she had never used, the rabies pole. Five feet of hollow steel rod with a handle at one end connected to a sturdy noose at the other.

Deploying the loop, Mandy turned and puffed toward Choop. Engrossed in gourmandizing the guts of a pit bull/wolfhound cross, the predator remained blissfully unaware of her as she positioned herself behind him.

The instant he lifted his head, she dropped the loop over his muzzle, pulled it past his pointed ears, and, with the handle at her end of the pole, yanked it tight around his neck, turning a clamp to keep it that way.

That, she thought, should take care of the brute. He—the weird liver-sucking thing that had been Choop—couldn't hurt her so long as she kept the "control pole" between the two of them, and with her weight advantage, certainly she could keep him from hurting the dogs—God, what he had already done broke her heart, but there would be no more of it, no more—

With a banshee screech he leapt to stand on his hind legs, tall, twisting in the noose, turning on her.

—no more dogs killed—

The force of the chupacabra's black-eyed glare hit her like a physical blow or an illness. Stricken, nauseous, she felt her knees weakening—and he lunged, leapt, attacked, clawed at her, hurling himself against the scant sixty inches of steel that kept him from sinking his fangs into her. He might not weigh much but he was strong, preternaturally strong, and he was Choop, long arms and human hands groping—no, humanoid; he was a gray man with a sickle-spined back and an elongated face stretching into a sucking beak, a mosquito man—with scales. Reptile now, an upright lizard with a black forked tongue, hissing, dripping yellow drool, striking, and giving off such a stench that Mandy felt as if she must faint—but she must *not* faint or the dogs would all die.

She fumbled at the control pole's handle, trying to turn the knob, tighten the noose, to strangle the invader, the nameless, sucking—but he saw what she was doing. Humanoid again, he grasped his end of the rod in clawed long-fingered paws and tried to wrench it away from her. Strong. Far too strong.

Weight advantage, ha. Take care of the brute with the control pole? Choop was the one in control, swinging her in a circle around him while all she could do was cling, cling, and not let go, dizzy, faint, sick, must not pass out. Must save the dogs. Must save the dogs. Must save the—

Savagely he banged her against the wall. With a cry, losing hold of the pole, Mandy fell to the unforgiving tile floor, and the impact knocked the scant breath out of her lungs. Sprawling on her back, she couldn't move.

She could only lie there with her eyes wide open.

She saw Choop morph once more into a weird sort of hairless, feral gray canid. She saw him tower on his hind legs, oblivious to the noose still on his neck and the pole dangling. Sick with the knowledge that another dog would die, Mandy struggled for breath, and managed to beg in a ragged whisper, "No—Choop—don't do it…"

He didn't.

Instead, turning his gargoyle head toward the sound of her voice, fixing her with the stony power of his coal-black glare, he lunged straight at her.

Laughably, almost, it had not occurred to Mandy that Choop, with whom she had enjoyed a rather nice dinner, might now wish to suck out *her* liver. *Freaking cannibal!* she thought crazily as her date hurtled toward her with its shark mouth wide open, its gaping maw as big as the world, filling her vision, fangs aimed for her belly. Stark staring doomed and unable to move, she could not even scream—

Choop screamed.

Mandy saw his horrible white grin writhe, then skew toward the ceiling. As if she were watching a storm-dark sky and had seen lightning, a heartbeat afterward she heard thunder growl, snarl, roar. But it took her shocked eyes a moment more to focus, her stunned mind a moment more to comprehend: a pack of wolves, attacking Choop from behind, tearing his flanks, dragging him away from her. Although they might look like German Shepherds and Doberman Pinschers, Goldies and Newfies and Labs and big nameless mutts, they were all wolves at heart, and every one of them had sunk teeth into the chupacabra's back or haunches or hamstrings. When it tried to turn on them, the pole dangling from its neck wedged against the floor, preventing it. The power of its paranormal eyes could not reach its attackers.

They hauled the thing back from Mandy, mauling it, tearing at its flesh.

It screamed again. Agony.

Mandy closed her eyes. She rescued dogs, and now the dogs were rescuing her. She had wanted to save them, and they were saving her. The old, old, feral way. But she could not bear to watch.

Just as it was all over, just as she sat up, shakily, the door to the dog room burst open and Loony Calhooney, all featherweight five-foot-three of her, strode in, barking, "What the devil?"

"Betty," Mandy panted. She had forgotten that an alarm rang in the main office whenever anyone grabbed a rabies pole. She had also forgotten, if she had ever known, that any alarms that went off in the animal rescue also sounded in Betty Calhoun's home.

Looking around at Mandy struggling to her feet, dogs licking their red-stained flews, blood everywhere, two distorted, obviously dead canine bodies against the wall and—and most of all at the thing lying on the floor with the noose around its neck—Loony Calhooney said again in a softer, starker tone, "What the devil?"

A bit unsteadily, Mandy limped over to stand beside the old woman, both of them staring down at a scrawny gray-skinned hairless animal lying flat on its side, bleeding red runnels onto the tile, very still, looking no more dangerous than road kill.

"That's one of them things they shot in Texas," the old woman said almost in a whisper. "Saw it on the news. Killed sixty head of sheep in no time at all. How'd it get in here?"

"My fault. We were on a date, we needed something to do, and—" Mandy's hand flew to her mouth, partly to stop the insane things she was saying, but also because she had seen a slight movement of gray skin stretched over gaunt ribs.

Choop had breathed.

Within a heartbeat, instinctively, Mandy kneeled on the floor beside him, feeling the hollow of his neck. Yes, he had a pulse.

"He's alive!" she blurted. "We need to get him to emergency—"

"Whoa. Get *what* to emergency? Just because that thing can turn human, we should save it?"

Mandy felt her jaw drop, partly because she had never known Betty to say "whoa" in regard to saving any "thing," but mostly because Betty—what Betty understood—or knew… Speechless, Mandy gawked up at the old woman.

"Saw his clothes," Betty answered the look, jerking a thumb over her shoulder toward the mud room.

Vehemently Mandy shook her head. "He's just a—some kind of dog now."

"They tried to say in Texas that it was a coyote with a deformed jaw and with mange all over it. Bullshit."

"He's an animal," Mandy appealed. "Even if he's human he's still just an animal. We save animals, don't we?"

Loony Calhooney stared down at her with eyes that age had bleached nearly white, like flat full moons. "Am I mistaken," she asked, expressionless, "or didn't that so-called animal try to kill you? And didn't it kill those two?" She jerked her cleft chin toward the dead dogs. "And wouldn't it have killed every single living creature in the place if it wasn't for you tackling it with the rabies pole?"

"Even so," Mandy said, still kneeling by the monster that had tried to suck her guts out, pulling the pink silk scarf off her neck and folding it, applying pressure to a gushing wound in the creature's side. "Hurry, please, call somebody before he bleeds to death."

Betty Calhoun did not move, just continued to look upon her with moon-gray eyes. "It's the divorce, isn't it," she said, not as a question but as a statement. "Some women have the kind of heart that just won't quit. Can never get enough. Any sort of soul-eating heart-sucking bastard could do anything to you, anything, and you'd still want to bring him back."

Mandy jerked her head up, and if she had seen pity, or condescension, or scorn—but she saw none of those in Loony Calhooney's bleak gaze.

She saw an intimation of some larger understanding.

"You're crazy," Mandy mumbled, but she dropped the scarf.

"As if life isn't?"

Wordless, Mandy got up and placed herself by the old woman's side. There she stood over the grotesque bleeding thing and watched it die.

Bridge over the Cunene
Gustavo Bondoni

Botoso *was singing some innocent rhyme about the horrors* of the great change at the top of his lungs. It was a new phase, and Lara was fervently hoping that it would pass as quickly as the rest had.

It seemed only last week that the little five-year-old had contented himself with running around inside the stockade, happy to let his universe be defined by the log walls. But, suddenly, he'd become obsessed with the world outside. First, he'd gone through a period of curiosity about the Pale Ones, never going to bed unless he'd first been told a story about them, and the things that had happened during the change. He'd cover his head and pretend to be terrified, but never had nightmares, and always came back for more.

Then, seemingly simultaneously, every little one in the village had begun to sing the songs that their parents had sung. Songs about the Pale Ones, songs about the change. It was incredible how these songs, that had been buried for years, reemerged all at once. Nonsense songs, but their verses contained references to the horror of the times.

Lara noted that her son was looking at her quizzically. But he was silent at last, which was a relief. She could get back to mending the shirt.

"Mama," his thin voice piped up. "Do you think I could be the headman, some day?"

"Of course, dear," she replied absently.

"Just like Simao Zaboba?"

"Yes, dear."

He wandered off, and she breathed a small sigh of relief. There were clothes to mend, thatching to do. And he could be a demanding child sometimes.

§

He'd done this for all of his adult life. His predecessors had done the same. It was as natural as life on the veldt, and had been part of the cycle of life even before the great change, and would be part of it after the Pale Ones were a faded memory.

Simao Zaboba was at peace with himself, with the bright noon sun and the fresh June breeze whispering through the trees. He knew enough to be thankful for his role in the natural cycle. Twice a month, the offering was made, and twice a month, it was accepted. A pig on the full moon, valued for its brains, a goat on the new moon, desired for its blood; and safety, even a measure of protection, for the village all month long. It had always been thus, although in the times of his grandfather, the offering of a chicken or a cow were made on a less regular basis, to other, less tangible, spirits. But even those sporadic devotions must have had some effect, since the village had survived nearly unscathed, while others…well, others had been absorbed into the nests.

Today, he was leading a well-fed goat on a leash of metallic rope, enjoying the three-hour walk to the neutral zone across the river. Today was a clear day, and he could see forever, but knew that he would never see one of the Pale Ones during the day. Like all spirits that had once been day-walking humans, they were nocturnal creatures.

The bridge was a rickety affair, long poles lashed together with vines. His father had told him that the Cunene had once been bridged by dozens of concrete structures designed to last for generations. But these had been torn down in a desperate, failed attempt to stop the plague from spreading north to Angola. The village had avoided the change only because it was so far off the beaten path. By the time they'd been rediscovered, the Pale Ones had evolved, and had even reached the point where they could be reasoned with. Spirits were like that.

As they approached the neutral zone, the goat began to show signs of nervousness. It seemed to sense, somehow, that hundreds of its brothers and sisters had perished very nearby. Close enough that the smell of death was still present.

Or maybe it sensed something else. Something hungry.

Simao was unconcerned. He dragged the now openly resisting, panicked animal towards the clearing the way he'd done hundreds of times before. The stained ground and scattered bones seemed to give the animal added strength, and it left four furrows in the dust as its feet slid along.

He reached the tree and looped the end of the metallic rope around the trunk. As always, he double-checked the clasp; the consequences of the goat escaping were too ugly to contemplate.

Leaving the grunting goat straining against the unbreakable rope, Simao walked, as he'd done countless times before, back towards the village.

He wasn't expecting to see little Botoso crouching behind one of the bushes, because he'd never been there before. And that was probably why he didn't.

§

Botoso knew he was in trouble. He had no idea how in the world he was ever going to get back to the village. He had no idea where the village was. This was the first time he'd ever been outside the stockade without his mother or one of the other village adults to take care of him, and the sun was setting redly over the horizon.

But he wasn't frightened. He told himself that a future headman would never be frightened just because night was about to fall. He would laugh the night off, and keep walking until he found the river. He knew the river was near his village.

He also knew that he would make a great headman someday. He was smart and compassionate. After Simao Zabobo had left the clearing far behind, Botoso had emerged from hiding and immediately noticed that the headman had forgotten the goat. The boy knew how important goats were to the village—he was old enough to know that the village's very survival depended on the supply of goats.

So, he worked at the clasp tying the goat to the tree and began his walk back the way he'd come. At some points, it was difficult to decide which way he had to go, since one patch of low grass or clump of trees looked just like the next, but he wasn't worried. A headman would never get lost.

But he had. And now the sun was all the way down, and it was hard to see where he was going. The goat, sniffing the air, had been getting more and more restless, and, suddenly, it gave a mighty jerk and broke free of Botoso's five-year-old grasp, dragging the leash off into the darkness.

Botoso gave chase, following the tinkling of the metallic cord until an unseen hole in the ground sent him tumbling onto a patch of thorns. He lay there silently, listening to the tinkling which grew fainter and then died out, and to the night, which was suddenly alive with scurrying and wildlife sounds. He knew that some of those sounds weren't alive.

He told himself that he wasn't afraid, but the tears that streamed down his face seemed unaware of it.

§

Lara was frantic. She'd been waiting for Simao Zaboba outside the village ever since she'd realized Botoso was missing. Now, off in the distance, she could make out a dark, tiny speck coming towards the village from the south. She knew, she had to believe, that the speck, as it grew nearer, would resolve itself into two figures, a large, thin one, and a slightly rotund smaller speck less than half the height of the first.

As the speck grew into a smudge, her hope waned, but then she rallied. The headman probably made Botoso walk behind him, as a punishment. That's why she could only make out one figure approaching in the afternoon glow.

But even that hope soon faded. She ran out to Zaboba, stood before him, clutching his arm, getting her breath back and finally panted, "Did you see Botoso?"

The headman looked her over, perfectly still, his impassive gaze showing no emotion. "There was no one on the path. How long has he been gone?"

She hung her head. "I'm not really certain. I looked for him, to eat the midday meal, and he was nowhere to be found. We looked all over the village." Lara was holding back teas now, desperate, her nails digging into his motionless forearm.

Zaboba looked at her knowingly. She felt that he could see through her, that he knew her deepest secrets, that he knew she was holding back. Finally, she could hold back no longer. "I think he followed you," she sobbed, and broke down completely.

"This is grave news," Simao said. "Go gather the elders." He pushed her gently towards the village, and walked slowly after her as she ran, stumbling, to do his bidding.

Other than Simao Zaboba, there were four village elders, and they all looked gravely on as she explained her plight. Finally, Satumbo, a toothless old man, by far the oldest man in the village, broke the silence. "A boy lost in the night is a job for the father," he said.

"My husband is dead."

"The uncle, then."

"He had no brothers."

"Then, the boy is lost. The village cannot risk the men we have. No wife will let her man go. There is no way we can defend ourselves from the Pale Ones outside our walls in the night. The night belongs to them, and if we violate that agreement, we forfeit our lives."

Simao Zaboba spoke unexpectedly. "I will go," he said. "I know where the boy is. The mother must come as well—she will have a choice to make."

Lara swallowed. Nothing was more important to her than her son, but what Satumbo said was true: the night belonged to the Pale Ones. She was suddenly imagined herself being torn to shreds, her bones cracked for their marrow, her blood drained from her body, her brain sucked from her skull through a hole in the top of her head. But then the image in her mind changed, and she saw Botoso there in her place.

"I'll go," she said.

"You will go alone," Satumbo replied. "Simao Zaboba is much too valuable to the village."

"No, I am not. I am just a silly old man whose only value to the rest is that he leads a goat to a dangerous place once a fortnight. And besides, I will certainly return tonight. I speak the language of the Pale Ones."

"The Pale Ones will kill you when they see you."

"It may be so, but I don't think so. They have changed since your childhood. And even since mine. I will be all right." He turned to the still-open gates of the village, retracing the steps he'd taken to return to the village that afternoon. He didn't look back to see whether Lara was behind him.

And he didn't seem at all surprised when she appeared beside him. Only Lara knew that she almost hadn't come. Only she seemed to have noticed that no matter how confident the headman had been of his own return, he'd said nothing about her.

§

It was a typical night. The veldt was cool and the sounds seemed somehow louder than they did from inside the village compound. That was ridiculous, of course; the open-topped wall of logs wouldn't have done much to filter the sounds of the nocturnal animals—the hoot of an owl, or the scurrying of rodents, or the buzz of insects. But it still seemed that the sounds were louder out here without the wall.

They'd been walking, their way illuminated only by the starlight and the knowledge of Simao's feet which had tread this same path for thirty years, for two and a half hours. At first, she constantly called out for Botoso, but, as they neared the bridge, Simao Zaboba told her to be quiet. Sound carried a long way on these grassy plains, and soon, the sound would carry all the way to the nest.

He didn't know where the nest was located, exactly, but he suspected that it was just a little beyond the clearing in the neutral zone—a clearing that was less than half an hour away on foot.

The night sounds seemed to get louder and louder the farther they got from the village, as if the animals, far from the noise and smell of human habitation, grew bolder. But Simao knew it had less to do with the actual noise than the fact that he was listening harder, trying to distinguish the sounds that didn't belong to the night. The sounds that meant that there was a something out there walking noisily on its two hind legs—something that hadn't been designed to prowl in the darkness, despite having originated near there very same plains millions of years before.

Something that, despite not being human, would have the arrogance and fearlessness that had, until the great change, allowed humans to walk the night knowing that no matter how much noise they made, no matter what they stirred up, it could be dealt with.

But now, with the few surviving humans huddling behind thick walls or in underground bunkers as soon as the sun went down, only the Pale Ones walked the night that way. They could be easily heard by someone who knew what to listen for. And it wasn't long before Simao Zaboba distinguished the telltale sounds. His heart sank when he realized that the noise of multiple Pale Ones milling around was coming from the clearing where he'd left the goat that afternoon. It came from their destination.

He looked over at Lara, but she seemed lost in her own thoughts and not to have heard anything out of the ordinary. Her features were set, and she was grimly putting one foot in front of the other. She thought that he would know where to look.

She was right. He knew exactly where the little boy would be, but he dreaded what they'd find once they got there. He began to hope that they would be intercepted before they arrived, dreading each step. Soon, his fear had grown to the point where he was only reluctantly putting one foot in front of the other. By the time they were a hundred paces from the clearing, Lara was dragging him along.

Even in the dark, he could tell the clearing was crowded. Darker shapes could be made out in the darkness, and Simao Zaboba felt as though someone was running cold hands up his spine.

"Welcome," a voice said out of the darkness in front of him.

Lara jumped, but Simao had known it was coming. The word had been spoken in their harsh guttural language, the language that the villagers feared and reviled. They called it Palespeak. The Pale Ones themselves called it English—it had been the tongue of the southern land before the change. Only the headman and a few others could speak it.

The voice went on, "We suspected you come soon." It was a ragged, sighing voice—as if it had been unused for so long that it had to be dug up from deep within the Pale One's thorax. And yet, the speech was clearer than what he'd heard when, as an apprentice, he'd accompanied the old headman to make the agreement that exchanged an occasional goat and pig for their lives. During that meeting, the Pale Ones had spoken in grunts and single, almost incomprehensible words—and it had been impossible for them to understand any but the most rudimentary concepts.

Simao knew that how he responded could make the difference between life and death, but he also needed to understand the situation a little better. "I make fire to see," he said, glad he'd practiced his Palespeak all these years, despite never having had to use it.

His pronouncement was met with hissing and an unseen step forward from his right. Zaboba tensed, but the original voice replied before any action was taken against him. "Small fire," it said.

"Small fire," he agreed. One of his precious, irreplaceable matches was used to light a torch.

The clearing was bathed in flickering yellow light. The Pale Ones looked much worse for the wear. Nothing with skin as tattered and decomposed as the inhabitants of this clearing had any business being animate. Their once-mahogany skin, already pallid from the change, had become even more gray with the years. They looked like dolls made of stained rags.

Zaboba looked around desperately, searching for a smaller figure. His gaze was attracted by a commotion behind the nearest Pale One.

"Mama!" a high-pitched voice screamed, and suddenly a small brown bullet shot from the shadows and buried itself in Lara's stomach. She cried and bent over to hug him, protecting him with her arms. "Thank you, thank you," she was saying, to no one in particular, without thinking about it, just repeating the mantra—happiness and disbelief mixed.

"Thank you," Zaboba told the Pale One in front of him.

The other acknowledged, inclining his head. "We no eat little ones. Little ones grow, turn big ones. Bring us food. Other nests eat little ones, eat big ones, too. Other nests die out. No food."

Zaboba was shocked at this. He couldn't believe what he was hearing, couldn't believe the sophistication of the Pale One's thought processes. But he had no time to dwell on it then. "We leave now," he said, bowing.

"No."

Zaboba realized that the semicircle of Pale Ones in front of them had expanded, and was now a complete circle, ahead and behind. They could not leave unless they were allowed to. There was no way they could break through that line unscathed—and even a scratch meant the end of human life, and the beginning of a twilight existence as a Pale One. He turned calmly back to the spokesman.

"We no have food," the Pale One said.

And suddenly, Zaboba lost his calm. He understood that what had been his worst fear, in the back of his mind, had actually come to pass. He knelt beside little Botoso and, trying to keep the fear and urgency from his voice, said, "Where's the goat?"

And Botoso, sensing the fear, began to cry. "It ran away. I tried to catch it, but I fell." And, finally, accusingly, "You forgot the goat."

Zabobo turned back to the Pale one.

"We no have food," it repeated. "Give food."

Lara turned to him, eyes wide, understanding. She seemed on the verge of panic, so he calmed her down. "Do not worry," he said. "I will stay. I am an old man, almost fifty summers. The village does not lose much."

Gratitude flashed on her face, but was almost immediately replaced by doubt and then fear. "But how will I find my way? It is still a long time until dawn. What happens if we get lost?"

"You must not become lost."

"What happens?"

"If you get lost, you will both die." He cursed the moonless sky. Even the small illumination from the barest crescent might have made the return trip possible. "Once you leave the neutral area, you are fair game unless you are on a clearly defined path towards the village. If you are anywhere else, other members of the nest will take you, since they have no way of knowing you are from our village."

And Lara knew it. She cried softly, silently, as she accepted what she must do. Botoso, who had lifted his head to see what was troubling his mother, suddenly crying again as he found himself transferred to Simao's care.

Simao took a tight grip of Botoso's hand. He knew the boy would have to be kept in check.

"Will you take care of him?" Lara said.

Simao nodded.

"What will become of him, an orphan? His options will be few."

"His options," he replied, "will be one. He has seen the Pale Ones, and it seems he will survive the encounter. He will be headman. I will take him on as an apprentice."

Pride flickered across her face, but lasted only a fleeting instant. She had remembered that she would not be there to see it. "Tell them," Lara said.

"One will remain," he told the leader of the Pale Ones, who nodded in reply.

A rustling sound behind caused Simao to turn. The Pale Ones behind had disappeared.

"Ones who go, go now."

Simao Zaboba took a tight grip on Botoso's hand and began to walk towards the village. At first, Botoso came readily, but then realized what was happening.

"Mama!" he said.

But it was too late by then. The circle had reformed, with them on the outside. The headman dragged the resisting boy towards the village. He was even thankful for the boy's calls for his mother, as they somewhat drowned out the screaming. At first, a single cry of protest, then a series of long, drawn out screams of agony which grew hoarser and hoarser. The final scream was a ragged cry, mercifully cut off in the middle.

The boy seemed to understand; his struggles stopped.

But the sick feeling in Simao Zaboba's stomach wasn't caused by the sounds of a pretty young mother being torn to edible chunks behind them. It was caused by the knowledge that the Pale Ones had, in their way, discovered farming—or at least a way to get small but sufficient quantities of live food without having to hunt for it. At present, they needed the village to supply their meat, but how long would it take them to figure it out for themselves? After that, the village would serve no purpose other than as a breeding ground for their favorite dish—or, worse, the site of one spectacular nighttime binge.

His reverie was broken by a slurping and panting noise from the feeding ground behind. He shuddered and hoped it would fade soon.

But sound carries a long way over the veldt.

Brown John's Body

Winston Marks

*E*rd Neff wanted as little to do with his fellow men as possible. So, he lived alone in his big cash-vault. Alone, except for John...

Erd Neff dropped a thin bundle of currency into the $100 bill drawer of the flat-top desk and kicked the drawer shut with a dusty boot.

He flicked the drip from his hooked nose, which was chronically irritated by the wheat dust of the warehouse, then he wiped his fingers down the leg of his soiled denims. Across the twelve-by-twelve, windowless room, John stirred awake from the noise and began nosing in the debris of his filthy cage.

"Time for supper, John?" Neff tugged at the twine at his belt and examined his three-dollar watch. He pinched a dozen grains of wheat from a two-pound coffee can and let them sift through the wires of the cage. John pounced on the grain hungrily.

"Wait a minute! What do you say, dammit?" Neff's hand reached for the marshmallow-toasting fork that hung from a hook on the wall. He touched the points, filed needle sharp. "What do you say?" he repeated, twanging the tines like a tuning fork.

John skittered to the far corner, tearing new holes in the old newspaper with frantic claws. Cowering against the wires he spat half-chewed flecks of wheat trying to say the magic words that would spare him from the fork. "Tinkoo! Tinkoo!" he squeaked, straining to make the two syllables distinct.

Neff hung up the fork, and John turned to lick at the old scabs clotted from earlier jabs, taking sullen inventory to be sure there were no new crimson leaks in his louse-infested hide. Until two months ago, he had been just one more gregarious specimen of Mammalia Rodentia Simplicidentata Myomorphia Muridae decumanus. Now he had another name. Like each of his predecessors in the cage, he was a large, brown rat called John—after Erd Neff's despised and deceased father. Neff named all his rats John.

"Well, don't get fat."

John finished the grain, pawed the air and squeaked, "Mur!"

"More, hey? You talk fine when you're hungry."

"Peef, mur, mur!" John begged. He did well with his vowels, but "l" and "s" sounds were beyond him. He said "f" for "s". "Ls" he ignored entirely.

Neff gave him one more wheat head. "Okay, get fat!"

He turned to the door, lifted the inside, mechanical latch, shoved with his foot and snatched his revolver from his hip-holster. The vault door opened ponderously, revealing an empty warehouse. Neff peeked through the crack between the hinges to clear the area concealed by the door itself.

One hoodlum hopeful had hidden there once. Spotting him through the crack, Neff had simply beefed into the foot-thick slab of fireproof steel. Inertia, plus surprise, had disposed of that one. Neff hadn't even had to shoot.

Tonight, there was no one. Funny. The wheat country was getting tame, or else the tin-horns had learned their lesson. It was no secret that Erd Neff never visited the local bank, yet it had been more than six months since anyone tried to hold him up.

The local bank hated him plenty. He was costing them. His five loan offices in the rich wheat county skimmed the cream of the mortgage loan business. Of course, nowadays most people paid off their loans, and the low interest rates he charged to lure the business barely paid expenses. Yet, he still picked up an occasional foreclosure. Farmers still got drunk, divorced, gambled, broke legs or committed suicide once in awhile, and Neff's loan documents were ruthless about extensions of time.

These foreclosed acreages he traded for grain elevators and warehouses when crops were small and operators were desperate. Then came the bumper years during and after World War II. Wheat on the ground and no place to store it but in Erd Neff's sheds. It wasn't cheap to store with Neff, and he had a virtual monopoly in Ulma County.

Neff swung the great door back into place with its *whoosh-thunk* that sealed in air, sound and nearly a hundred thousand dollars in currency. He levered the bolts into place and spun the expensive combination lock.

The vault, tucked away in the front, left-hand corner of the old frame warehouse expressed Neff's distrust and contempt for mankind. Concrete and steel. Bed, shower, toilet and desk. In this walk-in cash box, he was fireproof, bomb-proof, theft-proof and, most important of all, people-proof. There he consorted unmolested with the one mammal on earth he found interesting—John, the brown rat.

He slid the broad warehouse door closed behind him with a cacophony of dry screeches and padlocked it. The dusty street was deserted except for a black sedan which two-wheeled the corner a block away and sped toward him. Neff dropped his pistol back in its holster. "Now, what the hell—?"

He waited on the splintery platform, a huge man, ugly of face, short-legged and long-bodied with a belly swollen from regular overeating. His shaved head swiveled slowly as the police car leaned into a skid-stop.

Officer Collin Burns got out and stared up at the motionless statue in sweat-dust stained denims. Burns was half Neff's fifty-six years, tall and thin. He wore gray, a silver star and a big black hat. He said, "I'll take your gun, Erd."

"Now what? I got a permit."

"Not any more. It's revoked."

"For why?"

"There were witnesses this afternoon."

"Witnesses? What in hell are you—oh, no! Not that damned dog?"

"The puppy belonged to a little girl. You can't claim self-defense this time."

"He was coming down here chasing the cats away every day."

"So, you shot him, like you did Greeley's collie."

"Cats count for more. You know as well as I do, you can't control the rats around a warehouse without cats."

"You've shot five men, too, Erd. Three of them are dead."

"I was cleared, you know damned well! Self-defense."

"You're too handy with that pistol. Anyway, I didn't file this complaint. It was the child's mother, and she made it stick with the chief. Give me the gun, Erd."

"You got a warrant for my arrest?"

"No, but I will have in an hour if you insist."

"I got a perfect right to protect my property."

"Not with a gun. Not anymore."

"I just get these punks convinced, and now you want to turn loose on me again. Who put you up to this Collin?"

"You did. When you shot that pup. I'm not here to debate it. You're breaking the law from this minute on if you don't hand over the gun."

"Dammit, Collin, you know how much money I got in there? You know how much I pack around on me sometimes?"

"That's your business. You can use the bank and bonded messengers—they get along with dogs."

"Telling me how to run my business?"

"I'm telling you to give me that gun. You'll get the same police protection as any other citizen."

Neff sneered openly. "I'd a been dead thirty years ago, depending on cops."

"I don't doubt that a minute. You're easy to hate, Erd. Are you going to give me that gun?"

"No."

"You like things the hard way, don't you?" Burns got back in the squad car and drove off. Neff spat a crater in the wheat-littered dust and got into his own car.

Two minutes later he turned up Main Street and stopped before city hall. Inside the tiny police station, he dropped his pistol on the counter. Bud Ackenbush looked up from his desk. "You could have saved Collin some trouble."

Neff stalked out without a word and crossed the street to the Palace Cafe. He ordered a double-thick steak, fried potatoes and pie. He liked the way the waitresses scrambled for the chance to wait on him. Women didn't like him. He was ugly and smelled of sweat, and on the street, women looked the other way when they met him. All but the waitresses at the Palace. When he came in, they showed their teeth and tongues and wiggled their hips. He was a twenty-percent tipper.

The important thing was it got him his steak, really double thick and double quick. People could be real efficient. Like brown John. Prod 'em where they live and they'll do anything. Even talk to you.

"You look kinda naked tonight, Erd," Gloria kidded.

Neff wiped steak juice from his chin and stared at her breasts. It used to excite him, but now it was just habit. It was better than looking at red-smeared lips that smiled and eyes that didn't, eyes that said, "Don't forget the tip, you filthy bastard!"

Funny. Hang a gun on any other citizen in town and people would stare. Take the gun off of Erd Neff and people make cracks.

He did feel naked.

"I didn't order this damned succotash!"

"It's free with the steak dinner, Erd."

Go ahead, pinch my leg like the harvesting crews do. I'm free with the dinner, too. Like the ketchup. Like the mustard and the salt and pepper and the steak sauce and the sugar and the extra butter if you ask for it, just don't forget the tip.

Clarence Hogan, the fry-cook, came around the counter and leaned on the booth table beside Gloria. "You don't like succotash? How about some nice peas, Erd?"

Clarence was Gloria's husband.

Pimp!

"Put some ice-cream on my pie," Neff said. He looked up at Clarence. "No, I don't want any goddamned peas!"

They brought his pie and left him alone. He finished it and felt in his pocket for the tip. He changed his mind. To hell with Gloria and her fat leg! The steak was tough.

He paid the check and went out. The sky was pink yet. Later in the week, the sunsets would be blood-red, as the great combines increased in number and cruised the rippling ocean of wheat, leaving bristly wakes and a sky-clogging spray of dust.

Neff's busiest season. Damn that dog! Damn Collin Burns!

His hand brushed his leg where the leather holster should be. Damned laws that men made. Laws that acquitted him of homicide and then snatched away his only weapon of self-defense because he shot a yapping dog.

As he got in his car Collin Burns came out of the station. He tossed Neff's gun through the open window onto the seat. "Here's your property. The Marshal came in, and he changed everybody's mind. It's going to cost you a hundred dollars and a new pup for the little girl, probably. Here's the subpoena. Tuesday at ten."

"I don't get it."

"The Marshal said to let you fight your own battles."

Neff started the car and let the clutch out. The Marshal knew his way around. The transient harvesting crews were a wild bunch. If word got out that Neff was unarmed, packing thousands of dollars the length of the county, the enforcement people would have a lot of extra work on their hands.

He parked behind the warehouse, next to the railroad tracks.

He came around front, unlocked the big door, pulled it shut behind him and bolted it. The warehouse was jet black now, but he knew every inch of the place. He could fire his pistol almost as accurately at a sound as at a visible target.

He practiced on rats.

Holding a pocket flash, he worked the combination. As the final tumbler fell silently, a faint, raspy screech came to his ears, like a board tearing its rusty nails loose under the persuasion of a wrecking bar. He listened a minute, then he levered the bolts back, stepped into the vault-room, closed the door and shot the mechanical bolts.

Sure. Someone was out there, but they'd get damned tired before morning. He flicked on the light and touched the other wall switch beside it. The powerful blower and sucker fans cleared out the musty air and rat-stink.

John rustled in the cage, blinking at the sudden light. "Hi, Neff! Meat! Meat! Meat!"

Smart little devil! Neff sometimes brought him a scrap from his dinner, but he hadn't thought to tonight. He sucked at his teeth and pulled out a tiny string of steak. "Here. Bite my finger and I'll poke both your eyes out."

John picked the thread of gristle from Neff's finger with his fore-paws and devoured it, trembling with pleasure. Neff lifted the cage. "Okay, now let's have a few tricks."

At once John made for the can of wheat. "Get outta there!" Neff scooped him up and dropped him on the desk, snapping his tail with a forefinger. John whirled, laid his ears back and opened his mouth. At bay, the brown rat, Neff knew, is the most ferocious rodent of the two-thousand different species, but Neff held his hand out daring John to bite.

Neff knew all about rats. More than anybody in the world knew about rats. When you live among them for three decades you find out about their cunning wariness, fecundity, secretiveness, boldness, omnivorous and voracious appetites. Fools reviled them as predators and scavengers. Neff appreciated them for what they really are: The most adaptable mammal on earth.

John was smart but no smarter than the rest. Neff had proved this by teaching every rat he captured alive to talk.

Impossible they had told him. Even parrots and parakeets only imitate sounds in their squawking—yes, and pet crows. Animals don't have thinking brains, they said. They react, trial and error, stimulus and response, but they don't think.

Neff didn't know about the others, but he knew about rats.

Keep them hungry and lonely for a mate. Hurt them. Torture them. To hell with this reward business. Rats are like men. Mentally lazy. They'll go for bait, sure, but they'll go faster to escape pain—a thousand times faster.

And rats have lived with man from the first. They have a feeling for language like the human brat. Between partitions, inches from a man's head when he lies in bed talking to his wife, under a man's feet while he's eating, over his head in the warehouse rafters while he's working. Always, just inches or feet away from man, running through sewers, hiding in woodpiles, freight-cars, ships, barns, slaughter-house, skulking down black alleys, listening, hiding, stealing, always listening.

Yes, rats know about man, but rats had never known a man like Erd Neff, a man who hated all mankind. A man who chose a rat for a companion in preference to one of his own kind. Rats named John learned about Neff. They learned that his tones and inflections had specific meaning. They learned very fast under the stabbing prod of the marshmallow fork. With just enough food to keep them alive, their blind ferocity changed into painful attention. They learned to squeak and squawk and form the sounds into a pattern with their motile tongues. In weeks and months, they learned what the human brat learned in years.

"Stand up like a goddamned man!"

John stood up, his tail the third point of the support.

"Say the alphabet."

"Eh—bih—fih—dih—ih—eff—jih—etch—"

Neff lit a cigar and watched the smoke float away from the ceiling blower and vanish into the overhead vent in the far corner. He bobbed one foot in time to the squeaky rhythm of the recitation. He took no exception to John's failure with "l," "s", and "z". The other Johns had been unable to handle them, too.

"Hungrih, Neff. Hungrih!"

The big man picked out three grains of wheat. He noticed the can was almost empty. One by one he handed the kernels to his pet, waiting for John's "Tinkoo!" in between.

"Mur! Mur!"

"Lazy tongue! It's more, not mur!"

John dropped to all fours and retreated. Usually Neff slapped him in the belly when he used that tone. But Neff was bemused tonight. He kept listening for sounds, sounds that he knew could never penetrate the thick walls.

They were out there, he was sure. Another damned fool or two, flashing a light around, trying to figure out something. Neff remembered one pair who had even tried nitroglycerin. He saw the burns on the outside of the door the next morning.

Amateurs! Nobody knew for sure just how much money Neff kept in the old desk, and big-time pros wouldn't tackle a job like this without a pretty fair notion of the loot. For all they knew, maybe he mailed it to an out-of-town bank.

"Okay, fetch the pencil."

John jumped from the desk and moved toward the open door of the shower-stall where Neff had thrown the pencil stub. He paused by the wheat can, then scurried on to get the pencil. He climbed Neff's leg and dropped the pencil into the open palm.

"Smart punks up at State College. So, you can't teach a rat anything but mazes and how to go nuts from electric shocks, eh? Wouldn't they be surprised to meet you, John?"

"Hungrih!"

"You're always hungry!"

"Meat! Meat!"

"Yeah. You can sound your "es" real good when you say, 'meat.' Someday, I'll cut off your tail and feed it to you." He laughed, grabbed John by the coarse hair of his back and slipped him back under the cage.

Then he undressed down to his underwear, turned out the light and lay on the narrow iron bed. John rustled in his cage for a minute, then there was only the faint hum of the blower and sucker motors in the ventilating system. The incoming and outgoing air was baffled and trapped to kill sounds, and spring-loaded sliding doors poised to jam shut and seal off the room if anyone tampered with the exterior grilles in the roof.

The fans hummed softly and Erd Neff slept.

§

Sleck-thud, sleck-thud!

He was awake pawing the wall for the light switch, but even as his hand found it, and his eyes discovered the closed ventilator doors, a reddish vapor sank over his body. A single gasp and Neff was clawing his throat. Sharp, brown-tasting, acid-burning, eye-searing, nose-stinging!

He fell to his knees and clawed to the far corner, fighting for air, but the acrid stink stained his throat and nose. His eyes kept burning. The whole room must be full!

The door-lever! No, that's what they wanted. Blind! Gun's no good now. God, for a breath of air! Damned tears! Can't open my eyes! Air! Got to have it!

His throat refused to open. The stink, a little like iodine, a lot like a hospital smell but a million times stronger—raked at the tender tissues of his throat. Icepicks stabbed from his soft palate, up into his brain, his temples. He swayed against the door, caught the lever and heaved convulsively. The door fell away slowly. He stumbled forward, gashing his knee against the sharp jamb.

A light struck redly through his clenched, tear-soaked eye-lids.

"That did it. Get the gun!" The voice was high, almost girlish. A young boy?

A slightly heavier voice said, "Got it. Keep an eye on him while I find out why the fan stopped working."

"He's going no place. You were right. That bromine stuff really did the business. Lookit his face. Sure it won't kill him?"

"Don't care if it does now. We got the door open."

"What is this bromine, anyhow? Boy, it sure stinks!"

"It's a chemical element like chlorine, only it's a liquid. It fumes if you don't keep it covered with water, and the fumes really get you. They used it in gas bombs in the war."

"That was chlorine."

"They used bromine, too. I read it."

"Air!" Neff rasped.

"Help yourself if you call this stinkin' stuff in your warehouse air."

From the vault the deadened voice came. "This must be the switch. The other switch is for the lights."

"Look out! When you turn it on don't get dosed yourself."

"I only dumped a few drops in. There. It'll blow out in a few—phew, let me outta here. That stuff does—God, it's worse than the dose I got in the chem lab!" The voice grew, coughing and cursing. "Better wait a minute or two. How's our big brave dog-killer doing?"

On his hands and knees, Neff was on the verge of passing out, but doggedly he tried to place the voices. High school kids? Bromine. Sounded like a chemical they might filch from the high school laboratory.

A kick in the ribs reminded him he was still helpless. "All right, get back in there." They aimed him through the vault door and kept kicking him until he went. They hauled him up into his chair. He tried to strike out blindly, but his chest was full of licking flames that spread pain out to his shoulders.

Now rope whipped around his feet, hands, chest and neck, jerking his body hard against the castered desk-chair and cramping his head back. "Tie him good. No way to lock him in with this door."

Neff opened his eyes. The boys were wet blurs rummaging through his desk. "Look! Just look at that! We can't carry all that."

"Get one of those burlap sacks out there. By the door."

Footsteps went and returned. "Now, just the small bills. Up to twenty. No, Jerry, leave the big stuff alone. Who'd take one from a kid?"

"Okay, let's make tracks."

"Wait!" Neff said desperately. "My legs and hands. You've cut off the circulation!"

Something hard like the barrel of a gun rapped down on the top of his head. "I ought to blow your dirty brains out. Killing my little sister's dog, damn you. Damn you, I think I will kill you. Damn you, damn you!" the voice crested.

"Wait a minute Jerry," the other voice cut in. "I got a better idea. Here. Look at this."

Short silence. "Yeah! Yeah, that's just dandy. Look how thin he is. That's just what the doctor ordered. Okay, the top's loose. Stand by the door and don't let him get by you. Wait. Got your flash? Good! In the dark. That's real good. Which switch is it?"

"Throw them both."

"Okay. Flash it over here. Look out, here I come!"

"Hurry up! Look at that hungry, black-eyed little devil. That ought to fix up the son-of-a—"*Thunk!* The compression rammed heavily into Neff's ears. The bolts shot solidly into place from the outside, and the combination knob rang faintly as it was spun. Silence.

They'd go out the same way they came in and tack the board back in place. How long before anybody would miss him? Twenty-four hours? Hell, no. Nobody would bust a gut worrying that soon. Two days? Some weeks he was gone several days making the rounds of his loan offices.

A week? Maybe. Girls at the Palace would get suspicious. Tell Collin Burns.

But a week! They'd cut off the blower when they threw both switches. No ventilation. No air.

198

Neff strained at the ropes. His legs were pulled under the seat so tightly that his feet were turning numb. Hands were tingling, too. Dirty little sadists. Turning John loose thinking—

He had to get loose. Less than one day's air, then—

"John!" Thank God John wasn't an ordinary rat.

"John, come over to me. These ropes. Chew them, John. Come on, John. Come on, boy."

No sound at first, then a faint motion in the old newspapers.

"John, say the alphabet!"

"Eh—bih—"

"That's right. Go on!"

"Fih—jih—" The squeaking stopped.

"Come over to me, John. Come to me, boy."

He held his breath. The beating of his heart was so loud he couldn't be sure that John was moving. The silence was long. Even the rat was blind in this blackness. He must be patient.

Sweat began oozing and trickling down his face, his armpits, his back—even his left leg. No, wait! That wasn't sweat!

The throbbing in his legs was greatest at his left knee. The trickle was blood from the gash. It ran freely, now, the ropes backing up arterial pressure. Never mind that!

"John!"

The coffee can tipped over, and the racket made Neff start against his bonds. The rope sawed his Adam's apple.

Crunch!

"Leave that damned wheat alone, John. Come over to me, boy. I'll give you a whole bag full when you chew off these ropes. Hear that, John? And a chicken foot. I'll bring you a whole chicken. A live one. I'll tie her down so she won't peck you. That's what I'll do, John."

He was breathing heavily now. "Do you get me, John? Would you like a live chicken?"

"Yeff."

The crunching resumed for a minute then stopped. Neff remembered, there had been only a dozen or so grains of wheat left.

John would still be hungry. The thought of a chicken should do it. If not, he could threaten him.

Neff waited. Relax! There was all night to work this out.

Finally, he felt something at his ankles. "That's the boy, John. Up here and down my arms. They're behind me. Get the rope off my hands first. Come on boy."

It was John, all right. Neff could feel the little claws coming up his left leg.

"Come on, hurry up, John. Tell you what. I'll bring you a nice, fat female, just like yourself. A live one. You can live in the cage togeth——John, don't stop there!"

The claws had paused near his knee and were clinging to the blood-soaked cloth.

"No, no, John! Don't! I'll stick you with the fork. I'll stick you—I'll kill you! John, we got to get out of here or we'll both die. Die, do you hear! We'll suffocate! Don't do that. Stop. Stop or I'll—"

$

Neff's threats beat hard into the rat's brain, and now as the slanting incisors tore at the cloth and chewed the luscious, blood-smothered, hot meat, Neff's screams sent tremors through the skinny, voracious body, and the tail tucked down. The words made John nervous, but it was dark. And there was food, such wonderful food, so much food! They were harsh words, terrible, screaming words: but words are words and food is food, and after all—John was only a rat.

Short and Nasty

Darrell Schweitzer

*M**y friend, who will never read this, I'm writing this for* you. I want to tell you about the sound of the rats on the metal stairs. You'd appreciate that. Once, that would have been your sort of touch.

The rats. I heard them skittering after me as I descended into the darkness from the El platform at Ruan Street. At times the sound they made suggested not many creatures, but one, and not a rat either, but some sort of crippled, twisted dwarf: scrape-scrape, *thunk!* Scrape-scrape, *thunk!*

Ridiculous, *then.*

In the old days, we would have started this together like some collaborative Gothic novel, telling how we traveled comfortably by coach for some days in the winter of 182—while composing our thoughts in separate diaries with enviable elegance (alternating passages from such diaries forming the opening section of the novel) before reaching London and calling our old friend Sir Archibald Blank, with whom we had enjoyed cordial business and personal relations, lo these many years. That way the three of us could at least look forward to a cozy evening's chat by the fire, gently sipping brandy, our glasses unobtrusively kept full by the taciturn, enigmatic butler, who would figure hugely in the subsequent plot once the requisite weirdness began to manifest itself.

That was the old way, Henry, when we were young. Remember? When we two were in college together, when everybody else was reading Hermann Hesse, we were heavily "into" Gothic novels— Monk Lewis, Mrs. Radcliffe, and the ever prolific Anonymous—the early Romantics, De Quincey, Byron, Keats, Mary Shelley—in short anybody who seemed suitably exquisite, melancholy, and doomed for Art's sake.

Remember how we used to try to top each other's affectations, just for the fun of it, the outrageous frilly clothes, the sweeping gestures, the dialogue never heard outside of a bad costume flick: "I say, old chap, I think I shall take up opium. It's so *frightfully* decadent."

"I much prefer laudanum, old bean. The visions of Hell are much more vivid that way—"

Neither of us could have fooled a real Brit for a minute, by the way. Our accents were pure college theater. I suppose most of our classmates just thought we were gay.

Ah, with a sweeping sigh. We had joy; we had fun; we had seasons in the crypt.

I try to be funny, Henry, to take the edge off the pain. We laugh to avoid weeping. There is no other way. It is hard to go on.

This isn't even London. It's merely Philadelphia. And I don't have much time.

Henry, the years have a way of taking the glitter off our dreams. Think of some piece of a Mummer's costume, soggy in the gutter the day after New Year's.

Rats on the stairway. I walked down, into the darkness as the train rumbled away above me, into the rain-slicked street of boarded-up storefronts and rubbish, past the occasional furtive late-night pedestrian; no longer the would-be Romantic fop but a worn-out man huddled in a worn-out trench coat against the bitter wind and drizzle, not exactly young either, but slouching into middle-age, gray-haired and forty pounds heavier.

Now I was there because Gretta, your wife, had called me. She said you were dying.

"Shouldn't you call an ambulance, then?" I'd asked.

"He's—crazy. It's too late. He says, no. You have to come. *Now.* Please." She was sobbing then.

Rats on the stairway, amid the trash on the street. Scrape-scrape, *thunk.*

§

I came because I was afraid, for you Henry, yes, and *of* you in a way, but mostly out of an even harder to define *fascination,* which brought me there at such an hour on such a night despite everything, despite even the souring of our friendship and the ostensible strangeness of Gretta's—and your—request that I, of all people, should be with you in your final hour.

Remember? The last time we'd seen one another there were a lot of obscenities. I think you started it. It hardly matters. Maybe it was me.

I came because I wanted to know how much you *knew,* Henry. That was what I was really afraid of. You'd found out a good deal about me, of course. And I'd found out that you'd found out. But I still had my own secrets. Yes.

I came because I had dreamed of you, and in my dream, Gretta called on the phone and spoke exactly those same words in the same tone of voice. "Paul, you have to come. *Now.* Please."

Then, I rode the elevated train, in my dream, and there were rats scraping on the metal stairway above me as I descended from the platform; and I walked in the cold January rain; and Gretta stood white-faced and wide-eyed at the door. She ushered me in without a word, without a sound; up to the dingy bedroom where you lay in the darkness, oblivious to the flickering TV in one corner. The place was crammed with books on leaning shelves, and odd statues and metal devices: pendants and symbols and a single, staring metal mask above the bed. The whole house smelled of dust and mildew and decay. The ceiling had cracked and sagged dangerously.

I leaned over the bed, in my dream, and you struggled to raise yourself on your elbows. At last you got a hand on my shoulder and pulled yourself up. You tried to whisper something—and out of your mouth came the sound of the telephone ringing, and Gretta's distant voice begging me to come, and her sobbing followed by the rattle of the train, and muttered words in my own voice, and the *scrape-scrape-thunk* of the rats.

Then, I was at the door again, and once more Gretta ushered me upstairs, and you tried to rise, only this time you were visibly *smaller* as you lay there, fully two feet shorter than before.

You tried to speak, and the sound of the phone came out of your mouth.

And for a third time, I reached the door, and Gretta met me, and your voice was no more than a faint croaking. You had shrunk to the size of a dwarf, or a malformed child.

And again, and again, until you were no more than a white lump of flesh like a beached and dying fish flopping among the bedclothes, still trying to speak, your face distorted almost beyond recognition.

You squeaked and wheezed. I couldn't make out any words. The noise was like rats, scratching.

I awoke with a start, sweating, my sleep interrupted by the sound of the phone ringing.

It was Gretta.

§

When I saw her standing at the door, where I somehow knew she would be, I didn't say anything. But I remembered a lot. I remembered what it had been like when both of us were young. I remembered one night in particular, when she had leaned dreamily out the window of my car as we drove along slowly somewhere out in the country, and the wind and the moonlight made her hair seem like flowing gold.

That was one of my little secrets. You hadn't been along that night. We'd never told you about it. It was only a few weeks before your wedding. I thought of it as my hopeless, impossible last chance then, and I suppose it was.

Now her face was lined, and her hair wasn't yet gray entirely, but it was stringy. It had been a long time since the moonlight.

I nodded to her and walked slowly up the stairs, certain of what I was going to see.

§

There you were in the semi-darkness. I can't begin to describe what I felt, what I feared, confronting you at your pathetic end.

I don't think you were even aware of me as I leaned over and switched off the TV. You lay still, your breathing labored. Then, suddenly, you tried to raise yourself. I sat down beside the bed, leaned over, and you caught hold of my shoulder.

That was the worst part, you touching me, just then.

You struggled to speak.

"You bastard—"

I pulled away. You dropped back.

"Now, now, my dear Henry old chap, old bean, that's no way to talk to—"

"You slime-sucking bastard."

"Ah, Henry, we had such dreams in the old days. Remember? We were going to be great poets, novelists, playwrights, actors, and now it has come to this."

"Go to the devil—"

"Henry, at the very least, you always had a more impressive vocabulary than that."

"1 know—"

God, Henry, I felt all the rage pouring out of me then, all the useless words pent up for years. "Shit. What do you know? That I stole money from the firm? That I took it from *you*, my esteemed partner in that second-rate, second-hand costume rental business? You can't prove a thing, Henry, for all the hurtful things you've said, for all you have ruined our friendship with your own paranoia. I never took more than my due. Not a cent more."

Even then I couldn't say everything I wanted to. There was so, so much. Could I tell you how you'd been the millstone around my neck for so many years, how every time I looked in the mirror and saw myself a little grayer, a little more rumpled, I thought of you? Yes, you, and I told myself that I could have taken another path, walked another road in life other than the one Henry Fisher led me on with his promises and his absurdities and his so-called ambitions. You wasted the best part of my life, Henry. You, somehow, you dragged me down, and I blame you for it. You made me part of the mediocrity we are today. I cannot forgive you.

§

One more joke, Henry, the knife twisting in my gut. You accused *me*.

"I don't give a shit about the money. *I know what you did—*"

I leaned forward and whispered, "You know that I went to see Laura Howard? Yes, I did. She's very good. I thank you for recommending her to me."

I indulged in a little untruth, my friend. You merely mentioned that you'd run into her after so many years. You gave me the address of her shop. That was enough.

I never got over Laura any more than I ever got over Gretta. She was *very* special, more than another old college chum, Miss Occult 1970, whose burning ambition at nineteen had been to conjure up the ghost of Aleister Crowley so it could possess her and make her the greatest magician in the world. Now she ran a magic shop along Frankford Avenue, not far from your present hovel, behind one of those boarded-up storefronts. As your mind had gone progressively softer, as you babbled more and more about auras and past lives and all that New Age crap, you became rather a disciple of our old friend Laura Howard, didn't you?

I attended one of her, ah, sessions. At first it was all I could do that night to contain my laughter.

But no—

Afterwards, when all the suckers were gone, with visions of Atlantean past lives dancing in their pointy little heads, she just stared at me, like a snake, her gaze inscrutable and implacable. Something deep inside me told me that it was time to leave, that it was time to *run,* that my entire soul was laid bare.

"Hello Paul," she said softly. I couldn't make any sense out of her tones, her words, her gestures. They seemed a mixture of surprise and fondness and hatred and almost robotic apathy, all blended together.

We talked for a long time, about the old days, about you, and about Gretta, and sometimes she was almost like a confessor, someone I *could* lay my soul bare before, and at other times she was an inquisitor and I her helpless captive.

We went out for something to eat, not to a fancy restaurant, no, not in that neighborhood, but to this ridiculous hole-in-the-wall Japanese place which, in deference to the sophistication of the customers, served sukiyaki on a hoagie bun.

Then we came back, talked some more, and had sex. That, I think, was part of the spell she worked on me, something magical.

Afterwards she stared into my face in the semi-darkness—her eyes as impenetrable as a cat's—and she said, "You want something, Paul. You want it very much."

And I did. I was afraid to say it. But I did, just then, want a way to go back and reweave the strands of my life, to make everything better, to be rid of *you,* Henry.

Then, she told me. She told me the secret of your death.

"1 know what you did—"

You surprised me again by actually sitting up of your own accord. I could tell how gaunt and wasted you had become, like a ninety-year-old man with both feet and half your legs in the grave. I thought you were going fall apart then and there into a mass of bones and squishy goo. But you were determined to have your say.

"I know about my *death,*" you said. How you ranted just then, Henry. How your face was twisted with—was it simple hatred or elementary fear? "It has been growing within me like a seed, ever since I was born. Laura told me that. All that lives must die. *Death* is built in. When we're young, it's small, dormant, like a pinhead-sized tumor nobody's found yet. But it's there, slowly growing larger as we age, as our living tissue diminishes, until by the time we're old we carry around a great load of *death,* with little life remaining. Sometimes very old people can look in a mirror and see *death* staring back, *death* wearing an old man's face like a tissue-thin mask."

"She told me its name," I said. "I can make it come and go fetch, like a dog. All I had to do was whisper that name each night for a week, and I woke it up. So I did, every night before I said my prayers, thinking of you."

"*Why?*"

That took me aback. Suddenly, it was me who dangled there on the edge of the abyss. I fumbled for words.

"Why? Because you deserved it."

"No, why did Laura Howard do it?"

That was exquisite, my friend. Your deft touch from the old days. Artistic and agonizing. Just then you seemed pleading with me, despairing not that your death was devouring you from the inside out even as we spoke, or that I seemingly hated you, but because you had lost Laura Howard's friendship, because *she* had turned on you for some inexplicable reason.

I really wanted to comfort you then. My own hatred started to unwind. I wanted to make it easier for you.

"I don't know," I said. "I paid her for her, ah, professional services—I mean the secret, the name, the spell, what have you—but I don't think she cared about the fee. It's part of some machination of hers, probably. God knows what she is trying to do. We're just tools to her, puppets."

I felt helpless then. I rose to leave.

"I don't understand," I said. "Why *did* you ask me to come here tonight if you knew all this? Just to confront me? What good would that do?" I was angry at you again. "You were always a bit of an idiot, Henry."

"Yes, I was, but not this last time. I went to Laura, too, once I understood what was happening."

I paused in the doorway.

"She was as you described her, Paul, like an inscrutable snake, neither horrified that her old friends were murdering one another, nor pitying, nor anything at all. I don't think she's quite human anymore—"

"Henry, she's got more humanity left than you do just now, or I—"

"Shut up and let me finish. She told me something important. Something I found very comforting, all things considered. I think it's part of her scheme that you know this, so Goddamn you, Paul, you're going to hear it. She told me that my *death* was indeed like a little doggie out in the back yard which would come running after it had finished its business, after it had dropped the gigantic turd that is my rotting corpse. Then, it comes running. Home to Papa. *You.* And it's hungry."

I turned back into the room, ready to—I don't know what—ready to throttle you then and there with my own hands, for the satisfaction, so I could deny, negate everything, so I could shout in your face as you died, *No, no, you sniveling moron it's all your fault*—

But you were too quick for me. You died even as you sat there, eyes suddenly rolling up white, jaw dropping, and out of your mouth came the sound of the phone, of Gretta's voice, the rumble of the El, and the scratching on the metal stairs.

And there was something more, something crawling *inside you* under your skin, not like a dog at all, but more like a huge spider scratching to get out.

§

I screamed then and ran out of the room, down the stairs, colliding with Gretta. I hardly realized she was in my arms. We stumbled together to the base of the stairwell, bouncing off the wall, grabbing the railing, never quite off our feet. It was a weird kind of dance, and I was crazy then, as if the record needle in my mind were skipping and scratching all over the record, and everything was a jumble, a bit of that, a screech of this—and before I knew what I was doing I kissed her hard, passionately, not because I desired her anymore, but to *deny* it all,

Henry, to fling one last defiance in the sanctimonious face of time; as if for just an instant you'd never existed and she and I had been married all these years but we weren't old and poor and everything had turned out differently; as if, no, that wasn't it at all—as if somehow the three of us were still together and you were still my friend and we both loved Gretta and she loved both of us equally and the end we came to was beautiful and romantic and not just sordid—

She broke away, frightened.

"What's happened?" she said.

"I can't talk about it. I'll call you later—"

I think she thought the look on my face and the tone of my voice bespoke grief.

She was sobbing behind me as I ran out of the house, down the street in the cold rain, toward the rusty elevated platform.

§

Scrape-scrape, *thunk!*

It was waiting for me. I saw it once, wriggling between the steps almost at my feet. I caught a glimpse of it as it dropped down into the darkness below: something like a fleshy, scaleless fish with a human face, and with crab-legs and claws.

I ran the rest of the way up the stairs, onto the platform.

A black man sat at the far end of the furthest bench, smoking and reading a newspaper. He glanced up once, then resumed his reading.

Scrape-scrape.

I gazed down the steps in growing horror as I saw something moving on the landing below where the stairway turned. Something dwarfish and misshapen, but more human now, with arms and legs.

I wanted to run to the black man. But what could I have told him? What could he have done?

Down there on the landing, the thing stepped out of the shadows, into the half-light, and I saw that it had my face, hugely out of proportion to the body. Our eyes met. It spoke, clearly, with your voice, my friend.

"1'm all yours now."

§

I would have run then. I would have scrambled across the tracks risking getting fried on the third rail. But just then I saw that the train was coming. It was all I could do to remain where I was, clinging to a pillar and watching as the thing on the stairs ascended painfully, inexorably, the steps much too large for its stunted legs.

It was all I could do to hang on as the train's light got brighter and brighter, as I could hear the rattling cars draw nearer, blessedly nearer.

Then, I was aboard. The black man sat at the far end of the otherwise empty car, still reading his paper as if he hadn't noticed a thing. Just as the doors wheezed shut I saw the creature at the top of the stairs, glaring at me, croaking something I couldn't make out.

I think it had grown taller by then.

§

Of course, there was no such easy escape. Your *death* at the very least knew where I lived, either from your memory or instructions, or from some inevitable homing instinct.

When I got off the train at 69th Street in Upper Darby, I heard the same scrape-scrape *thunk!* on the stairs behind me. I glanced back once across the nearly deserted station and saw something shuffle furtively behind a locked-up newsstand. I heard it scraping on the concrete floor.

A cop stared at me strangely, but only at me.

There was a cab outside, thank God, but just as I closed the door something struck hard against it, tearing metal, and I looked out; and there, inches from my face was *my face* or a distorted parody of it, filled with hate, mouthing words, the body behind it hunched and powerful.

"Drive!" I shrieked at the cabby.

"Where to? I said. "W*here to?*" He hadn't seen, hadn't heard anything. I managed to give him my address correctly. He shrugged and muttered, "Jeez," and must have taken me for a drunk.

Not that my continued flight did any good. How the thing travels is something of a puzzle, alternately fast and slow, if undeniably relentless. Did it hang onto the outside of the El train? Possibly it doesn't travel at all, but merely gathers itself together nearby like a cloud of guilt each time I come to a halt.

Somehow the cab ride confused it, and bought me a little time, so that, in the approved Gothic manner, this document serves as my confession and the tale shall end with my demise.

You would have appreciated that. If only we could go back, be young again; if only we—*I*—could find the strength within ourselves to go on, to shape our own lives. Hatred is a mere admission of failure. If only we could still be friends and talk about this in Sir Archibald Blank's cozy study and feel that last, delicious *frisson*. Then, it would all fit. I wouldn't be afraid of dying then. If it fit.

Then, I might tell one final joke. I might speculate that the footsteps I hear on the stairs outside, that shuffling and thudding and crashing, could very well be two gigantic furniture movers delivering a grand piano to the apartment upstairs at four o'clock in the morning.

But that would wreck the ending.

Scrape-scrape, *thunk*.

This story is for you, old friend. It's the least I can offer.

Mother Lode

David M. Hoenig

Bring us in slow, Derek." Captain Narcisse Renault's fingers played over the console by her command chair. "Park us right alongside and match rotation at local coordinates, ten meters distance."

A woman of few words, she'd just said more than she had in a week. Since the third of our crew, Wraith, was mute, it was a good thing I didn't mind silence. It gave me time to think.

I didn't really need the Captain's directions, being wired directly into the *Pat Hand* as her pilot. I had direct input from all the ship's sensors, and they were sorted through a neural interface in my brain where they were translated into sensations like sight and touch. It all helped me 'feel' the ship when flying insanely dangerous missions. The asteroid we approached was rotating in all three dimensions, and had sharp, mountainous jags all over it which could shred our hull like it was made of puff pastry if I screwed up.

I didn't screw up.

I heard the Captain exhale softly. She touched a button on her command console, and spoke.

"Wraith?"

I made a minor adjustment to the attitude of the ship, perfectly matching the asteroid at the coordinates we'd abstracted from the computer file on the *Errant Thought*—I checked my board's readout—just under five days ago.

Wraith entered the bridge. An amazing engineer, he had served with the Captain on various ships for over twelve years. I'd worked with him for two years aboard the *Pat Hand*, though he was still something of an enigma to me. He'd lost his voice about seven years ago in an accident which had partially decompressed the *Hand* into vacuum. The damage to his vocal cords was irreparable, but silent or not, he was still a wizard with ship's systems. After two years on the ship, I wasn't sure which characteristic the Captain prized more, his technical skill or his silence.

"We are here, Wraith," she said to him, pointing at the main monitor which displayed the uploaded map we'd taken as salvage from the derelict nearly five days before.

The engineer grunted something indistinct, but damned if the Captain didn't somehow understand.

"I know."

Even after two years on the *Pat Hand*, I didn't have a clue as to what his sounds meant and that irritated me. I whirled around to face her. "Translation?"

She looked annoyed, probably at having to speak further. "He doesn't like the fact that there were only corpses on the *Errant*, and the only undistorted log entry in their computer was the one which contained the location of this asteroid and the strike at these coordinates. Frankly, I don't really like it either. We don't know what went on aboard that ship, but here we are anyway."

I saw Wraith nod vehemently in agreement.

"But Captain..." I glanced from one to the other, taking in both disapproving faces before continuing. "The derelict's log showed they had discovered a lode of platinum in that spot below us on this tumbling mountain, and that makes it worth mega. But we found their ship a hundred thousand kilometers and a couple of weeks away, moving out-system. If someone had found the data on this mother lode, they would've come back and started mining already, right?"

"Maybe. Or maybe whoever did it is a bunch of psychopaths and they get off on killing people and don't give a gene-modded trout's ass about the platinum. They could be holed up somewhere out of line of sight, just waiting for us to pull our pants down trying to get at the ore."

"Look, there's absolutely nothing out there on prelim scan, and the drill site which was documented in the *Errant*'s log is right below us and pristine. Remember, we found them pretty far away, and that's plenty of space for something totally unrelated to have happened. If they were victims of pirates or marauders, there should have been wounded or signs of a fight, and we didn't see any of that." I started ticking things off on my fingers. "There could've been disease, radiation, an imbalance in their life support..."

Wraith interrupted with an unhappy noise.

Renault translated. "An imbalance which later corrected itself?" Silence reigned a moment as she looked first at Wraith, then back at me. "Give me full scan." Her clipped tones cut off further speculation.

I turned my attention to the external sensors and explored throughout the entire spectrum the ship could process. When nothing dangerous could be found in a three-hundred-sixty degree look, I started probing the asteroid with active electromagnetic pulses. Reflections of those probes were also run directly into my sensorium, and came across like touch. Overall, the sensations through the neural link were actually pretty addictive. When I used them like this, I felt like I had the kind of vision Superman had only wished he'd had, and giant fingers to reach out and caress anything out there I wanted to.

"No radiation other than background," I said after a few moments' work. "There's something super dense about ten meters beneath the carbonaceous surface, and which measures roughly twenty by forty meters. Computer modeling says the best match in the reference log is for platinum." I was about to say more, but saw Wraith and Renault standing like statues, watching the thing on the view screen. I felt the silence of the ship like a spacesuit around me, and chose to respect it.

Nobody said anything for a few minutes, and then the Captain heaved a sigh. "Wraith, please go EVA."

He made an unhappy sound and looked my way briefly, then back at the Captain. I saw the moment where his resistance to her request faded into something like resignation. I wanted to say something reassuring, but I really didn't understand what was bugging him. Okay, the derelict's crew were dead, sure, but space *was* a dangerous place. If the *Errant's* log and my readings were accurate, our entire futures rested just under the surface of that asteroid, ready for the taking.

Before I could find the right words to say, Wraith nodded his acquiescence to the Captain, and left the bridge.

The engineer's reluctance made me a little self-conscious, so I accessed the sensors to scan everything again to make sure I'd made no mistakes the first time about any additional risks out there. After a check, everything still looked clear, and I reassured myself that Wraith's radiation exposure would be minimal over the hours he'd be outside the ship.

A few minutes after I'd finished my repeat look, my console camera showed Wraith suited and entering our airlock. He carried a compact device with multiple bulb-like containers on its surface. He cycled the lock, and went out into vacuum, tethered to the ship via an umbilical which would exchange his air during the extended EVA.

With tiny jets of compressed air that I felt more than saw through my link to the ship, he moved to the asteroid, settled onto it and connected himself via crampon to the rocky surface. I observed him deploy the drill he'd brought, and align with the center of the subsurface metallic mass. I then watched avidly as it began to eat into the asteroid with ultrasonic fragmentation, suctioning up and sorting the chemicals it took into the different collection bulbs.

After about thirty minutes, I saw the telemetry readouts shift when the composition stream from the drill changed to show nearly pure platinum being mined. My earlier disquiet with Wraith's reactions faded under the prospect of finding real wealth. *It was 'The Big Strike' some spacers were always going on about*, I thought.

I turned to face the Captain. "Treasure ahoy." I knew I had this idiot grin she hated on my face, but what the hell—I might be able to buy my own ship with my share of the take.

She only grunted something indistinct in reply. *The engineer's language skills were apparently catching,* I thought, and had to suppress a laugh.

Hours passed slowly as Wraith and his drill proceeded to work a healthy chunk of the platinum out of the asteroid. Coffee helped pass the time. Still, things stayed nice and quiet aboard the *Pat Hand*, and I eventually got bored watching the slow progress. The latest ore values we'd downloaded at our last port gave me something to do, at least: trying to figure out just how wealthy we were going to be. I looked over at the Captain now and again, but she seemed absorbed in something on her hand console. Curious as to what it was, I queried the computer and learned she was reviewing the video footage we'd gotten during salvage of the *Errant Thought*.

When Wraith's drill had amassed its full capacity—eight kilograms of particulate platinum, approximately ninety nine percent pure—he deactivated it, secured it to his suit, and released his contact. He kicked off and quickly made the trip back to us, re-entering the airlock.

I watched it cycle and re-pressurize. I was sick and tired of the morose quiet, so I whistled appreciatively as I turned in my chair to face her. "What a score, Captain! At current prices, we're talking one-point-three million credits just for what we've mined so far, and there's tons more waiting in that deposit!"

She shook her head. "We've got enough. We're leaving as soon as Wraith's back aboard."

"What?" I couldn't believe what I'd heard. "But it's right there for the taking! I mean, Wraith could head back after he rested up. We've got nearly two days before we'd have to change orbit even a bit! He could go back at least two or three times, even with full shift breaks in between."

"It's enough," she interrupted.

"Enough? We could each be richer than Ceres Colony if we just—"

"It's enough." I saw that her mouth was now just a thin line. "I don't like it."

"Don't like what?" The sharpness of my frustration came out overly loud even to my own ears, and I wondered for a moment if I hadn't pushed her too far.

She didn't say anything for a minute, just stared at the footage on her console while I waited impatiently for her to say something. When she did, her voice was softer than I'd expected. "You ever wonder how the crew of the *Errant* found this lode, Derek?"

"They must have been prospecting and found it, looking for a good score. Or maybe someone sold them the data."

"With how much that ore lode is worth, no way someone sold it to them. As far as prospecting, good enough, but tell me how did they know to do close scans on this particular rock?" She tapped her console distractedly. "It's nothing special: C-types make up about three quarters of all the asteroids anyway. Basically, there are gazillions of them around, and this one doesn't stand out particularly much from anything else in the vicinity, does it?"

"Okay, so I have no idea how they found the damn thing."

"And that doesn't bother you?"

"Heck no! They must've had some kind of lead, or else got close enough to this sucker for some other reason. It could have been pure luck—it's happened before!" I found myself waving my arms around, and brought them down self-consciously and lowered my voice as well. "Whatever, however it happened, they got the scan data on that platinum and went to work."

"This asteroid's a needle in a stack of needles, Derek. Let me ask you another question: having found the ore here, did they mine the goddamned thing?"

"Well, I mean, wouldn't they have...?"

"If they did, where was the platinum they found? We didn't see any on the *Errant*."

"How should I know?" I didn't like that I suddenly felt like I was on the defensive. I shifted in my seat.

"They had a drill like ours on board: you saw it on board, but no ore. Next question: did you see any sign of a bore-hole on the asteroid here?"

"No," I said, thinking about that. "But..."

"But it doesn't make sense, right? If they were here, and they had both the drill and the lode's location, why wouldn't they mine some of the ore before they left? And if they had, where was it? And why the hell were they headed out-system instead of in—where all the markets for the stuff are?"

I floundered, lost in her logic. "I don't know."

"Well, figure it the hell out before we go anywhere." She stood abruptly. "I'm going to check on Wraith."

I was still speechless as she left the bridge, but my mind was already turning the problem over like the *Pat Hand* on autopilot. I needed to break down the problem into bite-sized pieces. Did the crew of the *Errant Thought* actually drill here? "Computer, full scan mode." I linked in and my senses bloomed in that euphoric sense of unfolding it always did. "Show me hyper-tracking of all regolith disturbed during Wraith's drilling of the asteroid over the last three hours."

I waited as the computer compressed the sensor data into two minutes of time-lapse which showed the small amount of debris launched from the surface during the engineer's extraction of the platinum. "Based on asteroidal mass and gravity, project time course for all disturbed regolith and display in compressed mode. Also, account for what percentage of regolith might be lost and beyond local gravity's attraction."

As the computer pursued its calculations, my hand unerringly found my coffee despite my otherworldly vision. It was cold. Bleh.

And then I saw something in the data stream which made me drop the cup. "What the hell was that? Computer: replay sequence." In the speeded-up view of the sensor tracking I saw something I would have otherwise missed in real-time, but I had to review the sequence twice more before I was sure of what I was seeing. I heard the bridge door open just as I murmured: "But that doesn't make any sense, does it?"

"What doesn't make any sense, Derek?"

I withdrew from full immersion in the sensory equipment and turned: both Renault and Wraith had come onto the bridge. "Found something odd, but it's preliminary. Let me put it up on the main screen."

The scan data, unenriched by the subjective experience of senses fully enhanced, was far less exciting, though the display was adequate. I ran it through first at slow speed, then at the compressed rate.

Wraith made a surprised noise and pointed at the video.

To my surprise, I understood him before the captain. "Yes, exactly."

Renault looked from her engineer to me. "What?"

"I had the computer go back through Wraith's drilling and look at the regolith he'd disturbed. Now, the gear's designed to be nearly completely recoilless so as to avoid major displacement in zero gravity and shoving either the operator or the ore away. But there's inevitable scatter of regolith which happens. Since the kinetic energy of it all is pretty low, the debris that's kicked up during the drilling ends up coming back to the asteroid based on its tiny gravity field."

Wraith nodded when the captain looked his way.

"So I followed the little fragments with hyper-tracking, all those project orbits and paths and if anything was lost to space or if everything returned. That was when I saw this." I highlighted a tiny blip of a will-o-wisp on the screen and followed it as it moved in real-time along a linear path from out-system to the asteroid. Then, a few seconds later, highlighted another.

A sound like someone gargling gravel came from behind me, and I turned around to see Wraith animatedly jabbering at Renault.

"He's right," I said. The captain looked at me sharply. "No, I don't really understand what he's saying, not like you do Captain, but he's seeing things from an engineer's perspective. That track is linear and doesn't make much sense: that's what jumped out at me, too."

Renault frowned. "Explain it to me so I can understand. What are we seeing and why is it significant?"

I glanced at Wraith and he gestured impatiently at me to continue. "In full-immersion scan, those little bright sparks I've tagged are particulate platinum, tiny particles moving from out-system to the asteroid."

"From where?"

"Pretty much on a direct line to where we found the derelict, Captain. Correcting for drift and such."

"Well. Damn."

Wraith made a noise, his face unhappy.

"Neither am I," Renault told him, "but we're going back to them."

"Um, Captain?"

"What, Derek?"

"Do we really need to solve this? I mean, we have over a million creds worth of ore in our hold. Can't we go sell that before we retrace our steps to a dead ship we already tagged for later salvage?"

She thought about that for fully a minute. "No. Set course and go. I don't pretend to understand what we've found ourselves in the middle of, but I will be damned if I don't try to figure it out and make sure that what happened to the *Errant* doesn't happen to us. So get us there."

I thought about another plea to greed, but gave it up immediately as a bad play. Instead, I set course and engaged the drive and the ship began moving out-system. I set it on auto and announced: "I need some rack time."

"Go ahead. You too, Wraith—you look like you've been through the waste recycler. I'll stay here and mind the ship."

The engineer and I left the bridge together. On the other side of the hatch he tapped my arm and I turned to him. Close up, I could see the swelling around the eyes that had accumulated during his EVA and which hadn't yet fully resorbed in ship's gravity. He grimaced.

I tried to guess what was on his mind, knowing we might need to go to the old text standby which had served since I'd come aboard. "You still don't like it."

He agreed with a nod, and held up a finger.

"And?"

He pointed vaguely along the lines of our course with his finger towards the bridge.

"Right. Headed out-system to recheck…"

He interrupted my interpretation by assuming a resigned look on his face and dragging his finger across his throat in a gesture that went back before sea-going ships were a racy concept.

I licked dry lips. "Let's hope for better, huh?"

He shook his head and went ahead of me and into his own cabin without another look. I shivered, even though I was sure the temperature hadn't changed an iota under computer control, then went to my own and lay down. I didn't remember falling asleep.

The ship-wide emergency alarm woke me out of a dead sleep, even as I felt the resounding slams of bulkheads falling throughout the ship. I was out of my sleeper and at my emergency suit before the captain's voice came over the intercom.

"Get suited up—we're depressurizing! Hull breach in the lower storage bay, pressure doors are coming down!"

I wasted no time getting secure and on internal air supply, then hit my suit communications to the bridge. "I'm good. How are we doing?"

"We've lost air from the entire lower storage bay, but we're tight now. Go check on Wraith. He may be having real trouble."

Crap. I remembered he'd been in a decompression before, and had lost his voice in that accident. "I'm on the way. What happened?"

"No idea yet—go make sure Wraith's okay and then get up here, I want you on scan."

I rushed out and across to the engineer's cabin and hit the emergency override. When the door opened, I slipped in to see him just dog the neck toggles of his own suit and helmet and also go air-secure. His eyes were less puffy now, but they had darker patches below them that wouldn't fade until he'd get some serious rest, and they were wide open with fear at the moment. "You okay? Renault told you what's going on?"

He gave me a shaky thumbs up, but I could also hear just how fast he was breathing.

I went over and checked his suit, then clicked my helmet against his so he could hear me when I spoke. "You're all good and airtight, Wraith, and Renault says the leak's contained by the pressure doors. We're under control, so calm down." I waited a moment while making eye contact. I saw him swallow, and saw him make an effort to slow his breath. "She wants me up on the bridge to cover scan; you coming or heading down to the bay?"

Wraith hesitated a moment, then pointed downwards.

"I'll let her know. Uh, stay safe."

He moved close to me and grabbed my shoulder with one hand. Seen through our two face-plates, his expression looked grim but determined. Then he moved past me and out into the narrow corridor.

I went to the bridge, and because there was equal pressure on both sides of that door, it opened and let me in.

Captain Renault looked tired and a bit strung out, and I couldn't recall ever having seen her that way before. "Get plugged into the scanners right away, Derek."

I moved to my station and did. The unfolding of my senses, then— "Whoa."

"What?"

"The lower cargo bay is empty of air, but I'm seeing something streaming out of there anyway."

"Let me guess; the platinum?"

"Damn it!" It was, of course. "But how did it happen?" I got the computer to replay the sequence leading up to the hull breach, looking for anything on hyper-tracking that might have taken a poke at us.

"So what happened, Derek?"

I ran the sequence compressed and the last few minutes before in real time. "Nothing external, Captain. It blew out from the inside."

She played her hands over the console by her chair and didn't respond.

"Captain? Narcisse?"

She looked up at me. "What?"

"Uh, the cargo bay decompressed spontaneously. I mean, nothing hit us to hole the ship."

"I heard you. I was reviewing the scan footage from the *Errant Thought*. Remember they had some airless sections?"

I nodded. "But the crew weren't in them, and it was clear they didn't die in vacuum."

"Right, but we still don't know what killed them. No platinum on board, right?"

"Nothing on scan, or when we went through the ship."

"Exactly."

"But what does that mean?"

Wraith stepped onto the bridge just as the Captain shouted at me: "I have no goddamned idea, Derek! But I saw the same data stream you did, live, on the mined stuff which Wraith pulled in from the asteroid! It's ninety nine percent pure platinum, right?"

I nodded.

"Well, what the hell's the other one percent?!"

Her outburst—the first time I'd ever seen her lose her cool—left me feeling like I'd had a decompression accident myself, unable to breathe or speak for a moment. "I, I don't know."

She stopped stalking back and forth and crossed her arms as she looked at me. "Did you bother to analyze it?"

"No," I admitted uneasily.

"Well, I did while you were sleeping! *The computer can't recognize what the hell that one percent is made of!*"

I looked at Wraith and saw him nodding in agreement. My mouth went dry as we all looked at each other.

Then the engineer collapsed, and I realized he hadn't been agreeing—he was seizing, or something worse.

Renault was at his side before I could move. "Wraith. Wraith!" The bucking became more violent and she looked at me, face white. "Flush atmo, now!"

"What?"

"Do it! We're all suited, just do a complete flush. Override the emergency doors, send it all out the cargo bay!"

I felt sluggish as I shut down safety protocols through the computer and opened the hatches. When I'd turned back around, I saw the Captain had her arms around Wraith from behind, looped around his chest and she was dragging him backward off the bridge.

"Okay Captain, we're venting."

She looked up at me. "Now, get us turned around."

"What heading?"

"Ceres Station. I'm going to get Wraith plugged into Medical, see if we can figure out what's wrong."

I heard the order, but my brain felt like it was stuck in gear and I just sat there wondering if something similar had happened on the *Errant Though* before its crew had been lost.

Then the bridge door opened, and Renault looked up from her burden and her gaze found mine. I'd never seen a look like that on her face in the years I'd known her. "Go already!" she shrieked, and left the bridge with Wraith.

Then I was alone with the *Pat Hand* and suddenly I could move. I programmed in the new course and set thrust to maximum, and plugged myself back into the scanners. As my sensorium expanded to that god-like feeling I wasn't sure I'd ever get enough of, I could see the hole in the cargo bay clearly. It wasn't venting atmosphere anymore, and I confirmed the ship was a total vacuum, but there was still something coming from the breach.

And even as the ship changed thrust vectors to turn us back in-system to match the course I'd programmed for Ceres, I saw the particulate platinum change its direction as it emerged, and then finally it stopped. "Computer, hyper-tracking—where's that matter-stream headed, as if I didn't know?" The computer projected courses, even throughout the ship's changing attitude, that were bang-on for that damned asteroid and its lode of ore.

I shivered suddenly, but a quick check of my suit told me my life support was steady in the green. "C'mon, Derek, pull yourself together. It's all gone now."

I unplugged from the scan unit and used my comm. "Captain?"

No response.

I repeated the call. "Narcisse?"

Nothing.

"Computer: what is the location of Captain Renault?" The response, when it came, seemed to freeze my blood. "How the hell can it be unknown?" I touched my suit's environmental controls and raised the temperature a couple of degrees and hoped it would take care of the chill I felt.

I went to internal scan and after frantic jumping from camera to camera, finally found two suited figures lying on the deck just outside of Medical. I watched for a long time before I was convinced that neither was moving at all. Then, I dropped the pressure door outside the bridge.

A quick check showed I was halfway through my suit's air, and there was no way I'd make it to Ceres without more. The bridge's emergency supply was intact, and theoretically should have been completely sealed from the rest of the *Pat Hand*. I aired up the compartment, then compared the projected time to reach our destination with oxygen consumption rates and liked what I saw.

I unsealed my suit, breathed deeply, and leaned back in the chair. "Just get me to Ceres, baby," I told the ship. "Just that far, please."

About twenty minutes later I got her answer when I felt the first seizure hit.

Thanks for reading!

Thanks for reading. If you enjoyed this book, please consider leaving an honest review on your favorite store's website.

§

About the Editors

Kelly A. Harmon is an award-winning journalist and author, and a member of Science Fiction & Fantasy Writers of America. She is a former newspaper reporter and editor, and now edits for Pole to Pole Publishing, a small Baltimore publisher.

A Baltimore native, Ms. Harmon writes the *Charm City Darkness* series, which includes the novels: *Stoned in Charm City, A Favor for a Fiend, A Blue Collar Proposition,* and *In the Eye of the Beholder.* A stand-alone novel, *Blood Soup,* was winner of the Fantasy Gazetteers Award. Her short fiction has been nominated for a Pushcart Award and short-listed for the Aeon. It can be found in *The Pale Leaves* and *Gallery of Curiosities* magazines, *Beyond Steampunk, Occult Detective Quarterly, The Best Indie Speculative Fiction Volume 1,* and more.

She is co-editor with Vonnie Winslow Crist of Pole Publishing's first three Dark Stories anthologies: *Hides the Dark Tower, In a Cat's Eye, and Dark Luminous Wings, and* Pole to Pole's first four anthologies in the Re-Imagined series: *Re-Launch, Re-Quest, Re-Terrify,* and *Re-Enchant.*

Visit her website at http://kellyaharmon.com, or connect with her on Facebook.

§

Vonnie Winslow Crist, MS Professional Writing, has had a life-long interest in reading, writing, art, science fiction, fairy-tales, folklore, and legends. An award-winning author and illustrator, she is a member of the Science Fiction & Fantasy Writers of America, Society of Children's Book Writers & Illustrators, and Pen Women.

Her books include T*he Enchanted Dagger, Murder on Marawa Prime, Owl Light, The Greener Forest,* and *Leprechaun Cake & Other Tales.* Her speculative stories can be found in *Chilling Ghost Short Stories, Faerie Magazine, Killing It Softly 2, Chaos of Hard Clay, Fae Wings & Hidden Things, Amazing Stories, Cast of Wonders,* and elsewhere.

Editor of *The Gunpowder Review*, Ms. Crist co-edited with Kelly A. Harmon Pole to Pole Publishing's first three Dark Stories anthologies: *Hides the Dark Tower, In a Cat's Eye, and Dark Luminous Wings,* along with the first four anthologies of Pole to Pole Publishing's Re-Imagined series: *Re-Launch, Re-Quest, Re-Terrify, and Re-Enchant.* For more information, visit her website: http://vonniewinslowcrist. com/, blog: http://vonniewinslowcrist.wordpress.com, Fb page: http://facebook. com/WriterVonnieWinslowCrist, or http://twitter. com/VonnieWCrist.

Also Available in The Re-Imagined Series

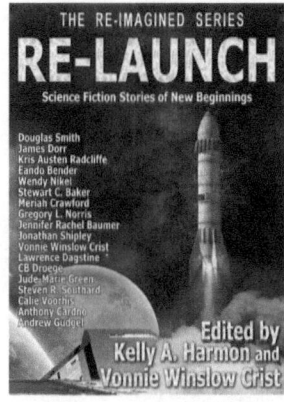  

Re-Launch
Science Fiction Stories of New Beginnings

Re-Launch reminds readers that new beginnings rarely go as planned and danger waits for the unwary on all worlds.

http://poletopolepublishing.com/books/re-launch/

Re-Enchant
Dark Fantasy Stories of Magic and Fae

Re-Enchant takes readers down twisted walkways to discover strange and magical places, people, and creatures.

http://poletopolepublishing.com/books/re-enchant/

Re-Quest
Dark Fantasy Stories about Magic and the Fae

Re-Quest takes readers on fantastical quests filled with adventure, magic, and danger.

http://poletopolepublishing.com/books/re-quest/

Available in the Dark Stories Series

Hides the Dark Tower

Dark Stories #1

http://poletopolepublishing.com/books/hides-the-dark-tower/

In a Cat's Eye

Dark Stories #2

http://poletopolepublishing.com/books/in-a-cats-eye/

Dark Luminous Wings

Dark Stories #3

http://poletopolepublishing.com/books/dark-luminous-wings/